The Rock Hole

Books by Reavis Z. Worthham

The Rock Hole

The Rock Hole

A Red River Mystery

Reavis Z. Wortham

Poisoned Pen Press

First Edition 2011
Large Print Edition 2011

10 9 8 7 6 5 4 3 2 1

Library of Congress Catalog Card Number: 2011920306

ISBN: 9781590588857 Large Print

Poisoned Pen Press
6962 E. First Ave., Ste. 103
Scottsdale, AZ 85251
www.poisonedpenpress.com
info@poisonedpenpress.com

Printed in the United States of America

This book is dedicated to the three women in my life.
My daughters Chelsea and Megan,
and the love of my life, Shana.
They keep me grounded and in the real world.

Author Note

Lamar County; Paris, Texas; and Hugo, Oklahoma exist, but they are used fictitiously in this novel. The same is true for certain businesses and other places that have passed with time. Center Springs exists, also, but it is the original name of a small community called Chicota. Other geographical references are correct. The Rock Hole on Sanders Creek was still there the last time I visited, but that was thirty-five years ago. All the characters, with the exception of Cliff Vanderburg, are the product of the author's imagination. Any resemblance to actual persons, living or dead, or to actual events or locales is entirely coincidental.

All towns and communities have stories and are bonded together by the people who live there, who drop by and only stay for a spell, and who pass through on the way to some other place. All have an impact on those with whom they have contact. Those stories are collected in memory, and are spun around kitchen tables, in front of the fireplace, on porches, in deer camps, or up at the store. Kids flow through these venues without notice, but they are sponges, and they absorb the stories as they are told. Eventually, they grow up and tell stories of their own.

With that said, step back with me in time to the good and bad of rural life at the end of an era. Welcome to 1964.

December 22, 2010
Reavis Z. Wortham
Telluride, Colorado

Chapter One

I came to live with my grandparents up on the Red River in the summer of 1964. Their hardscrabble farm sat exactly one mile from the domino hall in Center Springs, a one-horse settlement named after the clear-water spring that feeds Sanders Creek, which then drains into the Red.

When I climbed down the metal steps of that hot old bus outside the Greyhound station in the much larger town of Chisum, Grandpa and my grandmother Miss Becky were waiting on the sidewalk. I was so proud to see them I could have busted, Grandpa especially. There he stood in his sweat-stained old straw hat and overalls, with a tiny badge pinned to his blue work shirt.

I knew a revolver was in one of those big pockets, because he was the Law in Lamar County, though you couldn't rightly tell if you didn't know.

He hugged me against his big belly. Miss Becky was nearly dancing with excitement when he turned me loose to throw my suitcase into the truck bed among the bailing wire, empty feed sacks, and loose hay. He'd parked right at the curb, and the bus' front bumper was right against the tailgate. When the bus driver stopped a few minutes before, I could tell he was aggravated because the truck was in his way, but he didn't say anything.

"Why Top, you've growed a foot since we last saw you!" When Miss Becky hugged my neck, she smelled like the bath powder she kept in a round tin on her dresser

"C'mon, Mama, we have to go." Grandpa opened the door for us. "Get in hoss, and let's go look at a dead dog." He was always in a hurry to get out of town and back to the country. I crawled onto the dusty seat full of holes and Miss Becky gathered her long skirts and climbed in behind me.

"Ned," Miss Becky softly scolded him when he pulled away from the curb.

"Aw, Mama, it ain't nothin' but a dead dog and we're liable to see two or three in the same condition on the side of the highway before we get back to the house. It won't hurt him none."

"Well, y'all can drop me off at the house first, then."

"I intend to."

Ten-year-old boys are always up for an adventure, so twenty minutes later we let her out at the house and fifteen minutes after that I followed him through Mr. Isaac's chest-high corn. Grandpa led us between the rows with a hoe thrown over his shoulder and a 'toe sack dangling from the back pocket of his overalls. I wasn't sure how he knew where we were going until I looked down at his brogans and saw footprints leading through the rows in the sand.

I cocked my Daisy air rifle he'd remembered to bring for me. The BB gun's barrel was hot to the touch from the blazing summer sun. "Glad we have a gun." He always enjoyed kidding me. "You never know if you're gonna run across a booger-bear out here."

I rattled the air rifle to see how many BBs were left. "Is this your corn?"

"Nope. It belongs to Isaac Reader. I usually don't like being alone in another man's field. It feels like trespassing, but since Ike called me, here we are."

Turkey buzzards drifted on the thermals high above the thick corn stalks surrounding us. Locusts sang in the trees at the edge of the field. He stopped and wrinkled his nose at the edge of a tramped-down area in the corn. "Sheew. That stinks."

I almost gagged. The sight of what lay at our feet nearly made me fall out. Someone had used a heated two-handed screwdriver to torture a poor bird dog lying beside the cold remains of a fire. Dark stains on the blade and the German shorthair's wounds told us what had happened in the clearing. Burn marks made crisscross patterns in the animal's hide. Deep puncture wounds from the once red-hot blade still oozed fluid.

Despite the heat, a chill ran up my spine. I'd seen dead dogs on the side of the highway, but I'd never seen one intentionally mistreated. My stomach rose, but I choked it down again. The stink made my asthma act up, making me wheeze. I dug my puffer out of my jean pocket, stuck the atomizer end in my mouth, and gave the bulb a squeeze. My lungs tickled deep down inside and I began to breathe better.

"Bastard." Grandpa had a habit of talking quietly to himself. He hooked the sharp blade of his hoe under the stiff corpse and lifted it off the ground. Flies rose and buzzed all around us. "This one makes five now."

"Five what, Grandpa?"

"Just you never mind."

I waved flies out of my face as he knelt onto one knee and pulled a damp scrap of paper free from the sand. He unfolded the raggedly torn advertisement from *The Chisum News*. I got a peek at the drawing of a boy and girl playing catch.

He stood with a grunt and backed off a step.

I'd never seen anything so horrible in my life,

and I wished Grandpa hadn't brought me. Center Springs was always my safe place, where I didn't have to worry about anything except running outside, hunting, and fishing. That's why I came.

Another truck rattled down the dirt road and pulled into the shade beside ours. Grandpa slipped the folded clipping into the deep pocket of his overalls, removed his hat and wiped the sweat from his bald head with a blue bandanna. "That's your Uncle Cody's bird dog someone stole out of his pen last week. But you don't say anything to him about it. I'll tell him."

"Why?"

He stared down at me with those pale blue eyes of his. "Because I said not to."

Behind him, I saw the tops of several corn stalks twitch, but there was no wind. I started to say something about it, but a man got out of the truck and hollered across the field. Had I known someone was creeping through the field with us that morning, I could have told Grandpa and we might have ended what was coming for us right then and there.

He also might not have had to do what he did.

But at the time I didn't know I'd been slapped square in the path of a maniac who had it in for our family.

Chapter Two

A cold feeling of dread grew in Ned's stomach as he absently folded the piece of newspaper. Animal mutilations were stacking up in the river bottoms, but for the first time, the threat pointed toward children.

Ned shivered at the future in his sun-browned hands. Crows called in the distance. Blinking sweat from his eyes, he wondered if he'd soon be staring down at a child's body.

He rose with a grunt and slipped the paper into his pocket as Isaac Reader slowed to a stop in the shade beside Ned's own pickup. It was Isaac who found the dog the evening before and called Ned on the party line. Isaac slammed the door and hurried into the field.

"Dammit. I hoped I'd get through here before Isaac showed up." He rubbed a damp bandana over the back of his neck. Sweat plastered the faded blue shirt to his back. Top didn't pay much attention, watching instead the corn stalks moving behind his Grandpa.

His youthful imagination in overdrive, Top pointed the muzzle of his BB gun toward the booger-bear Ned had warned him about. It was a perfect way of avoiding the corpse at his feet. He shot at a corn stalk and cocked the gun again. Ned glanced down at his grandson, then back at Reader.

A short, talkative man, Isaac Reader moved with quick jerky motions, as if he'd been weaned on too much caffeine. He matched Ned in a way that only comes from a lifetime of farming together. Dressed in faded overalls and soft blue shirts, both men wore straw Stetsons which fell under the "absolute necessity" category like a tractor, plow, and a good sharp hoe. With the first norther of autumn, they traded the breathable straws for a warmer felt.

He talked as he bulled his way across the rows toward Ned, breaking and shoving through the cornstalks without consideration toward his own crop. "I told you on the phone last night it was something!"

Waiting until Isaac was within conversational distance, Ned drew a long-suffering breath and stared at the distant tree line along the nearby Red River. He hated to be yelled at and any conversation with Isaac drained all of his energy.

Isaac soon joined him in the rough clearing. "Gosh-a-mighty! That stinks, don't it?"

"He's pretty ripe all right."

The little famer noticed the youngster holding his BB gun. "Hidy Top. What are you doing here?" Before the youngster could answer, Isaac pointed to the dog. "Listen, I couldn't believe it when I found that thing laying here. It weren't here three days ago, because my hands chopped this entire field. I believe if they'd seen anything I'd have heard about it."

"It probably happened night before last. He swelled pretty fast in this heat."

"I don't give a fiddler's fangdang *when* it happened. I don't like *what* happened."

"Well." Ned pondered the dog's corpse.

He thought about burying it right there in the cornfield, but he knew Isaac wanted the animal gone. "I'll carry it off a ways down to the river, but don't you tell Cody how we found him. You know how he is. He doesn't need to know how his dog was killed. I'll find the right time and tell him you found it already dead somewheres down here. I don't want anyone to know about this."

"Listen, I ain't telling nobody nothin'."

The trio stood in uncomfortable silence for several long moments.

Isaac hated silence between men when, in his opinion, they should be talking. "It's a crying shame. Who would do such a thing?"

"I cain't call anybody's name right now, but I'm afraid we probably know him."

"You don't say."

"I do say. Strangers can't come in here like this without being seen by someone who'd talk about it."

"I can't believe anyone in Center Springs would do something like this. Who'd wire up a dog and burn it with a screwdriver like that? And why pull its toenails? It looks like he wanted to make a necklace out of it."

Ned agreed. "It ain't nothing but puredee meanness."

"Listen, look at it. The poor thing's been halfway skint. Why would anyone peel an animal's hide back thataway? Do you think it was alive when he did it?"

Ned cut his eyes toward Top, who didn't seem to be paying attention to their conversation. He was busy shooting at corn stalks. "I can see it right there Isaac. You don't have to tell me to look at it."

"Listen, you reckon it's them circus people over there in Hugo?" Isaac never did like the Carson and Barnes Circus people who wintered across the river in Oklahoma.

"They're not there in the summer." Ned knew Isaac had always been suspicious of circus people because he'd been afraid of clowns since they were kids running the bottoms in Lamar County.

"I know it, but there's always a few of those people still hanging around all year long. Maybe it's one of them freaks they carry with them, like the feller that bites the heads off'n live chickens."

"Now you're thinking about those little carnivals that come to town." Any other time Ned would have laughed at the familiar conversation. "The circus just has elephants and clowns and such."

Isaac shivered despite the heat. "I hate clowns. People can hide under all that paint and colored hair and you don't know what they're up to. I bet there's a lot goes on over there we don't know about. Maybe one of 'em went crazier than usual and they left him behind."

"I doubt it."

"Listen, don't tell Joshua or any of my coloreds about this. I'm 'possa have thirty hands here in a week to gather my corn and this could scare 'em off. I have enough trouble getting good hands as it is. They'll probably think its voodoo or something. You know how them niggers are. They'll think this field is haunted."

Ned nodded toward Top and frowned, hoping the man would get his intent. "Joshua is as Baptist as you are, Isaac. His mama got the name from the Book of Joshua in the same Bible you carry in your hand to the *white* Baptist church every Sunday. Besides, they're just folks like you and me, only their skin is a different color."

"Well, listen, I don't care. All I know is that

none of his people need to hear about this. They'll think the bogey-man lives out here and then I can't get anyone to ever hoe this field again."

"You're right. No one needs to know, black or white. I won't tell anyone, and you don't neither. Neither will Top, will you?"

"Nossir." Top pointed his air rifle toward the now still corn stalks and pulled the trigger. Satisfied with the snap, he cocked the rifle again. Neither farmer paid any attention to the youngster's shot.

Suddenly tired, Ned didn't want to talk any longer while stewing in the disgusting odor. He drew a 'toe sack out of his back pocket and handed it to Isaac. "I'll have to study on this some more. Here, hold this open."

Isaac knelt, making a face at the odor of decay. Ned took a long piece of bailing wire out of his pocket and looped it around the dog's hind feet, then used both callused hands to lift the dog's body into the sack. Isaac waved flies away from his head. One flew into a nostril and he jerked back in revulsion, shuddering and shaking his head. He gagged for a moment and then held the sack open.

Top giggled at the sight.

The loose weave of the burlap was no relief from the stench that settled deep into their sinuses. The shade called as they filed down the rows, Ned silently leading the way. Isaac followed, staring intently at the dry ground. Top brought up the rear, turning around now and then to be sure whatever had been moving in the corn wasn't coming after them. It was fun to pretend Indians were stalking the trio of pioneers as they made their way though the wilderness.

In the shade, Ned settled the sack gently beside the tree and exchanged the hoe for a shovel from his cluttered truck bed. Much to Isaac's agitation, Ned dug a hole in the soft sand.

"I thought you were gonna take him down to the river."

"I thought about it, but it's too hot to go off down there. Burying him here in the shade won't hurt nothing at all." Ned lowered the dog gently into the bottom of the hole.

"Well, I declare. I could have done the same thing myself."

"But you didn't."

Ned was thankful that Isaac had called when he found the dog. The scrap of paper would have probably been overlooked by anyone else, putting Ned's quiet investigation one more step behind. Finished, he refilled the hole and kicked at the sand around until it looked relatively normal.

Sweating profusely despite the shade, Ned stepped over to a hand water pump jutting three feet above the ground and primed it with leaf-stained water from a nearby rusty barrel. The water pump had been there most of his life, a place to get a drink during a hot day or to put fresh water into an overheating engine.

He worked the handle until pure cold water gurgled up from below. He immediately felt cooler after rinsing his sweaty face in the icy water, then handed Top a dipper. "You want a cold drink of water?"

"Yessir." Top held the dipper under the stream.

Isaac couldn't take his eyes off the drying sand of the fresh grave.

Finished, Top handed the dipper to Isaac. "Can I pump it for you Mr. Ike?"

"Sure."

Top used both hands to work the handle.

"Now I mean it, Ike." Ned dried his hat band with a bandana and put the Stetson back on his bald head. "Don't you say anything about this here killing or what we found today. No one needs to know but us. I'll tell Donald and Judge Rains later, but it don't go no farther."

For the past three years Sheriff Donald Griffin served the office, but Ned had little use for the man. Griffin was more politician than lawman and Ned considered him a criminal to boot.

In his opinion, there was nothing worse than a crooked lawman.

Ned intended to watch Sheriff Griffin as closely as possible, especially since he was a first cousin to the most notorious former sheriff in Lamar County history, Delbert Poole.

Judge O.C. Rains was the cantankerous county judge and a good friend to Ned Parker. The white-haired old man scared Isaac more than clowns. Using his name was a calculated move to quiet the farmer's loose tongue, though it probably wouldn't last. Isaac might keep his mouth closed for a day or two, but sooner or later he'd mention it up at the general store, or at the domino hall next door, and then it would be all over the county.

"Listen, I won't sleep a wink now for worrying. I reckon I'll need to keep the shotgun beside the bed for the next few nights." The introduction of a new idea on a subject often led Isaac into fits of worry that lasted for months.

"Well, it never hurts to be ready." Ned absently toed the dirt, watching a red harvester ant search for a way around his brogan.

"Listen. I heard Top here had come to live with you and Miss Becky."

"He sure did." Ned flashed his grandson a quick smile, though he didn't intend to get into his personal business. He was glad Top hadn't offered an explanation. Youngsters needed to stay out of adult conversations, in his opinion.

Isaac waited, hoping Ned might offer more information. When that failed, he tried tact. "Well, y'all will get a kick out of such a good-looking grand-boy."

"You're right." Ned opened the driver's door of his truck and put one foot on the chipped running board. "Get in son. Ike, let me know if you find anything else." Top trotted around the truck and climbed onto the dusty seat.

Four rows away, restless fingers dug into the sand, incredibly anxious to begin work but holding back until the time was right. Top slammed the door, and the man relaxed, melting back between the corn rows.

Isaac kicked a little more sand around on the grave. "All right, then. Listen. I'd like to know who would do something like this."

"Well, like I said. I'm afraid it's liable to be someone we know, or somebody from close around here. All I know for sure is that he's bad, Isaac, mean as a snake and you probably can't tell by looking at him."

Isaac started to say something else, but then his eyes traveled from Constable Ned Parker's pale blue eyes down to the tiny gold star pinned to his shirt beside the gallus of his overalls.

Tiny letters stamped around the small gold badge read:

Constable, Precinct 3
Center Springs, Lamar County
Texas

"Listen. You find him before he does this again, or hurts someone."

Knowing Isaac would stay and talk all afternoon if he had the chance, Ned slammed his door so it would catch and started the engine. "I intend to."

As they drove down the dirt road, Top looked through the open window at the crops drooping in the heat. "Grandpa, why would someone do that to a dog?"

Ned wished he hadn't brought the boy. It was a spur-of-the-moment decision sparked by his joy at having Top safe with him at home. And now he was obliged to hold a secret from his Uncle Cody. It was a bad start, and Ned felt a great weariness settle onto his shoulders.

"Like I told Isaac. It's nothing but meanness, I guess."

"That ain't right. You think that kind of feller would hurt a person if he took a notion?"

Ned thought about the clipping in his pocket and worried that the next victim might be a child. "He might. That's why some people just need killin'."

Chapter Three

Constable Ned Parker roused up from behind the wheel of his sedan parked in the scrub brush shaded by an oak in the Red River bottoms. He put on his straw Stetson and poked Deputy John Washington awake. “Here comes Doak. He’s driving that big block Dodge of his.”

Six-foot-six and nearly three hundred pounds of solid muscle, John Washington was the first *official* black deputy in Chisum’s history. Charged with keeping the peace among his people across the railroad tracks, his deep voice rumbled when provoked, warning of thunderheads on the horizon.

Big John shook off the late evening drowsiness and looked through the dusty windshield. He was startled at the whiskey runner’s speed. “By dog, he’s moving.”

“Doak likes to drive fast.”

Doak barely slowed as the two-rut track bent at a ninety-degree turn to the left between two cotton fields. The Dodge fishtailed in the dust and then accelerated on the straightaway. Twenty seconds later, he slid through a right to bring him directly toward Ned's ambush at the narrow plank bridge across a deep ditch.

"Here we go." Ned started the engine.

Doak was well past Constable Raymond Chase's patrol car hidden in the brush before he realized the Law had found him. Expecting Raymond to pull his Pontiac in behind for a chase, Doak downshifted, relying on the faster engine to outrun the lawman.

On the other side of the ditch, Ned's car shot out of the thicket at the last possible moment and slid to a stop to block the road. He killed the engine, opened the door in one fluid motion and used the sedan for cover.

Big John stepped out of the passenger door with a pump shotgun in his hands and moved quickly behind the car.

Doak stood on the brakes and steered right toward the cotton field, to make a run for the woods. He'd lose the car and the whiskey, but he was confident he could elude Ned and his deputies on foot, once he reached the safety of the thickly timbered bottoms.

For one brief moment Ned wasn't sure Doak was going to stop in time, thinking he'd lose control in the soft sand and dive nose-first into the ditch. But Doak was an experienced driver and he fought the wheel until the heavy Dodge slid to a dusty halt only feet from the bridge. He and Ned stared at each other through the bug-splattered windshield. Then the cloud of dust enveloped them all.

Ned waited patiently.

Doak shifted into first and popped the clutch in a last attempt to escape. His rear wheels dug into the loose soil, shooting dirt high into the air. Doak thought he'd make it, but he'd forgotten about Raymond behind him, who quickly punched the accelerator and clipped the Dodge's bumper, knocking the car completely around. It dropped tail-first into the dry ditch.

Ned stepped out from behind his sedan. "Go on and get out. You're buried to the hubs."

Doak opened his door and jumped out to run.

"Stop it! You know it's too hot for me to be chasing you and I'm too damned fat. Besides, you ain't gonna outrun this pistol anyway. Holler calf-rope and let's get this over with so we can get back in the shade."

The whiskey runner still wasn't convinced the chase was finished until he saw the twelve-gauge in Big John's hands and the look in his eyes. He knew the deputy wouldn't hesitate to shoot. He turned his head back toward Raymond, and then sighed. "Dammit, Ned. How'd you find me?"

"Don't matter none. Walk over there to Raymond and let him put the cuffs on you."

As a last act of defiance, Doak simply turned and laced his fingers behind his back. The young constable slid down in the draw and quickly snapped the cuffs on Doak's grimy wrists.

"Dammit, boy, them cuffs are too tight."

"We'll loosen them up some in a minute, if one of us thought to bring a key," Ned said from his side of the ditch.

Doak looked at the ground, dejected. When Big John saw the prisoner wasn't going to resist, he returned to Ned's car, opened the trunk, and traded the shotgun for a crowbar. He picked his way down the sandy embankment and put his hand against Doak's trunk lid, leaving a clear palm print in the dust.

"You got the keys to this trunk?"

"I wouldn't give them to you if I did, Washington. I don't deal with nigger lawmen."

Raymond casually reached out and thumped Doak behind the ear with the lead weighted sap from his back pocket. Raymond didn't hit him hard, but it was enough to glaze his eyes. A little harder and he would have been out like a light. The prisoner sagged against the car.

"Mind your manners." Raymond waited, hoping he could use the sap again. He pulled Doak out of the ditch to Ned's car.

Like a man about to open a Christmas present, Big John smiled as he wedged the flat end of the iron bar under the trunk's lock. He gave it a heave. The lock resisted for a moment, but when John's thick shoulders flexed, it popped open and the lid rose with a metallic groan. The sharp, raw smell of white lightning filled the air. John flashed a wide grin when he reached in and held up a jug of clear liquid.

"You ain't haulin' spring water, are you Doak?"

Ned joined him in the ditch, getting the cuffs of his dress pants full of dirt. He peered into the trunk. "Lordy mercy. Looks to me like you had two dozen gallons of white lightning in here. Too bad we broke most of your stock. O.C.'s gonna love this."

"That ain't mine, and it ain't enough for you to arrest me."

"What's there is against the law."

"I just have it."

"Naw, you're carrying it to sell."

Doak didn't say another word as John rummaged through the trunk. "All them other jugs are broke."

"Well, the one in your hand ain't." When

they found nothing else, Ned struggled back up the shallow bank and rejoined Raymond and his prisoner. "All right. You're going to jail, so why don't you make it easy on yourself and tell me about your still."

"Ain't no still."

"I tol' you he wouldn't say nothin'." John looked into the open window to check the back seat. "Doak's bottling this stuff from a spring in the ground. Tell us where it is and we can get rich selling natural spring whiskey."

"Screw you, you black bast…"

Raymond applied his sap a second time. The impact sent the whiskey runner to his knees. "I already told you to watch your mouth."

"Don't kill him." Ned put a hand under Doak's arm and lifted him upright. "You clear?"

Doak squinted to focus on the constable. He flipped his greasy hair out of his eyes. "Goddamn!" He shook his head to move the fuzz and swayed for a moment. "Yeah, I'm clear. But this half-pint son-of-bitch is going to give me brain damage if he don't quit beatin' on me."

Raymond snickered. "You ain't been beat, yet, but I'd enjoy the opportunity."

John swallowed an almost overwhelming urge to climb the bank and use his own sap on the side of *Raymond's* head so he could see how it felt.

Raised on the south side of the tracks, John was no stranger to brutality from white lawmen and he had no interest seeing anyone mistreated; red, black or white.

"You gonna tell us where your still is?" Ned waited, but only the cicadas answered from the surrounding trees while Doak stared sullenly at the ground. "Don't matter none. After last night's shower, there's only one set of tracks I can see right now and they lead right back to where we want to go, so I reckon we'll follow them.

"Raymond, radio Judge Rains and tell him we have Doak in custody and we're going on up to the still. Tell him where we are so he can have Sheriff Griffin send somebody out to pick up this prisoner. I think we're gonna need people to help carry and inventory the evidence, too."

"Shouldn't it be the other way around, so Griffin can tell the judge?"

"Probably, but I want you to radio O.C. first, like I said."

Raymond shrugged and led the prisoner to his car, shoving him none too gently into the back seat. Doak wasn't any trouble, because his head was hurting too bad and he knew tomorrow would bring one mother of a headache.

Masking his emotions, John turned and pitched the crowbar into Ned's open trunk. He unscrewed the ring from his own Mason jar and took a long drink of tepid water, trying to contain his anger. When he was finished, John slammed the trunk lid down and rejoined Ned.

Oblivious to the feelings he'd awakened in the deputy, Constable Chase keyed the Motorola and reported their arrest to Judge Rains. The procedure was completely backward, but Ned had no use for the sheriff and usually communicated with him only through his old friend O.C. Rains.

Ned had a plan mapped out by the time he rejoined them. "Raymond, you stay here with the prisoner until another car arrives. But keep your eyes open. I don't know how many men Doak has working for him. There might be a dozen or so bad outlaws out here for all I know. Don't let anyone pass in any direction unless they have a star pinned on their chest. Now, go on while me and John go find the still."

"Yessir." He left and backed his car into the trees. John watched to see if he was going to hit his prisoner again, intending to put a stop to it, but Raymond only killed the engine and leaned back to wait.

The late evening light was going fast and Ned wanted to get finished before darkness arrived. "We need to git."

They drove slowly toward the thick line of

trees in the river bottom, following Doak's fresh tire tracks in the dirt. The light summer shower the night before left the road clear of any other tracks.

In his rearview mirror, Ned saw Raymond get out of the car and close the door. He hoped the deputy would crack the windows later to vent the car, even though it wouldn't hurt Doak to sweat a little so late in the day. It might steam some information out of him.

John looked back over his shoulder. "Hope he don't cook Doak."

"I don't care if he does."

"He's a little too free with that sap."

Ned cut his eyes toward John. "He hits pretty fast. I'll speak to him about it later."

Big John only nodded. "I's just saying."

Raymond's free use of the sap tapped memories a long time buried. Though John had no problem with using force when necessary, he felt Raymond was a little to relaxed when it came to whacking at a rowdy drunk or an uncooperative citizen.

The tracks turned eastward across an alfalfa meadow. Ned drove slowly to avoid raising too much dust and giving themselves away, if anyone was looking.

After another mile, the brush thickened and they lost the trail. John got out and walked a zig-zag pattern until he found the faint marks through the dusty grass. He got back in and they bumped slowly through a line of trees and across a small glade. Past a downed barbed-wire fence, the almost invisible tracks pointed like an arrow toward the rapidly darkening woods.

Ned killed the engine at the edge of the thick woods near the river. The grass was crushed in a wide area and it was clear that other vehicles had parked there recently. Though the lane continued through the trees, he knew better than to drive any further.

"I smell smoke, so we're close."

John's sweaty face was blank as he quietly closed his door. Ned did the same and opened the trunk. John picked up a shotgun and handed Ned a double-bit ax.

Ned adjusted the pistol hanging on his belt, set his hat and wiped sweat from his own eyes. "Stay close until we see the still."

"Then I'll slip around the other side." John gently pulled the slide on the pump shotgun and checked for a gleam of brass. Satisfied, he slid it back into position with a quiet snick.

After working together for years, the lawmen operated without needless conversation. They crept into the gloom of the woods, following a well-worn game trail. The wood smoke lay close to the ground, mixing with the smells of rotting leaves, damp earth, and living greenery. They slipped through the understory plants until Ned saw a flicker of firelight from a small clearing thirty yards away.

He turned, but John had already vanished off the trail. Ned waited, giving the big deputy time to make his way around the camp. He watched the activity around the boiler in the clearing's center. To his right in front of a tattered canvas tent, a heavyset middle-aged man in faded overalls and a flop brimmed hat sat on a wooden box, carefully filling the reservoir of a Coleman lantern. A similarly dressed slender young man tended the fire.

Nearby, steam rose from the end of a shiny spiral of new copper tubing emerging from the boiler. Clear liquid dripped into a half-full gallon jug. Ned nodded when he saw the equipment. Large piles of split wood and crates of glass jars filled the clearing.

A fox squirrel overhead decided it didn't like the two strangers moving through the woods. The sudden ruckus caused by its scolding gave them away, and Ned couldn't wait any longer. When the moonshiners looked up at the sound, Ned drew his revolver and stepped to the clearing's edge, partially protected by a large tree trunk.

"Throw up your hands, boys!"

The younger man reacted with surprising speed. He dropped an armload of wood and bolted toward the woods. A massive arm shot out from the shadows and clotheslined him, only yards from a successful escape. His feet rose head-high and he hit the ground with a solid thump, lying there without moving.

Big John stepped into the firelight and pointed his shotgun at the heavyset man on the crate. "You wanna run too?"

"Naw, and I'm proud I didn't. Ned hollered to set still, so I did." He casually leaned over to place the lantern on the ground and rested his hands on his knees.

"Keep 'em where I can see them, Tommy." Ned recognized the experienced bootlegger. Without marketable skills, Tommy spent most of his life in and out of trouble with the law.

After satisfying himself that everything was under control, John knelt to handcuff Tommy. Ned holstered his pistol and cuffed Tommy's hands behind his back. "Ain't that Doak's boy laying there?"

Tommy shifted a chew from one cheek to the other. "Yep."

"Well, they favor. He should have sense enough not to run."

"Doak always told us to run if y'all showed up, but I knew better. I figured you'd shoot."

"Might have, but he was too close to John there. Y'all are under arrest."

"I figgered. It's a shame, too. We got this still working good."

"Smells like it." Ned walked around the area, making sure no one else was hiding nearby. He kicked a scattering of wood chips and nudged a crate of whiskey with the toe of his shoe.

In the distance, a siren grew in volume.

Disgusted, Ned picked up his ax from where he'd leaned it against the tree and raked the fire out from under the boiler. "Glad we got in here when we did. Those idiots would have warned y'all in another minute. When he gets here I oughta beat the whey out of him for running a siren on a dirt road. John, we'll let Griffin's hotshot load up all this whiskey, if he don't get lost on the way."

John finished securing the still groggy youngster and joined Ned, handing him a razor sharp skinning knife. "He had this stuck in his belt."

"Y'all been poaching deer too?" The hilt was dark with what Ned knew from experience was blood.

Tommy shrugged disconsolately. "Camp meat. The boy there likes to trap, too, down there near the creek. He makes a little extra money from possum and coon hides. We ain't been hungry here, but I reckon we'll have to get used to fried baloney now."

A tingle began along Ned's back. "Well, you

won't get anything else because you've fallen in with bad company. You need to find another partner. Doak ain't nothing but trouble."

John found an empty bucket and filled it from a fifty-five-gallon barrel of water. When he drowned the scattered fire, smoke and steam filled the clearing, stinging their eyes. They kicked dirt over the blackened wood until it was completely out.

"This is the part I like." Ned hefted the ax and smiled at the boiler. Tommy watched them glumly.

As he chopped large holes in the metal to let the steaming contents spill onto the ground, Ned couldn't help but wonder if he'd stumbled onto the individual responsible for the long string of animal mutilations in the area.

Chapter Four

The streets of Chisum, Texas, bustled with Saturday business.

With his ten-year-old grandson, Top, settled on the front row of the Grand Theater with an R.C. cola and popcorn, Constable Parker stepped from the darkness of the movie house into the bright sunshine. Beside the ticket booth, he adjusted the Colt 32.20 pistol in the worn hand-tooled leather holster on his belt. Some days he carried the heavier Colt .38, but the smaller caliber usually felt a little dressier when he went to town.

When he could see without squinting, Ned ambled down the hot street and around the corner. Sweat bloomed under the arms of his blue dress shirt, and the black slacks absorbed the sidewalk's heat.

The streets of Chisum bustled with Saturday business. In direct contrast, a familiar covey of loafers visited in the shade of crepe myrtles hanging heavy with blooms in the light summer breeze, not far from the statue of a confederate soldier peering south.

"Hello, men."

"Hidy, Ned."

"Hello, Willie, how's your mama 'n 'em?"

"They're fine. Come by and see her when you get the chance. It'd tickle her to hug your neck."

"I will. I could use a few of her teacakes."

He climbed the flight of steep granite steps leading up to the brass-trimmed glass doors. Townspeople on official business passed Ned, recognizing the familiar constable elected more than two generations before, only six years after Bonnie and Clyde passed through town on their way to soak up several ounces of lead near Shreveport.

His footfalls echoed against the foyer's tiny black and white tiles. Deciding not to take the granite stairs worn by generations of feet, he stepped aboard the creaky elevator and waited for Jules to take them to the third floor.

Jules had served as the elevator man since before anyone could remember. Proud of his job, he arrived at work every day in a freshly laundered, paper-thin white shirt and a threadbare suit coat so worn that it shined.

"Afternoon, Mister Ned." The elderly black man attempted to rise from the tall wooden stool Ned gave him years earlier when he noticed the old man spent the entire day standing in the elevator's corner. It pained Ned to see a man of such advanced age resting against the wall.

By his own estimation, Jules was some years past his hundredth birthday. He once told Ned that his mama was born a slave on a plantation in southern Mississippi and he'd hit the ground about the time the Civil War began.

"Howdy Jules. Keep your seat. How's Lily?"

"Tolerable well." Jules looked up from the floor and nodded his gray head. He didn't often make eye contact with the white folks, but he felt comfortable with Ned. "She's home cookin' sweet tater pie 'cause it's her birthday." He closed the sliding door by hand and then slid the accordion safety door into place before pushing the button. The elevator groaned and jerked upward, cables rattling overhead.

"Tell her happy birthday. She must be treating you right. You look good."

"Yessir. She's a good 'un. I don't know why she took up with me, but I'm right proud she did."

Jules had outlived several wives of lesser constitution. He was particularly proud of his new wife because she knew how to cook a proper sweet potato pie.

"How many wives does this make for you now?"

"Eleven, I 'spect." Jules laughed and shook his head. "Hope nothin' happens to this 'un, 'cause I don't want to go to Glory with a dozen women awaitin' on me up there. Heaven oughta give a man some peace and quiet, if he's earned it."

They chuckled at the thought of a dozen wives to keep a man company. Jules kept his eyes on the lights and when they reached the fourth floor, he opened the metal safety gate, and then the door. He held out a hand to stop Ned for a moment while he carefully adjusted the elevator by hand to even it with the floor.

"Step off now, Mr. Ned. I'll be waitin' on you."

"See you in a minute."

"Tell Mr. O.C. hidy for me." There was no other reason for Ned to visit the fourth floor on a day when they weren't having court.

"I will."

Judge O.C. Rains glowered through brushy white eyebrows when Ned walked into the stifling office without knocking. Despite his rolled up shirtsleeves and loosened tie, O.C. sweated profusely in the sweltering office, trying to catch up on the mountain of ever-growing paperwork.

The windows in his office gaped wide to capture even the smallest breeze. The ceiling fan's weak assistance did little to move the air.

Instead of the heat, it was the flies that were

driving O.C. crazy. In an effort to save taxpayer monies, the city council refused to pay for screens on the public building, and flies buzzed in and out without impediment. O.C. kept a flyswatter close at hand and killed over a dozen that lit on his paperwork that morning.

Ned closed the office's frosted glass door with a bang, rattling the large pane of frosted glass.

"Just feel free to walk right in, Ned. There ain't no need to knock or anything." O.C. slapped his wire swatter at a particularly annoying bluebottle fly.

Ned didn't bother to answer. He threw his hat on the wooden desk and reached up to click on the dented metal outlet fan sitting atop O.C.'s filing cabinet.

"That won't do more than blow hot air. I'd have already turned it on myself if I thought it'd do any good."

Ned sat in the only chair not stacked full of law books or papers. He didn't pay any attention to the walls covered with diplomas and photographs of O.C. with several famous politicians, generals, and presidents.

"I'm glad you're here, though. A good constable oughta make a fair hand at using a flyswatter. You can help me kill some of these flies. They're worrying the piss out of me today."

"I didn't come here to kill flies, but it looks

like you're doing a pretty fair job without my help." Ned nearly smiled at the scattering of insect corpses on the polished oak floor. "I'm here because I've got a crow to pick with you."

O.C. sighed and pitched the flyswatter onto the stacks of papers on his desk. He'd been dreading Ned's visit all week. The wooden chair groaned when he leaned backward. "All right. Go to pickin'."

"How come you piddled around and let Doak Looney out of jail? I had him dead to rights with whiskey in the trunk of his car."

"I turned him loose because I didn't have enough evidence to hold him for making whiskey. You know as well as I do one little ol' gallon don't make him guilty of running a still."

"I know he was guilty of carryin' white lighting. The still was his and we both know it. The sorry son-of-a-bitch was heading into Oklahoma with it when I pulled him over. Only trouble was most of it got broke."

"He wasn't at the still. He was in the ditch. You don't have any proof that he's making whiskey in your precinct, and by law I can't hold him in jail for just having one gallon of the stuff in his car. If that was the case you'd have to arrest half the county and a right smart number of my own lawmen. Hell, Hank Willis most likely smells like whiskey right now, and he's one of my best deputies. You get Doak with a whole load in his trunk next time, or find the still with him standing there puttin' fire under it, and I'll put him in the pen. But until then I can't keep the man."

"Then you oughta shoot two or three of those sorry deputies of yours and get me some decent help so I can catch the son of a bitch."

"Yep, I ought to, but shells ain't cheap."

"Well, I tell you what, the next time I pull Doak Looney over to check him out you can bet his trunk will be packed tight."

"It better be packed with his own whiskey."

"What are you saying?"

"I'm saying he'd better be guilty on his own."

Ned felt his neck redden. "Goddammit, O.C., the man's been making whiskey every day since he was in grade school! He's even teaching his boy to run shine. I know for sure he hauled a load across the river to Hugo last month because he stopped back by the Ranchhouse and got cut up some by Frank Lightfoot boys. He wasn't healed good when we brought him to jail."

The population of Hugo in southeastern Oklahoma leaned heavily toward Indians, mostly Choctaw, Creek, and Cherokee; remnant scraps of the Five Civilized Tribes in the Indian Nations. Frank Lightfoot had been in trouble with the law since he was big enough to walk. Both Ned and

O.C. agreed that Lightfoot needed killing, but unfortunately, it hadn't happened yet.

O.C. picked up the swatter and slapped at a fly a little harder than necessary. He and Ned had been having the same arguments for the past twenty years. It was their way to clear the air. "They shoulda cut his damn throat, but it don't make any difference. When Doak needed a lawyer he called Cal Philips over here with a pocket full of money. I had to let him go, and that's it."

"Cal Philips is as crooked as Doak."

"You're right, and it galls me to know Doak is back out free and clear, but I had to set a low bond. Any judge can charge Doak Looney with possession of moonshine, but there's no way in the world we could convict him of running a still or transporting whiskey with intent to sell unless he's caught red-handed with a whole trunk load and not one...single...gallon."

"He's selling whiskey to Sugar Bear across the tracks." Ned habitually rubbed his bald head. "Then *he's* turning around and selling it in that raggedy-ass juke joint not far from Frog Flats. We both know it. John Washington told me he suspicioned what they were doing, and we're probably going over there tomorrow night to see."

"You hear what I say." O.C. waved the flyswatter at Ned to emphasize his point.

"I heard you."

They scowled at each other for a while and Ned watched a fly light on O.C.'s thinning white hair. It made him feel better. They sat in silence for a good five minutes.

"I can't *stand* Doak Looney." Ned picked up his hat to leave.

"Me, neither."

"And that slack-jawed idiot keeps cranking out the kids."

Silence again. O.C. interlocked his fingers over his stomach and rocked back and forth in his creaking chair, staring at the ceiling.

"I have something else to talk to you about." Ned glanced at the door to see if it was shut.

"What?"

"Isaac Reader found Cody's bird dog in his corn field. It was tortured and might-near skint. I'm worrying myself to death over it."

"No reason to worry over a dog."

"I'm afraid it won't be a dog or a cat or a possum next time."

O.C. raised his eyebrows in question.

"You remember a couple of years ago somebody was shooting folks' dogs and barn cats when they caught them away from home. Then there were a couple of weeks when I got calls on somebody shooting cows and horses in their pastures."

"Now I remember. But they quit after a while, even though you didn't catch whoever was doing it."

"Right. I thought we were done with it, and I reckon we were through for a while. Now I believe he's back." Ned pulled a crumpled envelope out of his coat pocket and passed it over to O.C. The faint odor of decay still lingered on the newspaper advertisement. "Take a look at this."

With two fingers, O.C. pulled the newspaper clipping out of the envelope and spread it on the scarred desk in front of him. He waved at half a dozen flies that were immediately attracted to the odor. "You don't think he'll go to killing people now, do you?"

"I don't think anything yet, except this is cranking up a notch. He's liable to do anything."

"And you don't have any idy who it is?"

"Naw. Not much to go on except footprints, clippings and dead animals."

Law work in Lamar County usually amounted to whiskey stills, minor theft, drunks and family disputes, with an occasional act of amorous rage thrown in for good measure with some husband, wife or boyfriend getting worked over with an ax handle. Brutality wasn't new ground for either man, but neither had seen anything like the methodical cruelty of torturing and burning animals alive.

Ned watched flies bang softly against the glass transom above the door. "I'm gonna kick around a little bit, and see if any of the other boys have run onto anything like this. I'm taking Top to the rodeo tonight, too. I might hear something there. I'll try to find Big John in a day or two to see if he's heard anything from his people."

The almost mythical deputy operated virtually without oversight south of the tracks.

"Let me know what John says." O.C. studied the stained advertisement centered on his desk and wondering how anyone could be mean to animals and kids. "He may have heard something. It's liable to be one of his people and they're not talking."

"I will. How's Catherine doing?"

O.C.'s wife Catherine was chronically ill with a variety of maladies. "Purty good. She had a spell Wednesday night and I had to call Miss Sweet. She came over and set with her for a while. I don't know what she gave Catherine, something to swaller and a poultice, but she got easy toward morning."

Miss Sweet was one of John Washington's elderly aunts. Her daddy nicknamed his twin girls Sweet Cakes and Sugar Pie. But through the years, they became Sweet and Sugar. Both round and friendly grandmothers did a right smart amount of doctoring when anyone called. They mostly ministered to the colored folks on the south side of the tracks, folks who had more faith in them and their home remedies than in doctors and their expensive medicines. But Ned and O.C. had known them since they were kids. They knew their remedies worked.

"Catherine has some trouble breathing sometimes, doesn't she?'

"Yep. She has a little touch of the asthma. I think there's something down deep in her chest, but she won't let me take her to Doc Townsend. She says its nothing, but I don't believe she knows what she's talking about."

"Maybe I'll talk to Miss Sweet and see if she can help Top. He has the worst case of asthma I've ever seen. He'll probably have some trouble since he's moved up here with us, especially around ginning time."

Most people wanted to call the boy Cotton, for his thick mop of white hair, but he was named after his great-uncle, Texas Orrin Parker and shortened to Top.

"He's a keeper. Bring him by when you get the chance. One morning here pretty soon we'll go catch us a mess of catfish."

Ned's black dress shoes squeaked as he stood and shifted his weight. "Sounds like a good idea. You going to the rodeo tonight? They've got the fairgrounds open, too."

"I might drop by to see the calf scramble. Those kids chasing that calf always tickles me."

"I like to watch that little monkey riding the dog while it herds sheep across the arena. The poor little feller looks like he's scared to death and he just hangs on for dear life." They chuckled at the thought of the monkey holding grimly onto the dog's shoulder harness. Ned ran his hat brim through his fingers. "Well anyway, I'll be there."

"You sure you don't want to kill a few flies before you leave?" O.C. smacked another.

"Nope. I got plenty to kill at home, if I'm of a mind."

Chapter Five

On that Saturday morning when I was ten years old, Grandpa Ned dropped me off at the show about thirty minutes after the picture started, but I was used to it. I was grown before I ever saw a movie from the beginning. Even when I went with my girl cousin Pepper, the adults didn't pay any attention to the picture's start time. Uncle James bought our tickets and we all walked right in and watched the movie through the end. After the reel change, the cartoon and coming attractions, we watched to the part where we came in, and then left.

By the time I looked up and saw Grandpa Ned standing in the darkness, still wearing his hat and motioning for me to leave, I'd already seen Elvis and Ann Margaret in the same dance scene twice. I picked up my popcorn box and followed him outside.

It hadn't cooled off much, though it was close to dark. My grandmother Miss Becky, Aunt Ida Belle, and my cousin Pepper were waiting for us under the flashing marquee. Miss Becky was five-foot-four and a hundred pounds soaking wet. Five pounds was long hair in a bun on the back of her head.

I usually didn't have much to say to Aunt Ida Belle, even though she did all right by me. She was a stout woman who crinkled her eyes when she grinned. She gave me a little pat on the shoulder. Uncle James wasn't with them and sent word from his hardware store that he'd meet us at the rodeo grounds.

Pepper was my age, but she had a mouth on her like a sailor. Grandpa Ned called her a pistol. Blue eyes like Grandpa's and her long brown hair pulled back in a ponytail, she looked much older than our ten years.

I hadn't seen my tomboy cousin in a while, so I punched her shoulder and she hammered me back so hard my arm ached. She took my leftover popcorn like I'd offered it and stuffed a big handful into her mouth. I didn't care. I was about full up, anyway.

The adults finally finished talking and Pepper went with me and Grandpa in his '41 Chevy coupe while Miss Becky rode with Aunt Ida Belle so they could talk about woman stuff. Fifteen minutes later Grandpa parked in the grass lot beside the rodeo grounds and we climbed out. The sun dropped completely below the trees beyond the fairgrounds, and the carnival's gaudy flashing lights lit the sky.

The Tilt-&-Whirl made whooshing noises as it went round and round. Screams mixed with other carnival sounds of people having fun. I stopped for a moment in the dark lot to soak up the smell of fried foods and cotton candy mixed with the aroma of horses and manure.

Cowgirls with long hair and sparkling shirts walked their horses through the rows of cars and trucks parked on the grass, visiting with boys from the local farms and ranches while they unloaded their own mounts to ride in the Grand Entry. Miss Becky and Aunt Ida Belle arrived and joined several town ladies for a visit beside the cinderblock building where they sold tickets.

Grandpa stopped us beside the entrance gate. "There's Deputy Washington. Y'all hold up a few minutes while I talk to him about something."

I was excited to see Mister John. I hadn't been around the big deputy very much, but he made a fuss every time he saw me.

"Hidy, Mister Ned." John strolled up in his loose-jointed way, grinning down at us kids. He grabbed me under the arms and set me on his wide shoulder. My stomach flip-flopped. I could feel his huge muscles bunch under his pressed uniform shirt. No carnival ride on the midway was as exciting as sitting on John's massive shoulder high above the ground. I tried to see the lights in Hugo, Oklahoma, far to the north.

Pepper looked up at me, annoyed. She would have given anything to be lifted up, also. But there were limits to such things. Grandpa Ned wouldn't have cared if Big John hoisted her up to his shoulder, but you can bet someone would have seen it and started rumors about the black deputy picking up little white girls.

Instead, John ruffled Pepper's hair with his fingertips. "Evenin', Miss Pepper." She smiled and took his big hand in hers.

Grandpa watched both white and colored people funneling into the little midway. "Anything going on this evening?"

"Naw. I'm here making sure none of my people were over here acting the fool tonight."

"Well, it's good to see you. I wanted to talk to you anyway. Let's go over and listen to the Motorola for a spell. I need to ask you something."

He was talking about the police radio under the dash in his Chevy. Grandpa spent hours parked beside the house after dark, listening to radio traffic and watching the lights on the highway as cars hissed over the Sanders Creek Bridge a mile away. He always said a crook could outrun his Chevy, but no one could outrun his Motorola.

John swung me back to the ground. "Y'all look like you could use a snow cone." He raised his eyebrows at Grandpa, who nodded again. John reached into the pocket of his khakis and held out a handful of change. "Go get you a couple of strawberries."

Pepper squealed and jumped. I took two dimes from the scattering of coins in his palm, thanked him and we left for the concession stand. Pepper almost ran ahead, but I held back, watching Grandpa and John disappear into the dark parking lot.

"Come on." I tucked the Liberty Heads in my jeans and pulled her toward the parked trucks and cars.

"What are you doing?" She jerked her arm away. "Dammit! You're gonna get us in trouble. Let's go get a snow cone."

"I want to hear what they're talking about. When was the last time Grandpa just turned us loose like this and went off to talk with Mr. John?"

She hesitated. "Never. Now give me my damn dime."

"Nope. Come on. Something's got to be up. I'll give it to you when we get back."

"You fixin' to sneak up and eavesdrop?"

"It'll be fun."

She thought for a moment and grinned.

"Grandpa will give us an ass-whoopin' if he catches us."

"He won't." I led the way from the concession stand's lights. We took a route to keep several rows of cars between Grandpa and us.

When we drew close, I dropped to my knees and motioned for Pepper to do the same. We crawled through the dead grass and finally stopped not far away, with a pickup between us.

The dusty grass tightened my lungs. For years I was the only kid in our part of Texas to carry what we called my puffer, an awkward contraption designed to shoot vaporized medicine deep into my chest. I didn't go anywhere without it. I pulled out the plug in the nozzle, put it in my mouth and gave the bulb a squeeze. My lungs tickled and in seconds I could draw a deep breath.

Pepper watched me and started to get mad. "Dammit, you're getting clogged up and I'm getting my jeans all dirty. I'm gonna kill you."

"You won't have to if Grandpa hears us—he'll do it. Shut up."

In the shadows far away from the rodeo arena, I saw John's head above the car roofs. Enough light reached them so I could make out their features. "Nossir, Mr. Ned. I haven't heard about anyone killin' animals. You say they've been tortured?"

"Something like this happened off and on a

while back, but then it stopped for a couple of years. Now he's back and what was done to that poor dog was pitiful. Somebody jobbed a screwdriver in him a dozen times at least, and that wasn't the worst part."

"Lordy. You think it was coloreds or white folks?"

"He could be green for all I know. I'm going to check across the river in Hugo, but I don't reckon they'll be much help there, either."

"*Might* be an Indian." John considered the possibility.

I turned to Pepper. "Did you hear what he said? Indians could be getting ready to torture people." I had visions of feathers and tomahawks.

Grandpa took off his hat and wiped his head. "It might be anyone. Look around next time you're at Sugar Bear's joint."

"How many folks in Center Springs know?"

"Half a dozen. But Isaac Reader knows. I figured he'd let it slip at the domino hall, but he surprised me so far. I imagine it'll be on the party line pretty quick, though."

"I hope it ain't field hands. It could be some poor folks living down in the bottoms, though, but whoever they are, my people don't need that kind of attention."

"I'm more worried about where it's going." Grandpa told him about finding scraps of paper and advertisements.

The hair on the back of my neck stood up. This was a real police case Grandpa was working on, not some family argument in the middle of the night, or a drunk weaving down the highway. For the first time in my life, I realized Grandpa Ned was actually the Law, like Broderick Crawford on Highway Patrol. All those late-night phone calls were real police work.

I grinned wide when I realized I'd been on an actual case in Isaac Reader's cornfield.

Pepper tugged my arm. "Let's go! I keep smelling horse shit."

"That's 'cause there's a pile right next to your hand." When I turned back I could only catch part of the conversation because someone drove by with the car radio blaring.

"...be getting worse. I'll check around for you Mr. Ned. What you want me to do if I find out who it is?"

"Well. Tell me if he's white and I'll have O.C. write up a warrant. Y'all take care of it if he's colored. But think about this, I'm afraid he might start looking for a young 'un pretty soon and I can't take it if he hurts a kid. We need to stop him."

Pepper was shocked and we were both

suddenly very scared. "Shitfire. Kids? There's somebody after kids?"

"Shhhh."

Without another word, Grandpa and Mister John started walking back toward the rodeo grounds. I waited for another minute and slowly peeked over the truck bed. They stopped by the main gate to visit with a family on the way into the arena.

"They're gone." I knelt back down to dig the puffer out of my jean pocket and took another deep breath. Still on her knees, Pepper waited until I was finished, then doubled up her fist and hit me so hard on the side of the head the impact thumped my noggin into the truck beside us.

"Don't you *ever* get me into something like that again, dammit! Shitfire! This ain't anything like fun. Look at my jeans."

"Mine look that way all the time." I rubbed both sides of my Boy's Regular haircut. My head throbbed.

"Not in town."

"Didn't you hear? They're looking for a dog murderer. It may be a wild Indian and he may be fixin' to kill a person next."

"I don't care." She stood and stalked toward the lights. I followed at a distance in case she decided to whop me again. We were almost to the entrance when a voice stopped us.

"Howdy, Top."

We turned, thinking Grandpa doubled back on us. I was in for a surprise.

"Uncle Cody!"

In his mid-twenties, my favorite black sheep relative was something of a Choctaw outlaw, but because he ran a beer joint called Sonny's on the Oklahoma bank of the Red River. He called the little cluster of joints Juarez, after the Mexican dives south of the Rio Grande.

He leaned back on the fender of his shiny, brand-spanking new 1964 red-and-white El Camino, one pointy cowboy boot propped on the front bumper. Those half-breed trucks were new on the market, and I'd only seen them advertised on television. That low sporty truck made me feel different when I looked at it.

"Hey, gal."

"Hidy, Cody." Pepper gave him a wide grin. Most kids called him by his first name.

Uncle Cody tipped his straw hat back and stuck out his hand at me to shake like a man. Dark hair curled over his forehead and hung over his collar. The excitement of seeing him made me jittery all over. I wished I'd worn my own hat.

"Squeeze like I taught you, I don't shake hands with no sissies." I showered down with all my strength and he squeezed back. "That's the way."

My ears moved toward the back of my head as I grinned even wider. I loved Uncle Cody. He'd been gone for a while, to a country called Viet Nam where a bunch of people were fighting. A rocket shot down his helicopter while he was over there. It crashed in the jungle and only three Green Berets survived. No one knew where they were, and there hadn't been time to radio, so he and his buddies were on their own.

Led by my half-Choctaw uncle, with nothing more than pistols and what they had in their pockets, they struck off through the jungle. For the next twelve days, they dodged the bad guys, drank muddy river water and traveled at night by compass until they found a Vietnamese family who agreed to smuggle them downriver in the bottom of one of them flat boats they called a sampan. Lying under the boat's floorboards in the mud and filth, they hid from the Viet Cong soldiers who stopped them not five miles from the American lines, but the Vietnamese father convinced them that they hadn't seen any Americans.

After his tour, Cody brought back stories about little men in black pajamas and the phrase "it's heating up over there." I still hadn't figured out what he meant. Two months after turning in his uniform, he bought Sonny's honky-tonk, much to Miss Becky's horror.

"You kids having a big time?" He squinted through the smoke from a cigarette dangling in the corner of his mouth.

"We ain't hardly been here but a few minutes." I started to look at the El Camino more closely when something moved on the other side of Cody and I saw somebody was with him. I stopped and immediately knew Miss Becky wouldn't approve of her. The woman's red hair was thick, long and wavy. She wore red lipstick to match. I'd never seen a woman packed into such tight jeans, and the shirt she wore strained at the top buttons.

Cody cupped his cigarette. "You gonna hug me, Pepper?" She wrapped her arms around his neck and he raised her off her feet with his left arm. He wooled her around some and got Pepper to giggling, and that's when I recognized the lady as Calvin Williams' wife, Norma.

I gave a start. Somehow even back then I knew Calvin didn't know she was there. "Hello, Top." Her voice was soft as velvet. "I hear you moved in to stay."

Forgetting how to speak, I made a stuttering noise and stared at the dirt at my feet.

Pepper on the other hand bristled when Cody put her back down. It must have been some sort of woman thing. "You already get the supper dishes done, Norma?"

Cody laughed, and I smelled whiskey and saw the crows feet in the corners of his eyes. In the last few months I'd spent lots of time staring in the mirror, trying to make my eyes crinkle like his. I hoped some day they would. Then I'd look as cool as Cody in a Stetson, tilted back on my head.

Norma smiled at Pepper's attack. "No, honey, Cody took me to Reeves' café to eat, so I didn't have to wash dishes tonight."

"Calvin meeting y'all here?"

"You gonna ride a bull tonight, Top?" Cody winked at me, trying to head off another snipe.

"Naw. I'm just watching. I want to see *you* ride."

Pepper continued to glare up at Norma like she owed her money. I had a feeling Norma wasn't a stranger to that same look on women much older, and with much more to lose. She took it in stride and didn't react.

"We better go," Pepper finally said. "Grandpa's probably waiting."

Cody nodded. "That's a good idea. They're forming up for the Grand Entry right now. I'll drop by Uncle Ned's and see you in day or two, kids. We'll catch a few crappie or go dove hunting when season opens." The paper entry number pinned to the back of his shirt flapped in the breeze.

"Bye, Top." Norma tilted her head toward Pepper. "I'll see y'all later, hon."

A horse and rider trotted past. Cody dropped his cigarette butt on the ground, crushed it out, and blew smoke out of his nose. Norma took his arm and they bumped hips as they walked toward the rodeo grounds.

Norma threw her head back and laughed at something Cody whispered in her ear. It gave me a funny feeling in the pit of my stomach.

Pepper was still mad. "She's a married woman. If Calvin knew she was here with Cody, there'd be a killing." I half listened as we wove through the horses and cowboys on our way to the concession stand.

I thought about Cody. He was tough enough to fight little men in pajamas and run a beer joint in Juarez and ride in rodeos, so I knew he wouldn't worry too much about getting killed in Chisum. Calvin Williams was tough, but he wasn't any match for my Uncle Cody.

"So? It ain't none of my business, or yours, neither."

"You men are all alike."

I didn't pay any attention because my head was full of horses, dog killers, Cody, and redheads with smoky voices. I took another pull off my puffer, and we headed for the grandstands.

Chapter Six

Big John watched Ned and the kids walk through the gate into the rodeo grounds and turned to see a young gaggle of his own people pass on their way to the carnival. He walked toward the bright, flickering midway lights in his easy way.

A young black man waved a greeting. "Mister John."

John slapped the youngster on the back with a big hand and joined the moving crowd. "C.J., y'all all right this evenin'?"

"Yessir," said a willowy girl. "You here for the carnival? I know you ain't interested in the rodeo."

They laughed at the joke.

"You right, Miss Ruby Jean. I'm here to keep an eye on y'all."

"We'll behave," she answered.

"I know you will." John waved goodbye and peeled off as the group moved toward the Milk Bottle Throw. He knew what it took to be a good lawman, because for years he'd watched his dad, One-Arm George, act as the unofficial Colored Law south of the tracks in Chisum.

He also knew the struggle his dad suffered to keep the Negro population safe so many years ago.

On a moonlit night in 1934, One-Arm George stood in the shadows as six heavily armed white lawmen waited in the dirt front yard of an illegal juke joint on the colored side of the tracks.

Sheriff Delbert Poole and his men watched the customers through an open window. Music filled the yard, and he recognized the song called Red River Blues. It had recently gained popularity on the colored side of the tracks. "I've had enough shit out of you niggers! And I'm tired of coming over here. Y'all send out that feller who brought the young white gal in here tonight!"

George, a deacon in the Mt. Holiness Baptist Church, recognized some of his own neighbors in the crowd milling uncertainly inside.

Poole had beaten him there by mere minutes after he heard an underage white girl from the north side of town was in the after-hours juke joint with a black man. George sighed when the young girl bolted through the door and around the building to disappear into the shadows. "Oh."

"Naw, that ain't enough! I done missed my supper, so I want the dumb sonofabitch that brought her down here in the first place. Send him out and the rest of you can go on home." Poole motioned for his men to spread out.

"You'll kill him," a voice called from the interior.

"We won't kill him. We're just gonna teach him right from wrong!" The deputies snickered. "Send him out right now!" Poole held his men back with one hand and fired his pistol through the upper part of the open window. Women screamed. A shot echoed from the back of the house. Poole knew this man would try the back door first, so he had a deputy waiting out back. "Butch!"

"Nawsir, he run back in!"

Before Poole could respond, a backlit shape rushed out of the front door, firing a handgun toward the lawmen. The yard instantly flickered with flashes as Poole's men opened up on the running shadow. The gunfire lasted for more than thirty seconds and when it ended, the man lay dead in the yard while several others inside the honky-tonk writhed on the floor from the deputies' missed shots.

"Dear god," One-Arm George whispered over the screaming coming from the nearby building. He dared not rush forward, because he'd only be another colored target in the heat of the moment. He waited while Poole idly toed the fallen man.

"Now then, y'all remember this night and who y'are. I don't intend to come back over here again for such nonsense." Satisfied, Poole motioned for his men to climb into their cars and with barely a backward glance, they left the carnage behind.

George waited until they were gone before finally stepping out to help the wounded. By the time they'd tended to the living and removed the dead, he'd come to a conclusion. Someone had to take control.

George had an idea to calm the fears of the white population and gain control of the increasing number of incidents occurring on his side of the tracks. Allowing the people in their community to do as they wished only invited trouble from the suspicious white side of town.

The shooting electrified both sides of the tracks and for the next few days tensions ran high as every male in town, black or white, carried a gun…just in case.

Late one night a week later, after slipping down dirt back alleys and staying to the side streets in the white part of town, One-Arm George appeared at Sheriff Poole's back door, historically the appropriate place for business with a Negro man, but a dangerous place to be after dark.

The angry sounds of an argument met George in the unfenced back yard. He hesitated on the stoop until the sound of an open-handed slap echoed sharply through an open window and made his decision for him. A woman sobbed softly, and then became silent. George knocked on the screen door and then backed several steps away so the light spilling from the frame house could light him clearly.

A full thirty seconds passed before the door cracked open. Not recognizing the visitor, Poole almost shot the black man for standing there so late at night, until he recognized George by his pinned-up sleeve. Poole held a revolver beside his leg, but didn't lower the hammer.

"Sheriff, it's me, George Washington. Can I speak to ya for a minute please suh?"

"George, what the hell are you doing in my back yard this time of night? Have you lost your damned mind? You know better. You ain't got no business in this part of town. The first white man with a pistol in his belt is liable to shoot you."

One-Arm George stared at the ground. "Yessir. Sheriff, I don't mean nothin' by being here. I come to see if you'd let me help you."

"What can you do for me? Are you alone?" Poole peered suspiciously into the darkness beyond the splash of light spilling from the open doorway.

"Yessir. I needed to talk for a minute."

Still not sure he wasn't being set up for a

killing, Poole looked side to side and then stepped outside to talk. There was no thought of inviting George into the house. Behind him, George saw Poole's pretty wife standing ramrod straight at the kitchen table, tears running down her cheeks.

George knew Martha as the daughter of Chisum's well-known funeral home director, who hired one of George's cousins as a housekeeper. Martha married Poole against her daddy's wishes, and George once overheard the man complaining about the marriage and Poole's abuse of his young wife.

A fat baby sat on the wood floor at her feet, playing with a metal stew pot. Martha picked up the child and turned her back to the men outside, burying her face against the tiny body.

"What do you want?" In his undershirt, Poole kept the pistol beside his leg, always suspicious of people, and even more so in his own dark backyard.

One-Arm George nervously looked at the ground and then talked to the backlit shadow before him. "Sheriff, I'm not here to speak about what happened 't'other night at that ol' joint. That sorry fool carryin' on with that young gal shouldn't have messed with your men, but I think I have a way to stop such foolishness in our part of town, if you'll let me."

Poole didn't really care one way or the other,

but One-Arm George's presence in his neighborhood was something special. With his free hand, he scratched his opposite arm pit. "I'm listening."

"We ain't got no real full-time colored law on our side, Sheriff, and because of that, y'all have to come down every now and then. We've been kindly taking care of our business for the most part, but if you'll let me keep an eye on things, we'll keep our own trouble to ourselves. That way I can promise none of my people will cause problems in your part of town either, and if they do, I'll find out what happened and we'll deal with it amongst ourselves."

Sheriff Poole thought about getting mad. Who was this nigger who came to his house in the middle of the night to talk propositions? He could shoot him right there in his backyard without explanation. But then it occurred to him it was a perfect setup. He could point to fewer instances of trouble if George could maintain order on his side of the tracks, and the white voters would guarantee him another term come election time, feeling safer with the coloreds under control. If not, Poole could arrest George for disturbing the peace.

Poole would win either way.

"I'll tell you what, George. Let's try it for a couple of months and see if you make any difference. But if it don't, I'll bring my deputies back in and clean up for you."

One-Arm George's eyes flashed at the implications he'd already considered, but he stood quiet. It didn't do any good to make the White Law mad, especially when standing in the Sheriff's backyard after dark.

"Can I take care of things?"

"I done told you, yeah."

"My way, Sheriff?"

Poole stared at him for a moment, knowing what the man was asking. "As long as nothing gets on me."

"It won't. And if you do hear anything, instead of coming right over, please wait one more day. I might have to do a little sniffing around if we have trouble, but it'll get done. I intend to start Friday night."

Poole nodded without another word, mentally dismissing George and pondering the long-range significance of the encounter. Without another word, George left and Poole went inside to finish his argument.

For the remainder of the week George passed the word that the white law no longer dealt with their problems; he would. He also announced a weekend midnight curfew for the next two months until everyone got used to the new rules.

At midnight on Friday, One-Arm George tucked a worn .44 revolver under the nub of his left arm and locked the front door to the Baptist church. Juke joints lined a significant portion of M Street, so George took his first Walk directly down the middle of the cracked and potholed blacktop leading north to the stately homes across the tracks.

Stars in the clear sky twinkled over raucous laughter. Loud music floated through the screen doors and windows of the weathered buildings. Stopping on the warm blacktop, he waited alone in front of the first joint, staring at the door. It didn't take long for someone to look out and notice him.

"Good night," George called. The music stopped and through the windows George watched the patron's reactions. "Good night," he called again.

"Go home, grandpaw!" Laughter followed floated cross the yard.

George quietly stood his ground.

Feeling brave, a drunk with a giggling woman hanging on his shoulder staggered outside and stopped in a cone of light on the dried grass bordering the street. "You don't know what you're messin' with, buddy." He turned back to wink at his friends inside. His girlfriend giggled at his bravado. The rowdy, well lubricated crowd took the cue and hooted their encouragement.

"I don't believe I'm scared of an old preacher toting just one arm."

When he turned back around One-Arm

George had quickly closed the distance between them and the man was looking into the deep horizontal well of George's cocked .44. The barrel, less than two inches from his sweating forehead, was unwavering. The suddenly sober man clearly saw the blunt tips of the huge bullets in their chambers and knew another waited at the bottom of the black barrel.

"You don't know who *you* messin' with brother. I said, 'Good night'."

He swallowed, shocked suddenly sober. "Deacon, I believe I'll go on home now."

"That'll be jus' fine. Good night and God bless."

Moments later the joint was empty and the partygoers hurried down the broken sidewalk. A number of the club's patrons rushed ahead to pass the word among the other joints. One-Arm George meant business.

The remainder of George's slow walk was uneventful. He offered a pleasant good night to everyone he passed. Vehicles crept past, passengers gaping through the windows, awed by the lone one-armed Deacon with the big .44. Soon the street was quiet, and George made his way northward toward two sets of headlights parked on the road.

Sheriff Poole waited beside his dark blue Model A parked across the railroad tracks. Four deputies leaned against another car in the darkness, smoking and watching One-Arm George's slow progress. At least two colored drivers intended to cross the tracks ahead of George, but they made abrupt turns when they saw the waiting lawmen.

George's walk finally brought him to the tracks. He stopped with one foot on the rail, looking into an entirely different culture. He noticed the long shadows of pump shotguns leaning against the car and realized the bulky looking weapon cradled in Poole's arms was a drum-fed Thompson machine gun.

A shadow lay at their feet, moving weakly and moaning. It was the man George recognized from his encounter less than half an hour before.

"Evening, Sheriff."

"Hidy, George. Nice night for a walk."

George couldn't see Poole's eyes in the shadow of his fedora hat brim. "Yessir. Needed to make sure everyone was down and quiet for the night. I'll be walkin' about this time on Friday and Satiddy nights, and probably around ten during the week."

"That's real good." The sheriff took a deep drag on a hand-rolled cigarette, and the cherry brightened quickly. "Thissun was being argumentative this evenin'."

Someone snickered.

"He's hard-headed." George knew better than

to say anything else. Despite their earlier exchange, he felt bad for the man at Poole's feet, beaten for simply crossing a set of railroad tracks at night.

Relaxing, Poole leaned the Thompson against the car and slipped one hand into his pocket of his khakis. "Is that a pistol under your nub there?"

"Yessir. Can't never tell when you'll run across a bad dog out this time of night."

"That's a fact. You think you'd shoot it off here in town, if you saw a bad dog?"

"Only if it tried to bite me, Sheriff."

"Hope I don't have to come over there after any dogs."

"I 'spect you won't, now."

Poole finished his smoke and crushed the butt under his shoe. He motioned for the men to get in their car. Without another word they collected their firearms, slammed the doors, and drove off. Alone and expressionless, Poole looked down and ground his heel on the unconscious man's fingers. George felt his ears burn, but hid the anger flushing his face.

"You might want to get your trash off the road, and remember what I told you."

"Yessir."

Poole climbed into his car without another word, shifted into gear, and drove slowly down the street.

George waited until the coupe disappeared

around the corner and hurried down the street to send someone to fetch what was left of the drunk.

Each night thereafter, no matter the weather, George made his Walk, and word got around that he meant business with the .44. Some say it barked once or twice in the dark, but when Sheriff Poole or his deputies dropped by for a half-hearted investigation, no one knew what happened.

One-Arm George's popularity grew within the black population until he became a local legend. But when talk of electing a black sheriff to handle things in the south part of town arose shortly before Japan surrendered, George was found beaten to death one morning in the damp weeds beside the railroad tracks. The investigation into the murder lasted long enough for Sheriff Poole to look down at the body and grunt.

"Looks like someone killed another nigger." He closed the case by going home to eat breakfast alone, since his wife had taken their son and left.

Through the years young John Washington watched his father and realized how much respect came with his work. When O.C. Rains returned to Chisum after the war, he appointed John to One-Arm George's position, and an uncomfortable peace reigned, with a cautious nod from Sheriff Poole, who kept a close watch on Washington and his people across the tracks.

Chapter Seven

It had been a month since Grandpa and Big John broke up the still down in Plum Thicket, and he couldn't stop smiling. A photographer followed the highway patrol officer when he got the call about Doak's still, and *The Chisum News* wrote an article about the arrests. They ran the big picture on the front page of Grandpa, the deputies, and the steaming remains of the still.

Stacked in front of them, six hand-tooled saddles they found under a tarp proved the bootleggers had been doing a little side business in stolen goods. All in all, Judge Rains said his constables and deputies had done a good job and promised to end whiskey making in Lamar County.

The animal case was still up in the air, though there hadn't been another incident since the arrest. I heard Grandpa say that didn't mean anything, because there could have been things done they hadn't discovered. The woods are thick in the river bottoms, and a lot more could be going on in there than Grandpa knew.

It rained during the night, so the field was too wet to work. He was up early the next morning, shaking me out of bed.

"Get up, Top. Let's go to the feed store in Hugo."

I liked the old wooden store, because it smelled of sweet feed. It was also a chance to go to Oklahoma, though we could get nuggets or chicken scratch in other places if we wanted. Uncle Neal Box kept feed in the storeroom built onto the back of his store. Grandpa bought a sack or two from time to time, as much to support Uncle Neal as anything else, but he loaded the truck down to the springs when we went to Hugo.

Chisum had a feed store, too, but Grandpa Ned hadn't traded there since right after the war. The owner Ed Fergus overcharged Grandpa one time for salt blocks, ringing up the sale with the higher price of a mineral block. When Grandpa brought it to his attention the next weekend, Ed argued that Grandpa had bought salt. They disagreed for only a minute when Grandpa lost his temper and told Ed that he knew the difference between a salt block and a mineral block and Hell would freeze over before he ever set foot in his store again.

Hell was apparently still fairly warm that morning when we crossed the bridge over Sanders Creek. It wandered through bottomland groves of pecan, oak, walnut, and sycamores, and past shaggy fencerows divided by a patchwork quilt of pastures and fields.

Grandpa suddenly braked the truck and pulled over on the shoulder as we got to the other side. "Did you see that?"

"What?"

"That coyote hanging back there on the fence."

I stuck my head out the open window. "He's a big one."

"You stay here." Grandpa put the truck in neutral and got out.

I watched him step across the wet ditch. Grandpa stood between me and the coyote and talked to himself for a while. He flipped the body off the wire, stuck something in his pocket, and walked back to the truck. He didn't say a word as we drove on down the two-lane highway.

By ten o'clock we turned onto the highway at Arthur City and crossed the bridge into Oklahoma. The river below was thick with silt from the night's runoff. Sometimes it's so low you can walk all day on sandbars. Other times it's full to the banks and threatens to spill over the Texas side to flood Lamar County.

Across the bridge, the squatty, ugly cement, block beer joints were the first buildings we saw. Grandpa Ned noticed my interest when we passed Sonny's.

I was looking for Cody's El Camino, but he thought I was interested in the joints themselves. "You know why those honkytonks have sawdust on the floors?"

"They don't have regular floors?"

"Nope."

"Why do they use sawdust?"

"Because sawdust soaks up the blood."

I studied on that for a minute. "Why do people bleed in there?"

"Because men get to drinking and fighting. I don't want to ever catch you over here."

"Yessir."

"You know, you don't get into trouble if you're not where trouble starts."

The Hugo feed store was right outside of town. I liked it when we went all the way to Main Street because I always saw Indians. Caught between two different times, half the population was white, and the other half mostly Choctaw. Indian women in long skirts still walked the streets.

Dark Indian men dressed in overalls and flat

brimmed felt hats holding down shoulder-length black hair looked like our kinfolk in the faded black and white photographs Miss Becky kept in the cedar chest. I knew we had folks over there, especially in Grant, but we never had anything to do with them.

The store faced the highway and leaned tiredly on an ancient horse apple tree. It's really spelled bois d'arc, but up on the river we pronounce things differently and we called it a boardark. In the winter, big green fruit we called horse apples rotted on the ground around the trees.

Grandpa backed the truck against the feed store's splintered wooden loading dock. Several loafers held down the rough benches built against the wall, trying to stay in the shade. Two others leaned back against the unpainted wall in straight-backed cane-bottomed chairs.

Most people knew Grandpa, no matter where we went. He stopped to visit and I slipped through the wide double doors where the stacked bags of feed reached almost to the open rafters.

I climbed the sacks to the top level, carefully picking my way to one little spot where I liked to sit and look through the loft door at the whiteface cattle grazing nearby. The trucks and men were a long way down.

The only trouble was an Indian kid about my

age was already in my spot. I'd never seen such long hair on a boy. Even the Beatles' hair was shorter. Stepping carefully, I settled onto a sack beside him to dangle my legs over the void.

"How." I held up my right palm.

"That's not funny."

"How, again."

"How…about I push your ass off of here?"

We grinned at each other. He pointed toward the rafters about ten feet away. "Be careful. There's a big ol' yellow jacket nest over there."

"It was there last year, too. One of them stung the piss out of me before I could get down. Some feller down there put some chewing tobacco on it and it quit hurting pretty quick."

"That'll do it. My name's Mark." He must have noticed my puzzled look. "We're not all named Tonto. My last name is Indian, though. It's Lightfoot."

"I'm Top."

"That's a strange name."

"So is Lightfoot." We kicked our feet for a moment. "What are they talking about down there?"

"Cows, mostly. I was about ready to get down when you showed up."

"That's my grandpa there with the gun on his belt."

"I know him. He's a sheriff or something over in Texas."

"He's a constable. He's looking for a dog killer."

Mark pulled his hair off his collar to cool his neck. "I didn't know it was against the law to kill dogs."

"It is if they're tortured first."

"I didn't know the law worked dog killin's. Don't y'all have regular people killin's or cuttin's in Texas?"

"Yep, but it's mostly drunks who drive back from the beer joints over here that keep him busy. Those joints have sawdust on the floor to soak up the blood."

"I've been in enough of them to know that."

I was surprised someone my age had been inside a honky-tonk, but I didn't let on.

I heard Grandpa say he was going inside. He disappeared across the loading dock and the wooden screen door slammed behind him. A minute later two shirtless high school boys trooped into the storeroom and began loading our truck, lifting fifty-pound bags onto their shoulders as if they could do it all day without stopping.

Grandpa walked around the corner and stood there watching them for a moment, then he tilted his head up to see us. "You 'bout ready?"

"Yessir." I didn't think he knew where I was.

He squinted upwards. "Who's your friend?"

"Mark Lightfoot."

"Howdy, Mark Lightfoot."

"Hidy."

"You Frank Lightfoot's boy?"

"Yessir."

"Ya'll favor. How's your daddy?"

"He's fine, but he's going back to the pen again."

Grandpa raised his eyebrows at the news. "What fer, cuttin' up Doak Looney?"

"He got in a scrap at the Ranchhouse the other day and cut on a feller from Dallas for a little while. Sheriff Post from Hugo caught him coming out from where he was hiding in the Rawhide Cane breaks and revoked his parole, so he's going back in the pen."

"I'm sorry. It must be hard on you and your mama, being by yourself."

"Naw. He ain't much 'count anyway. We've always taken care of ourselves. Only trouble is, every time he comes back to the house for a little while we have another mouth to feed a few months later."

"Well, you don't follow him none. Let's go, boy."

"See ya." I grabbed a rafter and picked my way across the sacks.

"Yeah."

When I met Grandpa at the truck, everyone's attention was on two brightly painted Carson and Barnes pickups. It was unusual to see circus people in the summertime, but I overhead some men later saying they kept a year-round camp outside of Hugo and so the trucks were around all the time.

It was exciting to know wild African animals weren't too far away. The young guys loaded enough feed to sag the springs of the fairly new trucks. The circus people didn't have anything to do with the men on the dock, which surprised me, because I figured they'd want to talk about lions and such.

Before we left, Grandpa turned toward the loafers. "Y'all haven't heard about anyone killin' animals around here, have you?"

One wrinkled old toothless farmer spat a stream of brown tobacco juice off to the side. "What kind of killin' are you talking about? Killin' to eat, or killin' just for killin'?"

"Why, there ain't nothing wrong with killin' to eat, so I guess I mean for meanness." The man stared long and hard at the departing Carson and Barnes trucks as they left the lot. Then he gestured toward a wormy-looking farmer with skin so tanned it looked dirty. His hair stood on end as if someone hacked at it with a dull butcher knife. "Brady there was telling us last week about one of his calves."

Grandpa turned to Brady who sulled up and stared without saying anything. I could tell Grandpa had no patience for that kind of thing. "Well, what about your calf?"

"Sommun' cut hits tail plumb off."

"Probably a wolf or coyote chewed it off. I've heard bears will do that too, down in the Big Bend country."

"We ain't got no bears here no more and wolfs don't carry knives and they don't tie calves to fenceposts. That there tail was cut off, but that weren't the worst. He was gutted from his aisshole to his chest and lef' to stan' 'ere and die. He wusn't dead yet when I got there neither, and his guts wus strung out all underneath him. I shot him with m'pistol."

"Where'd it happen?"

"Out by my house."

"Where do you live, then?"

"'Bout ten mile of here."

Grandpa's frustration with getting the story piecemeal and backwards to boot was making his ears red. I noticed and before I could help it, I stepped into the conversation. "Any idea who done it?"

Kids weren't supposed to butt into adult conversations. "Be seen but not heard" was Adult Law and my blunder was huge. Every man on the dock looked at me like I'd grown an extra head while we stood there. It scared me and I wanted to disappear between the floorboards of the porch.

"If I knew who it wus, I'da already tak'n care a'it." The skinny farmer scratched his forearm. "Hit ain't none of yore business anyhow, boy."

I swallowed hard and backed up an involuntary step.

Grandpa's blue eyes flashed. He held me steady with one hand on my shoulder. "Well, I reckon it's *my* business." I'd never heard him use that tone before.

The porch got real quiet.

"Confound it, I ain't igner't. You're Texas law and 'at don't cut no ice with me. I don't have to tell you nuthin'."

"That's right. But if I think you know something you're not telling me, I'll have the Oklahoma Law here before you can say calf rope. I'm trying to get to the bottom of something is all."

"Now don't get mad, Ned," one of the men said from behind us.

"Why 'on't you jist go on back across the river?" Brady wanted to be tough, but everyone knew it wouldn't take much more to get Grandpa fighting mad.

Grandpa Ned looked a hole through the man for a moment. "I ain't mad…yet. Now, you men give me a call if anything else happens. There's some meanness going on and I intend to get to the bottom of it." He motioned at me. "Get in the truck, son."

Without a word I climbed in on my side. He stomped off the loading dock, jerked the door open, and got in. Before the engine caught good we went bouncing across the rough dirt lot while he talked to himself some more. "I god, now somebody's guttin' live calves."

The truck struggled with the load of sacks stacked solidly in the back. I waited for Grandpa to ream me out for getting into his business, but instead, he turned north.

"There's a café here. Let's get you a hamburger."

I knew then we weren't in town just for feed. Grandpa wouldn't waste time hanging around Hugo to buy me a hamburger, and he was mad to boot. Miss Becky always had dinner ready at noon, so I figured he was Lawing some more.

With no argument from me, we turned onto the highway and drove the rest of the way into the dusty little town where a shoe store, drugstore and the newspaper office on the main drag sat across from the hamburger joint and a notions store. The rest of the buildings on the street were empty.

I was already looking for Indians when Grandpa pulled the truck into a space in front of the café's screen door, but before I could get out, he put his hand on my chest. Then he jammed the shifter into reverse, grinding the gears for the first time I could remember and shot out of the parking place.

"I've changed my mind. We're going back to the house." He shifted roughly into first gear.

I didn't ask questions, but as we shot away, I caught a glimpse of a sign on the door.

No dogs or Indians allowed.

I turned and faced forward. Dogs were listed first.

Miss Becky was Choctaw.

Chapter Eight

Grandpa was in a better humor when I rolled out of bed on Saturday morning. "C'mon boy, we've got things to do."

A fresh breeze pushed through the screen. I stretched under the light weight of a thin sheet. Miss Becky's colorful quilt lay wadded at my feet. She always made the bed with the pillows at the foot, so we slept with our heads in the center of the room to catch even the smallest breeze through the open windows.

"Where we going?" I pulled on a tee shirt.

"Down to the river to dump the trash and then I need to go to the store and hire some hands. The cotton is ready and I want to start pickin' Monday morning."

Miss Becky sang a gospel song as she fried sausage in a cast iron skillet. She used the back of one hand to wipe the sweat from her forehead when I sat down at the table. "You're acting no 'count this morning. I thought you weren't ever gonna get up." She smiled to let me know she was kidding. "Grandpa has already fed and I've milked, gone to the garden, and gathered the eggs."

"I didn't hear y'all."

"You were sleeping too hard. I guess being ten is rough on a little feller."

I finished tying the laces on my P.F. Flyers and poured some blackstrap syrup on the hot scratch biscuits. A glass of milk waited beside my plate.

Cheesecloth covered two crocks of fresh milk on the countertop. One was bound for the icebox after she skimmed the cream from the top. She left the other out all day to separate so she could churn it for butter.

Miss Becky cracked an egg into the bacon grease. "I dreamed all night."

"I dreamed, too."

"What about?"

"Drowning in the Rock Hole."

She threw me a sharp look over her shoulder.

Protected by rough country, tall trees and thorny vines, the Rock Hole was a deep pool in Sanders Creek. One side was a rocky cliff about fifteen feet high, the opposite bank was a long, low sandbar. When kids weren't splashing the surface to a froth, fat bream and crappie made the water snap as they sucked bugs from the surface. Grandpa's little brother drowned in there when they were little fellers and he never got over his fear of water.

"I dreamed me and Pepper were jumping off the high side and I went under and was drowning in red muddy water."

"I heard you wheezing last night. That probably made you dream of drowning. But I don't want you down there without an adult. Make Cody go if y'all intend to swim."

Uncle Cody had been a sore point since Norma's appearance at the rodeo.

I had barely finished breakfast when Grandpa came into the kitchen. "Get the shovel out of the smokehouse. I'll pull the truck around by the barrels."

Out in the country there wasn't any trash pick up. After a couple of months of burning household garbage in a 55-gallon steel barrel, we had to dump the ashes and everything else that didn't burn.

I followed him outside and while he drove through the pipe gate to the burn barrel on the other side of the barbed wire fence, I opened the wooden smokehouse door. Grandpa kept his tools along the north wall, within easy reach. Trunks and boxes took up the south end.

The rough wooden shelves were almost bare, but November was hog killing time and I knew they would be full once again soon enough. I was mostly interested in more than two dozen dusty quart size mason jars full of clear white-lightning on the top shelf. Each one wore a piece of yellowed masking tape bearing a name, date and location of the still Grandpa had busted. I never knew if he kept them as trophies, or if Judge O.C. Rains asked him to hold them in case they needed them in court.

A clean jar with a piece of fresh masking tape shone like a diamond at one end, the new ring bright and shiny. I climbed the dusty shelves and took down the jar. Grandpa once showed me how to tell if homemade whiskey was pure by shaking the jar. Large bubbles formed and quickly burst in high-proof whiskey. Bad or dangerous moonshine made small bubbles that foamed and lasted.

Doak's whiskey made large bubbles and they quickly burst. For some reason I was proud of both Doak and Grandpa.

"Hurry up, boy!"

Replacing the whiskey jar, I grabbed the shovel and a hoe and hurried back outside. The truck was already backed up to the barrels. I went through the small gate in the fence, securing it with a twist of soft bailing wire so the cows couldn't nudge it open and get out.

He was waiting beside the tailgate, looking at his back tires. "I'm gonna need some new caissons pretty soon, but they'll get us to the bottom and back. Grab aholt and we'll histe this barrel first."

I threw the tools in the bed and together we lifted the barrel into the back. The second followed and in no time we were headed for the river.

Grandpa liked to look at the fields as we drove. Some were already picked clean. Cotton lint from the open-top wagons littered the ditches and looked like a light snow in the grass.

We didn't live but a mile from the river, so two more turns, a rumble across a plank bridge, and I saw the ribbon of water off to my right and the Oklahoma shore beyond.

Grandpa backed up to the river bank and killed the engine. I stepped out of the truck not five feet from the steep edge of the river flowing past, twenty feet below. From my tennis shoes down to the current, a sea of garbage nearly a hundred yards wide slowly gave in to gravity and an eroding bank People dumped everything from household trash to worn-out iceboxs and washing machines over the edge. Heavy rains cleaned the bank when the river swelled and washed it all downstream for others to deal with.

It didn't take long to tip the barrels over the open tailgate and pour out the burned cans and ashes in a rattling cloud of dust and breaking glass. We finished by raking out the loose hay and empty feed sacks from the truck bed, then kicked a stray can or two off the road, and the job was done.

While Grandpa talked to himself and looked across the river, I threw dirt clods at bottles and cans for a while. Then I shot at them with my BB gun. Grandpa watched from under his straw hat.

"You're getting pretty good."

I grew an inch with the praise. "I can hit what I aim at."

He pointed at a Mrs. Stewart's bluing bottle below us. "All right then. Can you hit that?"

I did, and he grinned when the blue glass shattered. "Now, shoot that snake."

I hadn't seen the water moccasin sunning itself on the rusty door of an overturned icebox not far away. Excitement got in the way of my aim. I missed the snake three times.

Grandpa laughed and reached into the pocket of his overalls. He pulled out the Colt 32.20. "They call that buck fever. Let me try."

The snake was a good twenty yards away, and I didn't have much hope that he'd hit it. He thumb-cocked the pistol and shot. The snake parted about six inches behind its head, falling on both sides of the icebox.

An explosion of motion to the right startled us both. A large wolf finally lost his nerve at the shot and bolted from his hiding place beneath a thick cedar. He raced down the dirt road.

"Wolf!" Grandpa cocked the little pistol again and aimed with his elbow bent like a cowboy in those flickering silent movies. The pistol cracked a second time and the wolf tumbled in the dirt.

My eyes must have bugged out of my head. "You hit him!"

"I intended to. Now stay right here. He may not be dead and he'll be dangerous if he's still alive."

I wasn't about to ignore his warning, because I didn't want to be eaten by no wolf. In the back of my mind I thought it could be a Texas werewolf.

Grabbing the tail, Grandpa cheerfully drug the carcass back to the truck. "Thissin' won't kill any more calves or chew off their tails. Let's go to the store and show him off."

He pitched the limp body into the truck bed, and we drove out of the bottoms to the main social hub of our community, two plank-walled general stores separated by a weathered domino hall that had never seen the business end of a paintbrush.

A loud, laughing Santa Claus to kids, Uncle Neal Box kept an eye on his one-room store from behind a wooden counter worn smooth by a lifetime of sales. He kept the store stocked with everything from food to dry goods. Farming equipment and hardware hung from the open rafters along with nursing buckets, well buckets, harness, and tack.

Fifty yards to the east, Oak Peterson's older and gloomier general store also housed the post office; a dark little spot in the rear protected by iron bars at the business window. I was always uneasy around Oak, because one eye turned out and I never knew for sure if he was looking at me.

Our family preferred Neal's store because he was family. And unlike Oak's store, Neal's place was built on a tall pier-and-beam foundation with a wide front porch. Grandpa liked to stand on the porch where he could look both ways down the highway.

You could always find a good game in the domino hall between. Sometimes three or four games rattled dominos, and the hall rang with laughter, cussing and good solid slaps on the homemade tables when someone made fifteen or twenty points.

"Make a nickel."

Click. "Made a dime."

Slap. "Twenty-five!"

"Dammit."

Center Springs was a pretty good-sized town back around 1870. It had a cobbler, a barbershop, livery, blacksmith shop and an honest-to-god brass marching band. But after a particularly long spell of rain and thunderstorms in 1908, the Red River drowned the entire river valley under silt and water. Most everyone washed away and only a handful returned.

Loafers on the two-by-six porch rails of Neal's store made up the majority of the crowd when we arrived. A few men leaned over the beds of trucks, talking and spitting and laughing. A circle of colored men squatted in the shade between Neal's and the domino hall, talking in low voices and drinking strawberry sodas, if they had a dime to spend.

Grandpa killed the motor and coasted into the parking lot paved with rusting coke bottle caps from the box beneath the cooler's opener.

Pepper sat on the top porch rail, eating a Zero bar and listening to Uncle James and the men talk. She ran down the steps before the truck was still. "Where you been?"

"Down at the river. Look what Grandpa shot."

She climbed up on the small step beside the spare tire and peered into the truck. "Shitfire. He shot someone's German Shepherd?"

"No you idiot. That's a wolf."

"Ain't neither."

"Is too."

We went at it while the crowd emptied off of Uncle Neal's porch and gathered around the truck to examine the carcass. The colored men craned their necks to catch a glimpse of the dead wolf, but none stepped into the inner circle of white folks.

"Glad you killed him, Ned." Sonny Choat drummed his fingers on the fender. He farmed land not too far from Grandpa's house. "I swear a bunch of wolves ran my dog up on the porch the other night, but my wife says they were coyotes."

"There weren't no others with him. That'un come a runnin' out from under a cedar tree while the boy here and I were dumping the trash. He tagged him with his BB gun while he run off, but I had to finish him when he got too far away."

Grandpa surprised me by stretching the story, and felt my face turn hot when Pepper shot me a look like she'd like to cut out my liver. "I bet you were running like a striped-ass baboon in the other direction," she whispered.

I elbowed her and saw Uncle Cody pull off the highway at the sight of a crowd around Grandpa's truck. He stayed behind the wheel and stuck his arm through the open window. "You got a booger-bear in there, Ned?"

I immediately forgot the wolf and went around to the passenger side of the El Camino. Pepper followed and we stuck our heads into the sweet-smelling interior to look around.

Cody gave us a smile and pinched Pepper's

nose between the knuckles of his index and middle fingers as a greeting. "Hey, y'all!"

"Howdy, Cody." Pepper had already forgotten that she was mad about seeing him with Norma Williams at the fair.

"Ned shot him a wolf this morning down by the river." Bryan Dollar always liked to be the first person to tell a story, no matter if he was involved or not.

"I been meaning to go wolf hunting, myself," Uncle Cody reached over to turn his radio down. "But I've been spending too much time at work."

"And at other things." Everyone laughed at Uncle James' comment.

"That too. I ain't married like y'all." Cody glanced at us and changed the subject. "There any dove out in your maize field, Bryan? I thought I'd go huntin' now the weather has cooled off."

"I saw quite a few last week when I was feeding. Come on out and shoot you a bunch if you want to."

"That's a thought." Cody paused. "I saw some hog tracks between the spring and the creek a while back. I thought I might camp out there to hunt birds in the morning and hogs at night."

"That'd be all right. I don't care if you shoot every hog in the county, the way they're rooting up my pastures. I'll tell Roland Roach you'll be out there at night after hogs, so he won't bother you."

Roland Roach had served as the game warden for as long as I could remember.

Pepper hung through the window to better see the inside of Cody's El Camino. "Don't you want to get out and see the wolf?"

"Naw, I've seen one before."

She stretched way into the car and started fiddling with the radio, turning it up so she could hear the Beatles over the static. Cody reached out without paying much attention, grabbed an arm and tumbled her headfirst through the window while he talked to the adults on his side. I rolled in right behind her and we flopped around on the seat like a couple of puppies.

"Scoot over." There was no way I was going sit in the middle next to Cody. It wasn't manly. Girls belonged between the men.

"Kiss my ass."

"Grandpa's gonna hear you one of these days."

He didn't, but Uncle Cody reached over and squeezed her knee, cutting off the argument. Pepper fiddled with the radio some more.

Grandpa turned to Cody. "If you want to do some honest work outside of that honky-tonk of yours, I'm hiring hands today to pick cotton. I can offer you the same wage for some honest work."

"Aw, I reckon I'll do what I know best. Besides, the last time I got into a work agreement with you, I think I got the worst of the deal."

"If I remember right, I offered a deal to gather pecans on the halves, and you didn't pick up but about fifty pounds or so."

"Um hum. I was fifteen and about broke my back picking up them stinkin' nuts. You didn't tell me I had to shell them, too."

"Yeah, I did. You weren't listening."

"I listen better now."

"I bet you do. You kids gonna get out of the car?" Grandpa leaned over and squinted through the window.

Pepper adjusted the radio, trying to get rid of the static. "I think we're gonna ride around with Cody."

Uncle James joined us at the car. "I think you're gonna get out. Is this a car or a truck?"

It made Pepper mad, but she knew better than to argue with her daddy.

"I guess it's whatever you wanna call it." Cody turned his attention to us. "Tell you what, y'all go on and stay here and if it's all right with everybody, you can go hunting with me next weekend."

I knew better than to say anything. Pepper started to open her mouth, but I gave her a good jab in the ribs and she shut up. "Shhtttt!"

Grandpa looked over at Uncle James. "I guess you were about their age the first time you went camping by yourself with your cousins."

"Yeah, that's what worries me." Uncle James scratched his head. "But we can't keep them in a box, I guess. All right, y'all can go. Now get out and go get you a cold drink and some peanuts."

We were out the door in a flash and I slammed it. "Thanks Cody!"

"Yeah, thanks!"

"Hey, you two," Cody passed a quarter to each of us through the window. "I'll see you next Saturday."

We threw another thanks into the wind and ran up the steps. Pepper beat me to the top. "You ever jab me in the ribs again I'll grab you by the hair of the head and pull you bald."

I pulled at my short cowlick. "No, you won't."

Emory Daniels stepped through the screen door eating a Moonpie. Everyone knew he barely had enough money to feed his kids, but there he was with a treat all four of his little ones would have cried for.

Pepper shot him a mean look, grabbed the wide Ideal Bread metal screen protector on the door and ducked under his arm. Emory frowned at her when she darted around him.

"I hate him. He's the most selfish man I've ever

seen. I think he's mean, too. I saw him whip his littlest one in here one time and Neal made him stop because he was hitting so hard."

"He always scared me, too. I try to stay away from him. One time I was throwing Coke caps outside and he got onto me because I might nick someone's car. I was only throwing them into the pasture over there."

I saw Grandpa and Uncle James wave Cody 'bye. Uncle James jogged easily onto the porch to visit some more with the men loafing there and Grandpa joined the colored folks in the shade beside the store.

We quickly lost interest in Emory Daniels, finding ourselves staring through the long nose-smudged oak trimmed glass cases holding Zero Bars, Baby Ruths, candy necklaces and wax bottles filled with flavored syrup.

A quiet voice drifted through the window propped open with a piece of broom handle to catch the breeze. "Howdy, Mister Ned."

I heard Grandpa's voice clear as day. "Howdy. Ivory, I hear ya'll are done with Don Allen's crop."

I glanced outside and saw Ivory Shaver squatting in the shade and whittling on a piece of pine. He stood, but didn't offer his hand. "Yessir." He nodded his head to the south. Smoke rose into the air from the cotton gin less than half a mile away. "That's his they ginning right now, I 'spect."

Some people's cotton needed more ginning than others. Grandpa Ned was particular about his crop and made sure his field hands actually picked the white fluff and didn't just pull bolls. Good pickers pulled the cotton from the bolls or husks, while landowners with more money than sense paid their hands for bolls and all.

Grandpa Ned paid for cotton, not trash. That's why he intended to hire Ivory and his family, because they picked fast, too. "Glad y'all are done. I need some hands come Monday morning."

"We're ready, sir. I was beginning to wonder when we were gonna go to pickin' for you."

Ivory had been dragging cotton sacks for Grandpa Ned ever since he was a young 'un barely big enough to make a full hand. When he married, his wife and kids did the same.

It wasn't unusual for Ivory and his family to work Grandpa's cotton. He fed his hands at noon, and fed them well. That was a selling point when you usually had to bring your own dinner. As an added bonus, he occasionally brought a sack of groceries by for the family and penny candy for the little ones, not counting a few clothes every now and then.

"Well, I got it in late this year. I had too much to do and almost didn't make it."

"Yessir. For a late crop, it looks good, though."

"We'll make it. How 'bout you get your family and some others who helped last year."

"Yessir. Everybody but Willamena can help. She's 'bout ready to have that baby, and I doubt she'd make it halfway down a row without fallin' out."

"Well, too bad. That gal can pick."

"Yessir. Most of the little 'uns will make a full hand."

"I trust you." Grandpa frowned at the ground. "Now don't you bring out Ralston. I had to lock him up last month. I imagine he's still mad and he'd probably kick dirt in the sack all day. I don't intend to pay for my own dirt."

Ralston was Ivory's wild younger brother. When he worked, he was a good hand, but most of the time he was sorry as the day is long.

Ivory grinned at his shoes. "Don't matter none. Ralston went to Dallas and got hisself thowed in jail down there. He can't stay out of trouble."

"I know. A lot of my own kinfolk have the same faults. I'll need about thirty hands, same pay as last year. I'll meet y'all here with the wagon at daylight Monday morning."

"We'll be here."

Saturday was the busiest day at the store, and customers were a steady stream through the screen door. When it was our turn for Neal to wait on us,

I spent my quarter on a Coke and some peanuts and worried about how to use the change.

We returned to the porch, and Pepper funneled peanuts into her R.C. bottle. Grandpa winked up at us as he passed and joined in on the commotion around a newly arrived truck.

Ty Cobb Wilson called to Grandpa through his open window as he and his brother coasted to a stop beside the porch. He'd known the Wilson boys since they first learned to walk. Hard workers during the day, he and younger brother Jimmy Foxx stayed on their tractors from sunup to sundown. If it was wet enough and they couldn't work, they spent their time hunting whatever was in season

Jimmy Foxx opened the passenger door. "Looky here, Ned." Men leaned over the back of the truck. "We caught these two up near Forest Chapel last night."

A low whistle floated across the parking lot.

From our high perch on the wooden rail Pepper and I looked down on two tawny half-grown cougars, stiff and stretched out in the truck bed littered with hay and empty feed sacks. Grown-ups stacked up around the truck to see.

Pepper disappeared from beside me and the next thing I knew she was crawling over the hood of the truck and onto the cab so she could get a better look at the panthers. I was shocked at her brazen move.

Uncle James reached over and raised the upper lip of the closest cat. White incisors flashed in the sun. Then he raised the animal's back leg. "They're the first lions I can remember in years. Both are females. I didn't even know we had panthers up here anymore."

"Never saw any larger tracks around our traps." Ty Cobb shrugged. "Maybe their mama had already weaned them."

"Guess we'd better keep an eye on the stock." Grandpa started back toward his car. "With wolves and lions around here these days, this may be a dangerous winter."

"Hold on, Ned." Jimmy Foxx pointed toward a pile of 'toesacks against the closed tailgate. "There's one more thing. Look under there."

Grandpa shot him a look and then pulled a 'toe sack to the side to reveal what was left of a dog. Everyone looked in silence for a moment. "You think the mama lion did this?"

"Nope. Not unless she's learned to build a fire and skin her meat. Someone spent quite a while working on this poor thing."

Uncle James and Grandpa exchanged glances. The men in the lot exploded in conversation and wondered aloud who could have done such a thing.

Pepper saw Grandpa's look and slithered off the cab. In an instant Grandpa's good mood evaporated.

Chapter Nine

That last week in October lasted an eternity because we were ready to go hunting. I doubt I learned much at school, and I'm afraid my grades reflected my inattention.

Grandpa was anxious, too. He urged Ivory's family to finish picking the tall cotton during long hours in the hot late season sun. No one got rich picking cotton, but it put food on the table for those poor folks living in unpainted shacks in the river bottoms.

One abandoned shack wasn't but a few hundred yards from Grandpa and Miss Becky's house. Bare wooden walls hung scabby with peeling newspaper that once served as wallpaper. The windows and doors had long ago disappeared.

The phone rang at the same time Grandpa got in from the field. Miss Becky handed him the receiver before he could even take off his hat. He talked for a moment before hanging up the handset.

He looked long and hard at the table set for supper. "G.W. says someone's squatting over there in the Howard place. I'll be back directly."

She put his plate in the oven to keep it warm. "Ira Mae called and told me they moved into the house last night. She said they're not much more than skin and bones."

"How'd she know?"

"Mary Sue called her."

"Well, I don't know how Mary Sue knows either, but all right. I'll go run 'em off." Grandpa didn't care much for G.W. or his wife Mary Sue, but he needed to do something about the call. He pinned his badge onto his shirt, slipped a pistol into the pocket of his overalls and left. He wasn't gone long.

I was working on a piece of pie when Grandpa came back through the door, shaking his head. Miss Becky was loading canned and dry goods into paper sacks on the table. I couldn't figure out why she was taking food out of the cabinet.

"Mama, make up a basket of food and clothes for those folks...." He saw the sacks on the table and gave her arm a squeeze as he went past. "They ain't got nothin' but the clothes on their backs and they're eating feed corn. I can't run 'em off the way they are."

"God love 'em. Any little 'uns?" She gathered

tomatoes off the window sill where she put them to ripen.

"Looked like a whole covey of kids to me. Top, get a couple dozen eggs out of the ice box and three of them gallon jars of milk. I bet they haven't had fresh butter in a while, either."

Miss Becky went into the bedroom and returned with her arms around a load of clean clothes. I finished my pie and we loaded everything into the truck. Miss Becky stayed behind, but I rode back with him. Grandpa stopped in the dusty yard near a steaming wash pot. The mother was a worn-out looking Indian woman with a baby on her hip and a snotty nosed little boy hanging onto the tail of her shapeless shift.

A bony white feller with a sharp, sad face stepped out onto the porch.

"Stay here." Grandpa killed the engine and got out to unload the boxes. The adults didn't meet Grandpa's eyes while they talked. Not even when he gave them the food and clothes. I glanced out the side window and watched half a dozen raggedly dressed kids staring at me. It was obvious they belonged to the Indian woman, and I could tell another one was on the way.

I smiled and waved, but none of them returned even so much as a grin.

Mark Lightfoot, the boy I'd met in the Hugo

feed store, appeared around the corner of the house. He nodded slightly through the windshield between us, but I could tell he was embarrassed.

The man finally mumbled something and offered his hand. Grandpa shook it and returned to the truck. The family gathered around the boxes in the dirt yard as we backed up and turned around.

"The kids wouldn't even talk to me."

Grandpa glanced in the mirror. "Folks sometimes don't talk much, especially to strangers."

"How long you gonna let them live there?"

"Awhile, I guess."

"G.W. gonna let 'em?"

"I'll talk to him."

"They don't have nothing. I've seen colored folks dressed better than them Indians."

"It don't matter how people are dressed, no matter what color they are. There are good and bad poor people, like there's good and bad rich folks. You don't go to judging them. I doubt they asked for things to be the way they are. They've had troubles a long time, but the man works for me now. Him and some of the older kids will be picking cotton starting tomorrow morning, so it looks like he's worth more than some lazy rich people."

He wasn't used to making such long speeches, so I knew I'd struck a nerve. "That wasn't their daddy."

"I know. You could tell them little 'uns were full-blood Indian."

"One of the boys was Mark Lightfoot. You remember him from the feed store."

"You're right. I guess that old boy moved in with the kid's mama when Frank went to jail. I just hope he knows who he's messing with. Frank Lightfoot's liable to kill him for just looking at his woman."

It was dark when we got back home. I called Pepper to make sure she was still on for the camping trip the next morning and heard Miss Whitney breathing on the other end of the party line. She was about ninety and liked to listen in on other people's conversations.

Pepper must have been waiting for me to call, because she answered the phone on the first ring. "Where the hell have you been?"

"Helping Grandpa. Why don't you see if you can spend the night over here so we can get an early start?"

"I can't. Aunt Tillie is here and everybody thinks I have to stay to keep her company. She's old and all she does is sit in front of the TV."

"We may find another victim of the Dog Killer this weekend." I didn't care if anyone was listening. I was hoping to do a little Hardy Boys investigation.

"Don't get me into anything that'll get me a

whipping. Daddy gave me one last week for cussin' and I don't want another'n while he's still thinking about it."

"Don't worry. We'll be mostly hunting. The worst thing that can happen is we'll get covered in chiggers and ticks."

"Miss Whitney, do you have any sulphur we could borrow to keep the chiggers off our legs?" Pepper could get mean sometimes.

Miss Whitney didn't answer, but I could hear her take a breath in shock. The phone clicked.

"Guess she doesn't have any. I'll see you in the morning." She hung up abruptly, like always.

I put down the receiver and went into the kitchen to see what Miss Becky had to eat. Even though it was late, she was making Grandpa's favorite, fried peach pies. "Miss Whitney was listening in again on the telephone."

"That poor old soul. Sister Jean wasn't so bad about snooping until Lefty died. Now she doesn't have anyone to talk to. Bless her heart, all she has to do is listen in, so y'all don't get on her too much about it."

I was grown before I realized "bless his or her heart' was a nice way to complain about someone without sounding mean, or to say they weren't quite right.

"But she was listening to me and Pepper talk."

"Were you talking ugly?"

"No, ma'am." It wasn't a complete lie. Pepper said the bad word, not me.

"Umm, humm. Well, then don't worry about her. Now, I want y'all to be careful out there in them woods with Cody this weekend." She sighed and looked out the window over the sink. She sighed a lot whenever she talked about Cody. "That boy. He's not much more than a kid himself, and I doubt he'll ever grow up." She flattened the dough with her glass rolling pin.

"He's grown now. He was in the army."

"Sometimes he don't act like it, and you can be full growed but still be a kid. Now you mind what I say. If he takes a notion to go across the river while y'all are out, or if he starts drinking, I want the two of you to come straight home." She dipped hot filling onto the dough, folded it, and crimped the edges.

"We'll be too busy hunting." I had no intention of coming home if Uncle Cody had a beer.

"Hum. Here." She handed me the mixing bowl after she scraped out most of the fruit. "Eat what's left so I can wash these dishes."

I forgot all about Miss Whitney and her nosey ways. It didn't take long to finish the bowl as Miss Becky fried the half-moon shaped pies. While she finished up, I went to sleep in the living room while

John Cameron Swayze strapped a Timex onto an outboard boat motor.

I was dreaming about drowning again a little after one in the morning when the crunch of tires on gravel woke me from a sound sleep. Grandpa heard it too and was up before I could clear the fog in my head. Once I shook out the cobwebs, I fumbled for my puffer and inhaled a deep squeeze.

A light mist began after we went to bed, and everything was wet and dripping. Barefoot and wearing nothing but his overalls, Grandpa flicked on the porch light, opened the wooden door, and looked through the screen to see who was in the yard. Carlo stood between the car and the house, barking at the visitor.

"Shut up, Carlo!"

I stopped in the kitchen door to hear what was going on. Grandpa's .38 hung loosely in his hand. He squinted into the car's headlights, trying to make out the driver.

"Ned! It's me."

"That don't tell me nothin'. Turn out them lights. Who's me?"

The headlights went out. "Sorry. It's me, Ty Cobb."

He sounded scared to me. Grandpa could

see Ty Cobb Wilson standing behind the open driver's door of his idling truck. He had one foot on the running board, in case he needed to jump back inside if Carlo tried to take a piece of his leg. Grandpa relaxed and slipped the pistol into the pocket of his overalls.

He pushed open the screen door and stepped onto the porch in his bare feet. "What's the matter?"

"Me and Jimmy Foxx think we done found a dead man in a culvert over near Forest Chapel while we was trailing a coon."

"Why do you *think* you found a dead man? He's either dead or he ain't."

"I 'magine he's dead, but he's hard to see. We thought we'd run the coon into a culvert under the road by the Forest Chapel Methodist Church. The dogs wouldn't go in and took to barking in the hole, so I thought it had balled up in there to make a fight. When I bent down to shine my light in the pipe, I could see a beard and teeth and it weren't no coon. I think somebody's done killed some feller and poked him up in there."

"Where's Jimmy Foxx?"

"I left him back at the culvert to keep an eye out. Walt Simms was passing by and he's waiting with him."

Grandpa was already turning around. "All right. Go on back and I'll be along directly. Tell

Jimmy Foxx and whoever else has stopped by to leave everything alone until I get there."

He saw me standing in the dark door in my underwear and grinned for a moment. "Well, as long as you're already up, get'che britches on and come with me. I doubt they found somebody poked up in a pipe. Get you a jacket, too. It's airish out this morning."

I was back in the bedroom and dressed before Grandpa could get his shirt and brogans on. I heard Miss Becky talking low without getting out of bed, asking what was going on. I was afraid she was going to put up a fuss about me going along, but Grandpa picked up his hat and waved toward the door. "Hurry up and let's go."

We were on the road in no time at all. The weather was more damp than cold, but I was glad for the jacket. I shivered until the car's heater warmed up enough to chase away the chill. The familiar woods on each side of the highway were eerie in the early morning darkness. I was seldom out so late, and it was an adventure to hear the coupe's tires hiss down the wet road as we rolled through the night. Lightning flickered far to the north in Oklahoma.

We drove west, past the store lit by a single light high on a telephone pole. Five minutes later we joined half a dozen trucks and cars parked with their headlights pointed toward the ditch. Even though it was early morning, several men milled around the lights, hands in their pockets, and hats pushed back on their foreheads. A heavy mist, almost like a fog, began to get thicker.

I could see the drops in the headlights. Grandpa reached into the back seat for his flashlight and got out. I followed, but at a distance. He got right to business. "Mornin' boys. Anybody else been in the ditch or messing around the culvert?"

Jimmy Foxx was the first to answer. "No, sir. I been here since Ty Cobb come back, so nobody else has looked in here yet."

Grandpa directed his light into the ditch and grunted at the footprints. "Well, y'all may not have looked in the pipe, but there's been a lot of feet down there in the grass. Don't matter though. From the smell I'd say any other tracks have been gone for a while."

He didn't wait for an answer, but carefully made his way down the wet slope and walked straight to the clay pipe. He bent down to shine his flashlight into the darkness and peered for a long time. "This booger's been dead a while."

The men around me nodded in agreement.

"Top, come down here." I couldn't imagine what he wanted, but I wove my way through a forest of legs and then half-slipped down the slope. "C'mere." I stepped forward until I was beside him.

"Squat down and tell me what that looks like to you."

Nearly overcome with horror, I did as I was told. The smell almost made Miss Becky's fried pie public once again. Taking the light, I pointed the shaky beam into the darkness and squinted without saying anything.

The men on the highway became completely silent. A night bird trilled in the trees beside the road, the only sound muffled by the heavy mist.

"You know much about goats, son?"

I glanced up and could see the twinkle in Grandpa's eye. "A little."

"See them teeth a-shinin'?"

"Yessir."

"See his head?"

"Yessir."

"What does it look like to you?"

"A goat, sir."

He laughed and straightened his popping knees. "He's right, boys. Somebody killed an old goat, probably got scared and stuffed it up in here."

The men around us hooted and began to harass the Wilson boys.

Jimmy Foxx scratched his head. "Well, if you ain't expecting a dead goat in a drain in the middle of the night, it might look like a dead man. And I didn't see no horns."

Grandpa struggled up to the road. "Y'all need to take this boy with you from now on, in case you see a dead calf. At least he can tell you what it is and you won't wake me up anymore in the middle of the night."

The hoorawing got louder. Ty Cobb and Jimmy Foxx grinned and toed the ground, taking the good-natured ribbing.

Grandpa motioned toward Ty Cobb. "Reach back in there and get a rope around something. I wanna see if it was run over, or stole and killed intentionally."

Relieved to get away from the ribbing, he quickly skinned off into the pipe with a lariat rope and backed out breathing through his mouth. His pants were wet and muddy from the knees down. "Sheewww! It's damned ripe in there."

"You ain't a-kiddin." I didn't know who said it, but everyone laughed like we had one of Ed Sullivan's comedians with us.

Jimmy Foxx joined him in the ditch and they gave the rope a good strong pull. It slid easy and they dragged the rotting goat out of the ditch and up on the shoulder of the road where it lay in the misty rain, lit by the headlights. Grandpa stared down for a long while, playing the beam of his flashlight over the carcass.

Someone behind me cleared his throat. "Say, this goat's been cut up."

The night bird stopped calling and something stirred in the dark brush along the ditch, beyond the lights. Suddenly grim, Grandpa shined his light there. We didn't see anything. Then his gaze went to the men around us.

"Yeah, it is. Boys, I got something to tell you." Looking sad, Grandpa finally told what he'd been finding in the bottoms to those men standing in the chilly mist.

The animals were getting bigger, but suddenly I wasn't as excited about the Dog Killer as I was before. It wasn't a secret anymore, and it had gotten scary.

Chapter Ten

I woke up to someone shaking me like a rag. When my eyes opened, I was buried up under two of Miss Becky's quilts. She must have covered me up after I got back in the bed. It had cooled off considerably during the night.

I cracked one eye and saw Uncle Cody grinning down at me. "Dang boy, you're gonna sleep the day away and we won't get any birds. Whadda think, Pepper? Should we leave this lazy bum here and go it alone?"

I heard Pepper's voice from the other end of the bed. "Yank the covers off of him and let's go."

"Don't you do it." I opened the other eye and looked out the window. It was barely light enough to make out the cows on the other side of the fence. "I ain't wearing nothing but my drawers and I don't think I want Pepper to see them."

She snickered. "I've seen you nekked."

"Not lately." I got a good grip on the covers in case one of them wanted to make a fight of it.

Cody leaned casually against the door fame with a thumb hooked in the front pocket of his hunting pants. "You know the difference between nekked and naked?"

Pepper played right along. "What?"

"When you're naked, you're doing something you're supposed to be doing. But when you're nekked you're about to get in trouble."

I couldn't help but laugh, especially after I heard Miss Becky holler. "Cody! Don't you go to putting ideas in those babies' heads with ugly talk. Y'all get in here and get you some breakfast so Top can get some clothes on. Pepper, come help me set the table."

Pepper stuck her tongue out at me, but she went. Cody threw my pants on the bed and followed her out. "Hurry up. I'm ready to shoot some birds."

I found my puffer under the pillow, gave it a squeeze, then quickly pulled on my clothes. By the time I got to the table they were already working on a big breakfast of boiled rice sprinkled with sugar, oatmeal, sausage, bacon, scrambled eggs, and scratch biscuits two inches thick. At his place at the head of the table, Grandpa Ned spread pear preserves on a biscuit while his coffee cooled in the saucer.

During breakfast he told Cody about the goat and I'd almost lost my supper. Everyone ribbed me about it, but I was proud I hadn't puked in front of all those grown men. The conversation moved to the animal mutilations and his concerns.

Grandpa looked at Cody a long time before he made his mind up about something. "Cody, there's one more thing you don't know 'cause I wanted to keep everything quiet for a while, but one of the animals I found was your dog Pal. He was misused pretty bad out in Isaac Reader's corn field."

I watched Cody's face. It got real hard and his eyes shined for a minute. He looked down at his plate. "I knew somebody took him. Pal didn't get out of the pen by hisself."

"I hate that it happened." Miss Becky got teary-eyed. She was tender-hearted about all living things, but especially toward dogs.

Cody gazed outside through the screen door. His were glassy. "So do I."

I didn't say anything, but the knot in my stomach eased for the first time since the day I came to live with my grandparents. I hated to keep secrets from Uncle Cody, especially about the day we found his bird dog in Isaac Reader's field. I was light enough to float out of the chair, but I just set there because of how heart-broke he looked on the other side of the table.

"Well, now the cat's out of the bag and it's still happening. I need some more eyes out there." Grandpa reached for another biscuit. "I don't know who's doing it, or why. But I want to catch him, so Cody, you keep the wax out of your ears in that honky-tonk you run, but let me handle it if you hear anything."

Uncle Cody nodded as he silently left the table and slammed the screen door behind him.

"I mean it!"

"I know it!"

Grandpa sipped the last of his coffee from the saucer. "I'm going to town for a little while to talk to O.C. Then I'm coming back to the field. I need to get the last of the cotton out pretty quick. The drizzle last night didn't help anything, but it ought to be dry by afternoon if the sun stays out."

I felt bad for hunting when Grandpa was trying to get his cotton in, but he winked at me and I knew everything was fine. We headed for the door while Miss Becky cleared the table. She didn't even tell Pepper to help, because she knew we wanted to get started.

Grandpa Ned joined us on the porch and handed me his double-barrel shotgun. The stock had been cracked and repaired back in the olden days and the blue was almost completely worn off the barrel.

"Here, Top. You can shoot this today. Remember to snug it up to your shoulder and she won't kick so bad." I pushed the thumb lever and broke the shotgun open to see if it was loaded. Grandpa was pleased. He nodded and grinned. "There you go."

I carried the gun into the yard. Pepper was sitting on the camping gear in the bed of Cody's El Camino and he was staring across the hood toward the river. He broke out of his silence when he saw me standing there holding a twelve-gauge.

"Lordy mercy boy. That thing is taller than you are. Think you can get it up to your shoulder?"

I aimed at a nearby sycamore, holding it too long. Even with my left elbow planted firmly against my side, the muzzle drifted toward the ground. Pepper snickered, but she didn't say anything. I knew she'd make her comments well away from Miss Becky's house.

Cody laughed. "Well, don't take too long to aim at them flying birds and you'll be all right. You might want to point it in the general direction of the sky when you pull the trigger, though."

Pepper's gear was already loaded. I threw my own quilts and clothes into the El Camino's shallow bed. We hardly knew what sleeping bags were, so bedding and feather pillows were the way to go against the evening chill.

I glanced into the back at enough gear for a

two-week African safari. Grandpa stepped off the porch and put his hand on the cab. "Now, Cody, you look after these young 'uns out prowling around them woods."

It made me mad because I knew we'd be fine, as far as I was concerned. I'd even stayed by myself for a night in the woods out back of the house before, so I considered myself an experienced camper.

"Don't worry, Ned. I won't let nothin' happen to 'em."

"You know what I mean."

"I do."

"You mind me, then. And y'all mind your Uncle Cody."

We could hear shotguns popping somewhere down in the bottoms. Cody heard them too. "Load up and let's go. Somebody's already down there stirring the birds up. We'll shoot us a few and then go find somewhere to set up camp."

Miss Becky dried her hands on a feed-sack dish towel and waved from the porch as we backed up to turn around. Uncle Cody shifted into drive and we crunched down the gravel drive. He had his hat tilted back on his forehead again and long curly black hair hung over his collar. I decided right then for sure and for certain I would grow up to look like him.

Pepper jabbed me in the ribs as soon as we hit the highway. "That shotgun is gonna knock you on your ass."

"Will not."

"Sure it will. They ain't enough of you to even hold it up, you little titty-baby."

"He'll do fine." Uncle Cody turned on the radio. "The only way to learn something is to do it. That old two-shoot gun might rock him some, but he'll get used to it pretty quick, and you watch your language."

That settled Pepper down and she tuned the dial to a rock and roll station and we listened to "Can't Buy Me Love" by the Beatles while he drove to the bottoms. Cody surprised us when he sang all the words. I didn't know he liked anything besides Hank Williams and Lefty Frizzell.

When we got to the field and Cody saw his hard-looking running buddies from across the river, he turned the radio up and grinned out the window. "Howdy, boys!"

Lane Miller's shirt sleeves were rolled up over his skinny forearms when he met us in the shade of a large oak. "Cody! 'Bout time y'all got here. Turn that shit down and help us shoot these birds. Don't these new cars get country music?" He waved at a dove darting overhead while those within earshot laughed. "Steve there can't hit nothing but his foot this morning, so somebody else is gonna have to do his shooting for him." He crossed his eyes at us. "Howdy, Top. Pepper."

Pepper grinned back at him without saying anything for once. I think she was feeling overwhelmed by all the big guys hanging around.

I saw a young man with a flat top haircut sitting under a nearby tree. We got out of the cab and joined a few guys milling around in the shade. I'd never seen anyone who had shot his own foot. Steve had his pointy toe cowboy boot and sock off and was examining his naked big toe. It was a little bloody, but the wound had already stopped bleeding.

I was disappointed. I expected his foot to be as full of holes as dead dove.

Steve looked up at the small gathering. "Damned plug is out of the shotgun. I borrowed this thing from a friend of mine, but he didn't say nothing about the plug being out. I'd already shot three times, so I was shoving a shell in it when it went off against the edge of my boot."

"You're lucky you didn't blow your damned foot off." Pepper forgot her earlier silence and realized she was away from her folks and in her element.

She knew Cody wasn't going to say anything, but her language around men she didn't know shocked the fool out of me. "Pepper!"

"Well, hell, he ought to be careful."

The guys laughed again, and Steve put his sock back on after realizing the toe was barely scratched.

Cody shook his head at Steve. "I swear. Boy, you're an accident waiting to happen." He thumped Pepper on the head. "C'mon kids. Let's show these yahoos how to shoot."

The field beside us began to shimmer in the rising heat.

We broke out the shotguns. Pepper knew how to load her Daddy's twenty-gauge pump, but Cody wouldn't let her put more than one shell in it at a time. It made her mad and she sulled up for a while, but he didn't care, and secretly, I was glad. It made me feel better about the ribbing I'd already taken from her.

We found a shady spot away from the cars and Cody's friends. He spaced us where he knew no one was in danger of being shot by a couple of kids. Then he loaded his own Browning humpback and joined the fun. When the first birds flew into range Pepper cheered up and started banging away.

Cody called it sky blasting. "Hey, girl! You gotta lead those birds some and I think you ought to at least shoot *toward* them. Don't shoot the whole bunch at once, either. Pick out one bird and shower down on him."

The dove acted spooky, like they'd been shot at before, which was likely so late into the season. They dodged and darted long before they got close to us, as if they knew ambush was waiting at the tree line. Shotguns thundered across the field. I kept missing the crossing birds and Cody told me I was shooting way behind them. The long, heavy shotgun slowed me down and made my reactions slow.

More shotguns sent the birds back our way. I sometimes found myself watching other men across the field and forgot to shoot, hypnotized that I could see them shoot and watch birds fall long before the sound reached us.

In no time at all Pepper went through two boxes of shells. Cody finally put his own shotgun down and counted the birds in his vest. "I'm limited out, so you guys are gonna have to do the rest of the shooting."

"What are you gonna do now?" I'd heard from the men up at the store about limiting out, but until then I hadn't realized you had to quit shooting when you reached a magic number.

"I'm gonna drink a beer and watch you guys hunt."

Pepper and I exchanged glances. I had my orders about Uncle Cody, but I had no intention of going home so fast. Besides, I wasn't sure beer constituted "drinking."

Cody fished a can out of his shooting vest. He picked off the feathers and dug around inside his shirt for the church key around his neck. Until then I thought he wore an Indian necklace, because I could see the woven grass cord sometimes when his top buttons were undone. He punched two holes in the can and took a long drink and sighed.

"Damn. That's good, even if it is rodeo cool." He looked at me and then at Pepper. "I got some Cokes and a few strawberries in the cooler back of the truck. I wouldn't forget you two."

A strawberry drink sounded good. Cody wagged the bottle opener at me with a twinkle in his eye.

It was good to be a man.

Pepper caught a flash of feathers and took a potshot at a dove crossing not far from where we stood. It folded and landed in a puff of dust. She looked around to see if anyone else had fired at the same time.

"You got him!" Cody whooped.

Some of the guys farther down saw the bird fall and cheered with us. Pepper ran out to retrieve it like when we were little kids picking up Uncle Mac's birds when he shot them from the shade beside his house. We passed the dove around for a moment and I was determined I wouldn't let Pepper outshoot me.

The double barrel can wear on a kid pretty quick. If the stock isn't snug against your shoulder, it'll leave a bruise that will last for days, too. Half dozen shots later, my first bird drifted into the pattern and everyone hollered when it fell. Uncle Cody put the bird with Pepper's and we went back to hunting.

Half an hour later he finally stood and stretched. "Let's get these birds cleaned. Then we'll go down by Visor Creek and set up camp. I don't want to be on the Red tonight, because I believe it's been raining out to the west and this ol' river can come up before you can say calf rope."

The rest of the hunters gathered around us as we cleaned the birds and aggravated Pepper for fun. She pretended to get mad, but she flushed red and it was obvious she liked all the attention. I'd forgotten all about Cody's drinking once the guys joined us, because everyone had a beer in his hand.

Feathers fluttered in the weeds by the time everyone was finished. Cody rinsed the birds off with some water from the cooler and put them into a galvanized bucket in the back of the El Camino. He pitched in a couple of handfuls ice and covered it with a wet rag. "That'll hold them until we fry them up tonight. We're gone boys. Climb in kids."

We waved bye at the hunters. They saluted us with beer and Cody punched the gas and steered toward the creek, leaving a rooster tail of dust and lot of cussing. Pepper and I couldn't stop grinning, because the trip had only gotten started.

Chapter Eleven

O.C. Rains' office wasn't nearly as hot as the last time Ned visited, but the windows were still wide open and a flyswatter lay close by. Because his hands were full, Ned kicked the door open and walked right in.

The judge looked up from his paperwork and frowned. "Don't you ever knock?"

"Don't need to. You wouldn't get up to open it anyway. You'd just holler to come on in, so there ain't no use in knocking." He handed O.C. two cold R.C. colas from the machine downstairs. "Here, pull these and rest a minute."

O.C. pitched down his pen and took the sweating bottles. He poked around in his desk drawer until he found an opener. "Thankee. What are you here for today?"

For the next few minutes, Ned told him about the dead goat the Wilson boys found in the drain, the dog they brought to the store and the coyote on the fence down by the creek bridge.

"This makes seven dead animals I know of right now." He held up seven fingers for emphasis. "Seven, and five of them have showed up in the last month or so."

O.C. leaned back and frowned. He took a long swallow. "I believe you're gonna have to show me some more evidence before I can charge Doak's boy with animal mistreatment."

"Don't bother. He ain't it. I believe you had him penned up here before the goat was cut up."

"Hell. I hoped we had the right one. You sure he didn't poke it up in there before you caught him at the still?"

"Positive. The goat was ripe, but he hadn't been in there that long. I'm still on the prowl."

"There wasn't any advertisements, were there?"

"Naw. But I found this one with the coyote on the fence."

He handed it to O.C. who studied the children's picture in the carefully cut newspaper advertisement. "This is like what you found under Cody's dog. Was the coyote treated the same way?"

"'Course it was, but this time it had been caught in a trap first. I could tell by its front leg Then it was skint like a squirrel, but the hide was laid back over it like a blanket. Damndest thing I've seen in a while, and that's saying something."

"Well, what are you gonna do now?"

"The same thing I always do. I'll kick around and see what turns up. Might even run over to Ragtown or Slate Shoals and talk to a feller or two. It's the only thing I know to do."

"Well, you need to do it then."

They sat in comfortable silence for a long moment. Then Ned cleared his throat. "You know, I'm thinking those poor animals I've found ain't the only ones out there."

"What do you mean?"

"I mean there are probably others I ain't found. I bet there are more animals he's killed just for the pure-d fun of it."

O.C. swiveled around toward the open window. It was his best thinking posture. "What others have you found?"

"This time around the first was a squirrel hanging from a rope under the creek bridge. He'd built a fire under it while it was still alive and I guess he set there and watched it twist and burn. He'd circled a coon in one of them Disney picture show advertisements and left it there with what was left.

"Then not long afterward Bud Sikes found a coon nailed to the side of his hay barn like you would tack up a skin, but it was still in one piece, its belly cut open and its guts hanging strung out. I imagine the poor thing hung there until it died. There was a newspaper advertisement of the bird dog trials over in Hugo stuck in its mouth. It wasn't long until I found Cody's dog, then the coyote on the fence, then another dog and the goat. The son-of-a-bitch is baiting me."

O.C. shook his head without turning around. He'd seen a lot over the years, but nothing like this. He shivered. "You don't think there are people or kids out there somewhere, yet, do you? Somebody left out in them woods you ain't found?"

"Maybe not right now, but the size of what he's killing gets bigger and bigger, and he keeps pointing at kids. And I don't know how to explain it, but he's doing more…damage to the things he's killing. Do you have any missing person reports I need to see?"

"I have a couple," O.C. said. He rummaged around on his desk and brought out a couple of sheets, but none of them were children. He handed them to Ned anyway. "You let me know if you find anything else. Let me know right then."

"All right."

"You been doing any other work?"

Ned brought O.C. up to date on the calls he'd cleared. They talked for a while about who was fighting, who was messing around and who got caught at it.

O.C. finally tired of law talk. "You gettin' your cotton in?"

"Ivory and his people won't be long now. The dampness last night cost me some time, but I doubt it'll be too much. Got some of John's kinfolk pickin' for me, too."

"You didn't hire Ralston, did you?"

"Naw. I know better."

"Well, if you see him hanging around the store out there, bring him in. I heard he cut up a Mexican across the tracks last night and then he run off."

"I'll keep an eye out, but I hear he's in the Dallas jail." Ned glanced up at the wanted posters papering the side of O.C.'s filing cabinet, half expecting to see Ralston's picture. "Speaking of outlaws, Frank Lightfoot's family moved into the shack down from the house. They're poor. We gave them some cornmeal for their supper with some other stuff. I hired them to pick, too. They're supposed to start work today."

"Indians picking cotton? You don't see many of them with cotton sacks on this side of the river." O.C. leaned forward and set his empty drink bottle on the desk. He rummaged through several stacks of files until he found the one he was looking for, then perched a pair of smudged reading glasses on his nose. "Frank Lightfoot. It says here he just got out of jail again."

"What? What fer? I figured they'd keep him for the next ten years."

"He did some talking and gave up a few boys who were doing worse things than him up there in Oklahoma. They're giving him time off for it, so he'll probably be back around pretty quick."

Ned shook his head. Sometimes the criminals were on the street before he had time to get back home from the jailhouse. "I swear. They must have one of them department store revolving doors up there in McAlester. Nobody stays anymore."

"Yeah, and it's getting worse. Maybe if we catch him we can keep him in Huntsville. Anyway, keep an eye out."

"I imagine he'll stop by and try to work that feller over who's took up with his wife. I'll be bringing him back in pretty quick. You know, O.C., you and I were raised in shacks. I didn't know what a wooden floor was until I was fifteen. But it ain't right this day and time. I live in a house with indoor plumbing and electric lights. Hell, I even have a television set that we can see when the weather is right. But those folks are barely getting by."

O.C. swiveled in his chair and looked up at the portrait of President Kennedy on his wall. "These are the 1960s and it ought not be that way. Kennedy said we'd be on the moon before 1970 and here people are still using outhouses, chasing down people making whiskey and dealing with whites who don't like niggers and both of them not liking

Indians. When you live off the land you'd think it'd be hard to hate another man for the color of his skin. What's next? You think those Mexicans will come up from down south? Who'll hate them?"

"Japs." They laughed.

O.C. reached into his back pocket and pulled out a worn billfold. He passed a couple of bills across to Ned. "Here. Either give it to them poor folks or buy them something to eat if you don't want to give 'em cash."

Without commenting, Ned folded the bills and put them in his shirt pocket beside a pack of Juicy Fruit chewing gum. He and O.C. had been through this same routine for years and the only people who knew were those they helped along the way.

Ned sat quietly for a moment. "Say, they're having a dance up at the gym tonight. Cliff Vanderburg and a few other boys are gonna start making music about eight o'clock. Y'all need to come out."

O.C.'s eyes lit up. "Good idea. I might take you up on it."

"Good. I'll see you tonight. Bring Catherine if she's feeling strong enough."

"Okey dokey." Both knew she'd never get out of the house. O.C. returned to the mountain of paperwork on his desk as Ned softly closed the door behind him.

Chapter Twelve

Uncle Cody drove us past Grandpa's cotton field. The opened bolls reminded me of melting snow. Dressed in faded and patched clothing, the colored hands spread out across the rows, dragging long canvas cotton sacks over one shoulder. The younger and less experienced workers pulled up the rear with sacks their own size.

The best hands worked faster and set the pace.

The Lightfoot clan was scattered back of the colored hands, not quite keeping up, but they made up for it through sheer determination.

The sun was rough. A couple of people straightened up and shaded their eyes, watching us go past, but I couldn't tell anyone apart except for Mrs. Lightfoot. Her thin cotton dress was stuck to her sweaty figure, and I looked away, embarrassed because I could see places where she pooched out.

Several of the smallest children played on pallets in the shade of a big tree. The smallest ones napped on a half-full cotton sack. Cody slowed to keep the drifting dust down. I waved at the little ones. A skinny teenage girl with a dirty rag wrapped around one foot kept an eye on the kids.

Once past Grandpa's field, the drive took us almost to the creek winding through the cool, dark woods. Getting closer to Visor Creek, things got pretty tight a couple of times when Cody squeezed us through trees growing close to the dirt road.

He drove us right up to our campsite in what was once the back part of Camp Travis during World War II. We called it the Army Camp.

In no time at all we set up camp right at the edge of a tiny clearing surrounded by tall pecans, red oaks, hackberries and white elms. Grapevines thick as my arm grew up the trunks, sometimes in thick groupings so dense we could barely force our way through.

We helped Cody pitch his moldy canvas tent that weighed more than a Brahma bull. While he held up the umbrella frame on the inside, we passed him the aluminum legs. Once the six-foot tent was up, Cody showed us how to tuck everything in tight on our cots to make army beds.

While I gathered wood for the campfire, Pepper took the bucket down to the spring to get water that bubbled up into a pocket of green ferns and moss. Tiny frogs hopped in all directions when anyone approached. While she was down there, Pepper pulled a few wild onions growing nearby in the damp ground.

Cody was mixing cornmeal to cook in his Dutch oven when she got back. "I'm gonna make some cornbread, and y'all know that's good."

"What are we gonna do then?" Pepper put the heavy bucket on the ground.

He lit a match and touched it to the stacked kindling. I had piled up leaves and small sticks, so the fire caught quickly. "We're going hog hunting."

Somehow he read my mind. I'd wanted to hunt hogs since I'd read *Hound Dog Man.* Our trip already reminded me of the adventure described in the book. I even brought a big knife, like the kind the kid carried in the story.

You never knew when you'd need a knife.

It took a while for the fire to burn down. When the coals were right, we rolled the dove in flour and fried them in about an inch of Miss Becky's hog lard. The cornbread was ready at the same time, and we ate it from the Dutch oven, loving the crunch and clean taste of the wild onions.

Cody finished and leaned on one elbow and picked his teeth with a little cedar stick he shaved to a point with his pocketknife. "I've always liked this little camping spot. When I was a kid your Grandpa Ned used to bring me down here. He liked to hunt squirrels when the leaves were falling. A couple of times he brought along Mr. Epp Parker. Did y'all ever hear tell of him?"

I looked at Pepper, but she shook her head and we turned back to Uncle Cody. "Well, Mr. Epp must have been way up in his nineties when I was about your age, and he was pretty spry. He didn't live in any one place. He drifted from one family to another, staying when someone offered a pallet beside the fire.

"He told a lot of stories to us kids, but the one I remember best happened when he was around fifteen and lived with his family on the Llano. A bunch of Comanches came through and burned them out. They killed his mama and papa and took Mr. Epp captive. They planned to kill him, but he got loose from being tied up and ran away in the dark.

"He ran down the riverbank with the Indians not far behind. He could hear them screaming and carrying on and knew he couldn't outrun them so he headed for a holler log he knew of. He barely beat them there and crawled inside. Since it was dark, they figured he'd kept going. He lay there and counted thirty-two Comanches as each one put one foot on the log to jump it. Once they passed by, he slipped out into the river and floated downstream all night until he found a family of settlers who took him in."

A whippoorwill called nearby and we lay there for a while, enjoying the night. Cody and Pepper cleaned up what dishes there were, and I took one of the lanterns and filled another bucket of water from the spring.

Back at the fire, I found Cody loading a rifle I recognized from war movies on television. "That's a carbine." For a moment I thought he'd decided the whippoorwill was a real Comanche about to lift our hair.

He nodded. "This clip holds fifteen shots and it has open sights. It's what we need for hunting hogs in the dark. Where's your pig sticker?"

"Right here," I put my hand on the hilt of my knife. It had been on my belt from the time we'd set up camp.

"I wish I had a knife to carry." Pepper sighed to make her point.

"Well, I know. Everybody needs a pocket knife." Cody reached into his back pocket and brought out two Old Timers. "Here's one for each one of you. Y'all keep them sharp and they'll serve you for years." Pepper squealed and hugged his neck.

I opened the razor sharp blade.

"Each one of you give me a penny."

"What for?" I dug in my pocket.

"Don't ever give anyone a knife. Sell it to them

for a penny so they don't have to pay in blood. A free knife will cut you."

"All right." Cody traded us a couple of 'toe sacks for the coins. "Here, girl. I want you to hold these and the lantern so we can see. Top, you carry the flashlight and if the pigs are down by the creek, we'll put the sneak 'em and shoot us a fat sow."

Pepper stuffed the burlap bag deep into her back pocket to keep her hands free. The remainder hung nearly to her feet. "What are these 'toe sacks for?"

"We may be able to catch a few little piglets for Miss Becky. I reckon it'll be easier to carry them in a sack."

We followed the sandy road through the meadow. It ended at the timber lining the creek. Our tiny group startled a big owl once. It thrashed through the limbs and flew away in the moonlight.

Pepper jumped. "Shitfire. That scared the piss out of me."

I didn't admit it, but the owl scared me, too. The talk earlier of Comanches made me jumpy. We didn't need Pepper's lantern once the moon was up. She blew it out and we walked a while longer. I couldn't tell where we were, but Cody soon stuck out his hand to stop us.

He spoke quietly. "Hold it, troops. We're almost there. Now, here's what we'll do. Top, you walk in front of me real easy and I'll follow you. Pepper, keep one of those wooden matches in your hand, and as soon as I shoot, you stop and light the lantern."

"Why can't I shoot? I'm a good shot."

"Not tonight you ain't." Cody scratched her head with his fingertip to ease the sting of his words. "Wounded hogs can be dangerous, so I'll have to do the shooting. All right, let's go and be quiet."

The trail was bright and I could see Cody when he held his hand up and whispered. "Listen."

Soft grunts louder than the crickets told us hogs were rooting nearby. I imagined we were creeping up on wild Indians. My pretending ended abruptly when I suddenly heard a deep, much louder grunt.

The entire moonlit meadow was full of hogs. I felt the hair rise on the back of my neck and jumped when Cody put his hand on my shoulder.

He whispered in my ear. "We won't need your flashlight. I'll shoot the one right there with the little ones."

The rust-colored sow rooted in front of us, surrounded by her young shoats. She stopped to test the wind with her nose, and then went back to work. The grass roots tore with a ripping sound every time she pushed deep with her nose.

Cody reached out, took Pepper's arm and

pulled her up beside us. "All right. They're close enough to catch two or three of them shoats once I shoot the mama. When she's down them little ones won't know what to do. They'll stay close, so when I holler, y'all start grabbing them. This'll be like the pig scramble at the rodeo."

Pepper stared at him with shock. "You're gonna kill their mama? Them little things will starve to death if you do."

Cody bent his head close to her ear. "No they won't. She's weaned them already. See them? They're eating the same things they're mama is turning up. Now, close your eyes until you hear the shot and then don't take off running until I tell you she's down for sure."

"I ain't standing here with my eyes closed."

Cody sighed. "The muzzle flash will blind you when I shoot. Close your eyes so you guys will still have your night vision."

"You gonna close yours too?"

I could see Cody's white teeth when he smiled. "Sure will."

"Then how are you going to shoot?"

I sighed like Uncle Cody. "He'll close his eyes before he pulls the trigger, stupid."

"He's right. But they're gonna hear us if we stand here talking like a bunch of old women at a quiltin' party. So you two shut up and get ready."

Cody took a knee and aimed. I closed my eyes. The shot split the night and I could see the muzzle flame even through my eyelids. He whooped. "Got her! She's down! Get them pigs!"

Pepper must have listened because she acted like she could see pretty good when she opened her eyes. The shoats scattered at the commotion. One ran straight at me and it was nothing to reach down and pick it up, only I grabbed mostly squeal and wiggle. It was worse than anything I'd ever held onto.

Beside me, another one started squalling. Pepper had it by the back leg and was holding on for dear life.

"Hold what you got!" Cody laughed big at the noise.

My squealer kicked as I dragged him over to Pepper. She pulled one of the 'toe sacks from her back pocket and held her own piglet with one hand. I finally got my pig's head inside the sack and pulled it over him like I was putting on my pants. He quieted right down, but Pepper was still in a fight, so I grabbed her pig's other back leg. We lifted the shrieking thing up and sacked him pretty quick. Another shoat darted between us. Pepper fell on it and they rassled in the dirt. Cody was on the other side of the dead mama, waving his arms and hollering, and keeping things stirred up.

Pretty soon the third shoat joined the others

in the 'toe sack and we tied the end. We giggled hysterically from nervousness and the piercing squeals shooting right through our heads.

Suddenly Cody fired two quick shots. "Goddlemighty!"

I couldn't see him very clearly in the moonlight, but something in his voice let us know something wasn't right. We turned and saw Cody running away from us like the Devil himself was chasing him.

"You kids run for those trees, now!"

I'd never heard that tone from him before. All the squealing had aggravated a mean old boar to the point that he had every intention to eat whatever was causing the commotion. Four hundred pounds of mad hog erupted through the brush, white tusks glinting and popping in the moonlight. The coarse hair along his backbone stood up like a mad dog's hackles.

We froze in absolute fear when I realized the the boar might turn on us with his razor sharp tusks, especially if the sacked pigs started in with their squealing again.

"Goddlemighty!" Cody waved his arms shouted to draw the boar's attention, and it worked. "Hey hey hey!!!"

The boar ducked his head and charged. Cody shot again at the boar, but its neck, armored with a layer of gristle and thick hide, turned the shot and it plowed the dirt off to the side. Cody must have wounded the boar with the one of his shots, though, because it didn't run right. He crawfished after Cody on three legs, but it didn't slow him at all, because he was mad.

Cody ran directly up to a tree with low growing limbs and jumped. His left boot caught enough purchase on the rough bark for him to grab a branch with his free hand. Somehow he kept hold of the carbine, squirreled up on the limb, and started shooting. I was amazed at how fast one man could shoot a semi-automatic rifle.

After using one bullet on the sow and three more on the boar, he still had eleven shots left. The boar attacked the tree, slashing at the tree with his sharp tusks. Cody emptied every last bullet into the furious hog from above in a quick, rolling stream thunder, and the boar finally went down. Everything was quiet for a few minutes. I heard Cody eject the clip and slap another into the rifle.

With the danger past, Pepper knelt down to light the lantern so we could see. "Shitfire! Snake!" She jumped up ran off without the lantern and her sack of piglets.

Following her lead, I took off in the other direction. "Water moccasin!" I hadn't really seen the snake, but it had to be a moccasin.

"Goddlemighty!" Startled and halfway out of the tree, Cody fell with a thud in the soft sand beside the boar.

His moving shadow made me think the boar wasn't dead after all and was attacking Cody. I grabbed my big knife out of its sheath and gave it an overhand, backward throw as I ran off, in case I might get lucky and slow the boar down.

The hilt of the knife thumped off Cody's cheekbone, instantly raising a mouse big enough to earn the name.

"Goddlemighty, boy!" I was halfway down the meadow when I heard him laughing behind me. People usually don't laugh when wild boars are eating them, so I slowed down to listen. "Hold it! Hey, kids! Come on back." He snorted some more. "I saw your snake when we went past a minute ago and it was only a chicken snake."

Pepper stomped back down the dirt road, working up a pretty good mad. "Shitfire and save the matches! You coulda told us there was a damned chicken snake in the road. You know how I am about snakes! They can make me hurt myself."

"I never saw such." Cody laughed. "You had five hundred pounds of mad boar hog not twenty yards away while y'all stood there like a couple of stumps, and you're more afraid of a little ol' snake." Cody rubbed his mouse and looked thoughtful.

"Besides, I was more concerned with y'all getting hurt. Watch your language and tell me how many pigs you caught."

"Three." I tugged at the heavy sack.

"Miss Becky will be tickled to death with all this meat." Cody examined the hogs with the flashlight. He looked sad. "Well, now we've gone and done it. We can't leave them laying here. We're gonna have to gut them so they'll cool and then take everything up to the house."

Pepper stomped around for a while longer, working off her mad. Gutting hogs wasn't at all what I wanted to do, either. The idea of a hog hunt had been great up to the point where we had to do something with them. I wanted to go back to camp, poke the fire, and sleep on my cot, but we were committed to the meat.

Cody checked the safety and put the rifle on the ground. "Here, Pepper. Bring your lantern over here so I can see what I'm doing. Top, go find your butcher knife and let's see how sharp it is. I'm gonna teach y'all how to field dress wild game."

None of us was squeamish about blood and guts. We'd been part of hog killings ourselves. But this was the first time we'd ever been elbow deep in the job. Usually at hog killing time, we mostly watched and fed the fire.

Hog killing began by shooting them right between the eyes while they were still in the pen. After bleeding them where they fell, the men drug them out, hoisted them up by their back legs and lowered the carcasses into a stained clawfoot bathtub full of near-boiling water to scald the hair off. Then they hoisted the carcass up again and gut it before someone cut them up.

It was different in the field. Cody started by slitting the sow's belly from her tail to her neck. With Pepper holding the light, Cody reached inside and cut everything loose. Then we rolled her over and pulled out the innards.

The boar was worse. His hide was tough as leather and he stunk. Cody showed us how well he was armored with a layer of gristle, even under the sharp knife.

"Look here at all these scars. He was a fighter." Long hairless scars crisscrossed the bristly chest and sides.

Cody showed us how the boar's tusks locked together and sharpened themselves each time he closed his mouth. A long line of spit dropped onto the sand from its open mouth. Ugly beyond belief, I didn't want to touch the nasty thing, but Uncle Cody had other ideas. He handed me his own skinning knife after sharpening it again on a whit rock he carried in his pocket.

"Now, you saw me clean the last one. This one is yours."

Pepper held the light. "Glad I'm not a boy."

Uncomfortable but game, I made the first cut through the chest and had to really bear down to get through the skin. The knife slipped and I cut too deep, nearly getting into the stomach and the edge of one intestine.

Pepper groaned. "Whew! You're not very good at this."

I offered her the knife but she refused to take it. For the next few minutes I did my best, but it was too much for a ten-year-old.

"Here, I'll help you." Cody finally did the hard part and the bloody job was finished. "You kids stay here and I'll go get the truck. When I get back we'll see about loading these guys up. Glad I brought a come-along." He handed me the carbine. "Now y'all stay put. Keep this, 'cause there may be a coyote or a wolf come by here with the smell of all this blood. Aim careful if they do and make sure of your target. Don't shoot me by accident."

Pepper's eyes got big, but before she could answer, Cody trotted outside the circle of our lantern. We listened to the night while the sacked piglets grunted quietly to themselves. There is no silence in the river bottoms. Crickets, frogs, night birds, and completely unknown sounds filled the air, sounding even louder once Uncle Cody was gone.

"You know, we can't see squat past this lantern light." I was feeling a little creepy at what might be out there beyond our secure circle of light. "Let's blow it out so we can see. Wolves could already be eating the sow over there before we even knew it."

Pepper snorted. "They'll most likely try to eat us since we're pretty much covered in blood."

"Don't worry. I'm here." I turned off the lantern. The sounds got louder.

She punched me. "That idea was as good as bringing a big knife to cut Cody's head off with."

"I didn't do any such of a thing. I was trying to save him."

"Well, don't try to save me. I'd druther have a wolf gnaw my arm off than to have you hit me in the face with a sword."

"You're a girl. You don't know nothin' about gnawing and knives and such."

"Kiss my ass. I know I ain't raised no mouse under Cody's eye."

"You couldn't have done it, because you were running in the other direction when you saw that snake."

"I wasn't expecting it."

"I wasn't expecting no five-hundred-pound pig neither."

"Well, be quiet so the wolves won't hear."

"They can smell, too."

"You ain't helping my nerves any. Let's just be quiet."

I took out my knife and thumped it into the dirt for a while. I quit when I couldn't see after clouds rolled in and covered the moon. Then it got really dark.

"What's that sound?" Pepper asked in a whisper.

I listened. It sounded like footsteps moving toward us through the grass. I imagined a dozen different things were sneaking up on us: everything from Indians, to bears, to the dog killer.

Pepper moved closer. I could feel her shaking. "Does that sound like somebody breathing?" she whispered.

"I think it's somebody walking."

It was then we distinctly heard a soft chuckle.

Pepper gave a nearly soundless scream. "Light the lantern."

"I ain't got no matches!"

"Shit. Use the flashlight, fool!"

I remembered the flashlight, but it was somewhere on the ground nearby. I was feeling through the grass, half expecting my hand to touch something hairy, or that another hand was going to grab mine, when the El Camino's headlights flickered through the trees.

Cody drove up and got out quickly. "Hey! Where y'all at?" His voice sounded scared.

I gave up on the flashlight and stood up. "Right here. We couldn't see out there with the lantern on."

Uncle Cody found us with his light, but the little beam didn't do much to light up the bottoms. "Good thinking. I got nervous when I didn't see any light."

Pepper jumped up and ran to Cody. "We thought we heard somebody out there."

"Well, there ain't nothing there."

"I can't find my flashlight," I said.

He worked his beam on the ground around us. "I don't see it."

"I laid it right there."

"You must have left it laying somewhere else."

I knew where I'd put the silver metal flashlight. And now it was gone. "I had it when you left."

"Well, I don't want to waste time finding it in the dark." He didn't realize how scared we'd been, and neither of us told him. "Y'all come on and let's histe this sow up in here first."

I stared into the darkness. I hadn't lost my flashlight. It had been took from right beside us.

Cody drained the beer he'd been holding between his legs and threw the can into the dark. Pepper shined Cody's extra flashlight on the truck and using the cab as an anchor, he attached a come-along to a wide canvas strap he'd run through both open windows. We unrolled the cable and wrapped it around the sow's back feet. Cody started cranking at the come-along, gaining a few inches with each pull.

Cody did most of the work because it was heavy. "Whew. This thing must weigh three hundred and fifty pounds. Here, Pepper, you take a turn."

She had to throw her whole body into it and when she gave out, I took over. We finally got the hog into the small bed and pushed her around until there was room for the boar. We helped some, but I think I was more in the way than anything else, because I kept trying to see what was in the darkness around us. The tailgate groaned like it was going to give out before we had him loaded.

Tired, sweaty, and bloody, we finally finished. Too long for the bed, the hogs lay with their heads hanging off the tailgate. Cody looked at his watch. "Lordy mercy. It's only eight-thirty. Throw them pigs in on top there and let's go."

The El Camino rested low on her springs, so we drove slowly back to camp. I kept expecting to see somebody with my flashlight caught in the headlights. But the only thing we saw was an armadillo.

It didn't take long to skin out of our dirty clothes. We washed up at the little brook down from the spring. It was dark under the trees, but the path was easy to follow. Our hands were hardly dry before Cody was ready to go again. He popped another beer and checked on the piglets. You could see them moving around in the burlap toesacks.

"You guys will be safe in a pig pen before daylight."

We drove to Miss Becky's house. She was still up and the windows glowed when we pulled up the drive. She heard us and the porch light pushed back the darkness and she peeked through the screen door.

"Cody? What are y'all doing back here? Is everything all right?" Miss Becky didn't expect us back and it scared her. She also didn't like it when kinfolk showed up late at night. It usually meant trouble or a death.

Pepper and I boiled out of the truck before he had time to answer. "Come take a look at these two hogs we killed. We brought you a mess of pigs, too!"

Miss Becky hurried off the porch in her night-gown to look into the truckbed. "My lands. Y'all brought home a lot of work." She immediately took control. She'd been rendering hogs since she was little, on a little scratch farm in Grant. "Here, you kids put two of the shoats in the hog pen and

I'll look at them in the morning. Leave the other'n in the sack. Top, empty the slop bucket in the feed trough while you're down there. I'm sure she'd weaned them already and they're probably hungry, poor little things."

We took our time at the hog pen, turning two of them out of the sack. They grunted a couple of times and huddled up in one muddy corner for safety while we waited, hearing the adult's voices in the yard. When we figured she was finished chewing on Uncle Cody about his drinking, we carried the remaining pig back up to the house and put the sack in the truck bed.

Not looking any worse than when we left, Cody backed the truck up to the smokehouse door, and they attached the chain hoist to the hogs. In no time they hung from the rafters. Miss Becky propped the carcasses open so they'd cool during the night.

I finally noticed the car was gone. "Where's Grandpa?"

"He's out." It was Miss Becky's way of saying Grandpa was doing law work. "Y'all want to come in and sleep in a good bed tonight?" She knew there was no way we'd stay.

Cody tilted his hat back. "No, ma'am. The troops and I have a good camp waiting for us down on the creek, but thanks."

She gave us kids a looking over and finding little else wrong, sent us inside to wash up again. Cody had on a clean shirt and was waiting behind the wheel while we cut two huge slices of coconut cake and hurried outside.

"You two eat more than any kids I've ever seen." The porch light went out and we headed out again. "Pepper, why didn't you bring me a piece?"

"I did."

Sitting between us, she shared her cake with him. I'd never noticed her graceful fingers before, despite the broken and chewed off fingernails. She looked a little different in the dim light of the dashboard. There was something embarrassing about watching her feed Uncle Cody one bite at a time, and I was glad when it was gone.

He slowed the truck and turned up the gravel drive leading to Uncle Henry's house on top of the hill overlooking the highway.

Pepper brushed the last of the crumbs off her lap. "What are we doing here? You got a wart you need taking off?"

Everyone knew about Uncle Henry's power of wart removal, but no one could answer for sure how he did it. Some thought he prayed warts away, closing his eyes and rubbing his fingers around and around in a pattern. Others said his body oils made them disappear.

"Naw." Cody turned into their steep drive. "We're dropping the other piglet off with Aunt Mamie." He stopped at the back porch and turned off the engine. A single bulb lit the yard. Cody lifted the sacked piglet out of the bed and we clumped up the wooden porch steps. Pepper rapped on the screen, and Uncle Henry opened the door.

He stood nearly six foot seven and was shaped like a pineapple. I saw him mostly in the spring because he had the closest storm cellar to Grandpa's house. Over the years we made several hurried drives in the middle of the night to his hand-dug cellar, thinking a cyclone was going to blow us away before we got there. There were always a couple of other families with the same idea. We'd stay under the ground until the storm blew over, or the men thought it was safe to go home.

In her nightgown, tiny Aunt Mamie peeked around her tall husband. She was a little gray-haired woman with a heart as big as Texas. She hugged all three of us while Uncle Henry simply smiled. "My lands, Becky called and said y'all were on the way. What are y'all doing out this time of the night?"

"We've been hunting and thought you could use a pig." Cody handed Aunt Mamie the sack.

"Y'all get in this house."

Pepper hugged Uncle Henry's ample belly stretching his undershirt. Pulling at his suspenders and grinning up at him, she suddenly became a little girl again. "You got any new puppies?" she asked.

Aunt Mamie was always taking care of something. A month earlier a litter of newborn puppies squirmed in a box beside the wood-burning stove in the living room. Their mama had been run over on the highway below the house. Since they were far from being weaned, Aunt Mamie fed them with an eyedropper every few hours, but she said it was no step for a stepper.

"Naw, hon." She put the sack with the softly grunting piglet on the plank floor beside the door. "Our new mama-dog hasn't found any puppies in a while, but looky here."

We knelt beside about thirty peeping chicks, tiny yellow balls of fluff in a shallow cardboard box near the stove.

Cody bent over and hugged Aunt Mamie. "*Found* some puppies?"

Aunt Mamie poked him in the side with her elbow and cut her eyes at us as if we had no idea where babies came from.

Cody laughed and settled down on the worn horsehair sofa. He and Uncle Henry talked farming for a while, and then with a grin Uncle Henry asked how business was across the river. "I might need to get over there and take me a dose of medicine or two."

Uncle Henry hadn't had a drink in his entire life. Aunt Mamie acted like she was mad, but I could tell she was putting us on. She left and returned with a plate full of cookies.

We didn't stay long after the plate was empty. It was getting late and we'd already interrupted their nighttime routine. Cody had something on his mind so we hugged some more and promised to come by soon for some mincemeat pie.

The lights went out before we got to the end of the driveway. Instead of heading toward the bottoms, Cody turned left on the two-land highway and cruised past the store and the gin, still running under the lights. A man in a wagon moved the big vacuum pipe around the surface of the load, sucking the cotton up to begin the separation process. Smoke boiling out of the chimney from the burning cottonseed hulls hung low to the ground.

I dug the vaporizer out of my jeans and took a puff.

Chapter Thirteen

I wondered why Cody decided to take the long way until I saw the lights of the little frame school. There was a dance going on in the wood frame basketball gym, and the grass yard and playground were full of cars and trucks.

Like every Depression-era gym built by the WPA, wooden bleachers on each side of the basketball court were capped by a stage opposite the entrance. The open doors and windows gaped wide for ventilation. "Your Cheatin' Heart" filled the air, and we could see people dancing on the maple basketball court.

Cody's eyes twinkled in the lights of his dashboard. He shut off the engine. "Let's have a little fun before we go back to camp. I hear your great-Uncle Cliff up there on stage, and he don't play very often any more."

He got no argument from either of us. A large crowd of men and women milled outside the entrance, talking and laughing. Pepper and I wove past the adults and slipped in through the open doors. I looked back over my shoulder and saw Cody join a group of men beside a truck. The glint of a bottle flickered in the dim light and then someone blocked my view.

Age made no difference on the dance floor. Kids spent the evening wandering or playing chase through the older folks' legs. Young couples and singles lined the walls nearest the wooden bleachers watching the dancers.

Uncle Cliff hunkered over his beat-up guitar on the wooden stage, his legs crossed at the knee. He must have been seventy then, gray-haired and bony, singing softly into a microphone. Lined face hidden by a worn out, shapeless felt hat, he wasn't there to be seen, but to play music so folks could enjoy themselves.

Local musicians backed him up with guitars, fiddles and one big standup bass. The songs switched between waltzes, two-steps, and an occasional Western swing when it suited them.

He slowed down for a bit and got away from dancing songs. When he sang "Old Blue," a song about a dog and a boy, everyone stopped to listen. One line went, "...old Blue died hard, digging little holes in the front yard." It made me want to cry, but I held it back. Several women dabbed at their eyes when he got to the part about lowering Blue into the grave with a silver chain, and when the song was over everyone clapped, whistled and whooped like it was the best song in the whole world. Uncle Cliff didn't say anything at all. He started a fast two-step and the floor once again thickened with dancers.

Pepper and I stayed together for a while, feeling a little out of place at first. I still didn't know a lot of the adults there. Of course Pepper knew everyone since she'd lived in Center Springs all her life. We hung around the door, and after a while half a dozen older local boys surrounded her. A couple of them gave me a look, but I held my ground and gave it right back.

Cale Westlake, the Presbyterian preacher's boy was one of those. "I didn't know you were coming by." He was a head taller than me and two grades ahead.

"Neither did I," Pepper laughed. "But I doubt I'd have told you anyway."

He took Pepper's arm and turned his back on me. His lackeys laughed and shouldered me aside.

She frowned at Cale but she also looked like she wanted to talk to him. I wandered off toward the refreshment table set up underneath the goal farthest from the stage, and one of the ladies dipped me a cup of polly-pop. Limp crepe paper hanging from the goal rustled each time a breeze pushed through the door.

Uncle Cliff and the band started a Bob Wills tune. I took the strawberry punch and wandered back outside. A group of women giggled and laughed not too far from the door, one or two were sneaking a little dip of sweet Garrett snuff.

I saw Cody's hat behind the truck. About twenty men stood around the pickups backed up with the tailgates down. Uncle Cody perched on one, holding court.

I wiggled through the adults and took up a safe position beside a fender.

"That old boar had me running across the meadow like my head was on fire and my ass was catching." The men chuckled.

"How'd you get up that tree without dropping your rifle?"

"Damned if I know. All of a sudden I was sitting up there in that tree like a monkey, shooting as fast as I shot at them gooks over in Nam."

"He just ran up the side of the tree." Horrified that words had actually emerged from my mouth, I couldn't believe it had happened again. My mouth engaged all by itself.

Everyone turned in my direction and though one or two of them scowled, the rest laughed.

"Did you see it?" asked T.D. Stacker. He was

one of those solid farmers who worked, went to Sunday services, and sometimes snuck a beer when he was with folks who knew when to keep their mouths shut. His boy Butch was in one of my classes, but I hadn't seen Butch inside.

"Yessir. I had my hands full of squealin' piglets, but Cody shinnied up in the tree using nothing but his feet. I've never seen anyone do that before."

Uncle Cody chuckled. "You won't ever again, either. The only way to run up a tree is for something to be chasing you."

I figured their good humor was all lubrication. T.D. lit a cigarette and looked down at Cody's cowboy boots dangling above the ground. "I can't imagine how you did it with those slick soles."

"Dug in with my toes."

The men were having a great time, not caring one whit if there was a dance going on because they weren't there to rub bellies with their wives or girlfriends. They'd suffer the consequences later without complaining, for the chance to sit outside with the other men.

"I recollect the time you and I went up on the creek to do a little hog hunting," Edwin Lohman told someone I couldn't see in the dark. Edwin was the only man I knew back then who had been divorced.

"We didn't quite make it down to the creek."

"Yeah, we did. Except we kept going across into Juarez. In fact, I believe we wound up over there at Cody's place before he owned it."

"Yeah, there were hogs all right, but it wasn't the kind we were hunting..."

Cody caught Edwin's eye and cocked his head in my direction.

Edwin gave me an annoyed look, but then followed Cody's lead. "Who's watching the club for you this evening?"

"Neal Box said he'd keep an eye on things for me so I could take the kids hunting this weekend. I can't believe anyone would run a store all day and then my club at night."

"He probably wants to show you how to make some pocket money." Edwin glanced behind me and started to ease his way out of the circle.

Cody laughed. "As long as he does a good job, I'll let him take my place any time."

"He's probably doing a better job than you ever did." A big hand rested on my shoulder and I looked back to find Grandpa Ned standing there, dressed in his constable clothes. His soft felt Stetson and badge almost glowed in the reflection of the yellow schoolyard lights.

Judge Rains was with him. Still dressed in his dark judge's suit, the only difference was the pinch-crown fedora covering most of his silver hair. I was always afraid of him. I'd met him several times over the years, but it was my first time to see him outside of his cluttered office. He nodded to the group. "Evenin', boys."

"Howdy, judge."

A couple of the men slipped off the tailgate and stood out of respect. Two quietly disappeared into the darkness.

"I thought y'all were hunting tonight." Grandpa kept his hand on my shoulder.

"We had to rest awhile. Top and Pepper 'bout wore me out killin' everything that walks or flies, so we had to come in and unload." He leaned toward me. "Tell your Grandpa about our pig hunt."

I was embarrassed, but I launched into the story anyway, forgetting the men and talking to Grandpa. Everyone listened to my version and laughed at all the right places. It made me feel about ten feet tall.

Judge Rains cackled. "Say, y'all need to take me with you next time. I'd love a chance to sleep in the woods again."

"We'd be tickled to death. We're going back out here in a little while. Come go with us."

"I reckon I'll take a rain check."

Grandpa Ned grinned down at me. "Sounds like y'all were pretty busy. Well, you boys stay out of trouble out here, and y'all ought to hide them bottles a little better."

"Good idea, Tom, Edwin." The Judge nodded at each man. "I don't want to see any of you fellers in my courtroom Monday morning."

"Yessir, judge."

Grandpa gently shook my shoulder. "Cody, you keep your wits about you and be careful with these kids tonight."

"Yessir. We were fixin' to leave after we listen to Uncle Cliff pick for a minute or two."

"You can probably hear him better inside."

"That's a fact."

"All right. Y'all be careful."

I followed Grandpa and Judge Rains back through the doors because Uncle Cody didn't get right up. On stage, Uncle Cliff and the band played a waltz. Even Pepper was dancing in the corner with Cale Westlake. I could see her laughing and throwing her head back. It made me feel better to see Cale was counting his steps.

Judge Rains saw them also. "Am I looking at Darrin Westlake's boy?"

Grandpa shook his head like he does when he's disgusted. "Yeah, and I don't believe he has the sense to know the difference between come here and sic 'em. I'm afraid he's gonna follow right along behind his sorry daddy."

"I'god, I'm tired of seeing these people come through my courtroom one after the other over the years. Maybe I could get a squeeze chute and vaccinate them against having any more young 'uns."

I lost their conversation as they drifted toward the refreshment table to join a knot of men standing nearby. Cody stepped through the propped open doors and was immediately swarmed with women. I stayed by the wooden bleachers and watched him work the crowd. He couldn't take three steps at a time without someone stopping him to talk or hug his neck. He laughed big and hugged them back each time.

Henrietta Lewis, in her seventies and destined to be forever unmarried, passed me on her way to the refreshment table. "Why, Top! My lands, honey, you've grown a foot since the last time I saw you. We're gonna have to put a brick on your head."

I'd seen her earlier and ducked as she went by, hoping to avoid the big spinster woman, who could smother a kid between her giant breasts. She hugged me and made a fuss over how much I'd grown. Then she left me smelling like gardenias from the cheap perfume she wore.

I looked for Uncle Cody again and saw he had Calvin Williams' redheaded wife Norma hemmed up in the corner by the stage. Then I knew for sure why we were there.

Uncle Cliff stepped down for a few minutes and the younger musicians played a Lefty Frizzell tune. Pepper and Cale danced to "Saginaw, Michigan" on their way past, finally brave enough to leave their corner of the gym. In her red button-down shirt and jeans, with her hair pulled back in a long brown ponytail, she was rapidly losing her tomboy look.

I also noticed a couple of small bumps in her shirt I'd never seen before. I was embarrassed by the revelation, but when she passed, we grinned at each other like we didn't have good sense.

It infuriated Cale. He stopped counting his dance steps and scowled at me. "What are you grinnin' about sissy-boy?"

"What do you mean sissy-boy?"

He sniffed the air. "You smell like my grandmother."

It made me mad to know I smelled like gardenias. I felt my eyes start to burn. "Kiss my ass." It shocked me to realize I spoke those words.

"Let's go outside you little piss ant. I've never liked you anyway."

"Oh, shit." Pepper tried to pull Cale away.

It was like watching a boulder roll downhill. You can see it happening, but there's no way to stop it.

"Don't." Pepper put her hand on Cale's chest.

"He wasn't making fun of you. Top really *was* looking at me."

"I'll knock his top off all right. Let's go." He swaggered out the door, looking back over his shoulder at me. "C'mon titty-baby."

Three of his toadies slouched out of the bleachers and followed Cale through the door. They all grinned wide, because each one had been in my position at some time and knew what was coming.

There was no backing out. If I crawfished, all one hundred and ten students would be talking about me on Monday morning. I was also afraid I'd start crying when I got fighting mad, and there's no way to make yourself look brave with tears leaking down your cheeks.

Pepper let go of Cale and grabbed my arm. "You stay in here and I'll go out and talk to them."

"Won't do any good. If he doesn't fight me tonight, he'll do it later. I'm not gonna be called a titty-baby."

Oblivious to the drama unfolding under their noses, people laughed and couples danced. Uncle Cliff returned. He picked up the pace, and the dancer's faces flushed as he swung into a fast two-step.

I followed Cale's boys outside. Looking back over the decorated gym, the last thing I saw was

Cody grinning down at Miss Norma in his arms. They were having a big time. Despite what was about to happen, I couldn't help but envy Cody. I wished I was dancing with a redhead instead of going outside to meet Cale.

I'd walked inside like a man after telling stories to grownups about hunting. I came back out scared and sick inside; a kid again.

They weren't waiting like I expected. They showed some sense because the grownups were still out there in the yellow light spilling through the doors and windows. I thought I was home free because someone had run Cale and his buddies off, but as I stepped off the concrete step and caught a whiff of cigarette smoke, I saw one of Cale's toadies standing at the corner of the building. He motioned for me.

I had barely rounded the corner, when a cannonball hit me. The next thing I knew, I was in the dusty grass, wondering what had happened.

Sparkles of light flashed in my eyes and I heard Pepper in the distance. "Don't hit him again, you son of a bitch! He wasn't ready. You're not fighting fair!"

"There's no such thing as a fair fight, stupid."

I could already feel my eye swelling shut. The sound of a slap reached me. I got a hard kick in the ribs and it knocked the breath out of me. Then a body landed with a grunt right next to my head. It was Cale and he was holding his blood-spurting nose and squalling.

Suddenly people were stepping and falling all over me. I rolled over to push myself up, but someone fell on my back. The fight went on for a minute with several more punches and then everything quieted down. Pepper knelt next to me, crying, and the music still poured through the open windows.

A hand grabbed me under the arm and helped me stand. "You all right? You got sucker-punched pretty good there."

My head was spinning and I finally took a deep breath. "How…how?"

"That's the first thing you ever said to me."

"Mark?"

"Call me Chief War Cloud now. This your sister?"

Pepper grabbed my chin to look at my eye. "No, I ain't. Shit. Will you hold still? I want to see how bad you're hurt."

"You look like his sister," Mark said conversationally.

"Naw. I'm his cousin. Who are you, War Cloud?"

"Mark Lightfoot. My family moved into the shack down from Mr. Ned's house."

Pepper turned her attention toward Mark.

"You ain't hurt, are you? Somebody caught you a good lick."

He rubbed his ear. "I'll be all right. Hope you don't mind me joining in."

I was still feeling woozy. "Where did Cale and them go?"

"They changed their minds and ran off. I don't think they've ever tangled with a Choctaw before. We've always been outnumbered by you white-eyes, so we learned how to fight early. Good thing I was here."

A panicked voice shouted from the direction of the parked cars and trucks. "Fire!"

People boiled from the gym as the cry was repeated inside. We stepped around the corner to see what was going on. I expected the gym or schoolhouse to be burning, but people pointed toward a glow to the east. It wasn't the rising sun they pointed to and it wasn't lightning either.

Judge O.C. stepped out the door. "I believe it could be your house, Ned."

Grandpa followed him, but didn't say anything. I think he was trying to figure out exactly where the fire was. Then without a word he took off running across the playground with Judge O.C. right behind. They jumped in his car and the engine barely turned over before Grandpa jammed it into gear, throwing dirt and gravel into the air.

The tires squealed when he hit the road. Someone's headlights shined through his open window and I could see the radio microphone in his hand and knew he was calling Chisum for help.

Both Pepper and I were almost lifted off of our feet when Cody grabbed each of us by an arm. "Come on everybody! Get something to fight the fire. We'll need help before the trucks get there!"

The volunteer fire department was stationed in Powderly, another tiny community about ten miles up the road.

Instead of trying to get into the cab with Cody, Pepper and I jumped into the back. The bed was still dirty from the hog carcasses we'd hauled, and the coppery smell of the hog's blood by the tailgate was so strong it was almost a taste. I looked up to see Lightfoot's ponytail fly as he rolled over the side with a thump. His eyes twinkled with excitement.

Cody drove like we were in a race car. We shot down the highway behind Grandpa. With our backs against the cab to stay out of the wind, I fished the atomizer out of my pocket and took a puff.

Pepper slid over and put her arms around me. "I'm sorry."

"Don't matter none." I was embarrassed since Mark was sitting right there. "I'm sorry to shake up your romance."

"That's all right. He had his hand on my ass most of the time anyway, and I kept telling him to quit. I didn't like it one damn bit."

Mark held his flying hair with one hand. "I knew I enjoyed beating on him for some reason."

Pepper frowned at him, but didn't say anything. It didn't take us long to get to Grandpa Ned's house. I stuck my head over the cab and was relieved to see the fire was still a distance behind the house. Miss Becky stood on the grass beside the highway with a cloth jacket over her nightgown, waving a flashlight at us. Grandpa braked and pulled over beside her in the oncoming lane. Cody squalled to a stop in the middle of the highway. More cars stacked up behind us.

"What's the matter, Mama?"

"Oh Lord, Ned! I heard that poor Indian woman a-screaming bloody murder down there at the shack. By the time I looked out the winder, the house was afire and someone was hollering for help and screaming, 'God save us!' and, 'No, please, no!', and then it just quit."

Grandpa simply stomped on the gas, throwing gravel all over the yard and Miss Becky. She waved her flashlight at Cody. "Tell him I've already called Chisum!"

He waved to show he'd heard, then made a gun with his right forefinger and pretended to shoot like little kids do when they're playing. "You got it?" Miss Becky patted the deep pocket of her jacket and nodded. Cody waved again and floored the accelerator.

I looked over at Mark. His face was completely blank. I wondered how he could hear something so horrible without reacting. I didn't know until much later his entire life was one tragedy after another.

Once again Grandpa's brake lights lit up as he slowed to turn left onto the dirt road leading to the shack. The sedan's back tires barely gripped the soft sand enough to keep him from slewing into the bar-ditch. He brought the car under control and then floored it.

We followed close behind, leading a line of trucks and cars. Headlights flickered in the dust raised by over two dozen vehicles. Ahead, the weathered shack was completely swallowed in flames licking high into the air. I wondered why bundles of clothes were scattered across the dirt yard.

Grandpa slammed his brakes. Cody slid us to a stop beside his car and opened the door. We started to get out but he held a hand toward us. "Y'all stay back there." His short tone stopped us cold. I didn't move.

Grandpa looked over his shoulder and reinforced the order to us. "You heard him."

Judge Rains stepped out of the passenger side and held out his hand. "You men hold up, don't worry about the fire. Stay right where you are."

"Listen, Judge, we have to do something."

He gave Isaac Reader a sad look. "It don't look like there's anything *left* to do."

I could tell the men stood there against their better wishes, but Grandpa and the Judge had spoken. I was glad Uncle Cody had parked so far away. Even from our distance the heat was almost too much. The fire was more powerful than any I had ever seen. It roared through the engulfed house and smell of smoke mixed with the odor of cooking meat was strong as the north wind pushed it toward the cars.

They walked slowly toward the nearest pile of clothes. For the first time I saw Grandpa's pistol hanging loosely in his big hand. It sent a tingle down my spine. He knelt by the mound. An ax handle stuck up at an angle.

Pepper moved in the bed of the truck to look over the cab. "Shitfire. That's some*body*."

The pile of clothes suddenly changed shape before my eyes and I gagged when I realized the smell of roasting meat came from burning bodies. I leaned over the side of the El Camino and gagged again.

"It's Mama!" Mark jumped over the edge of the truck bed.

Cody put his hand against Mark's chest to hold him still. "Stay right here. How do you know, son?"

"She only has one dress." He didn't try to go to his mother's body. Instead, he stood there and leaned into Cody's hand, tears running down his cheeks.

Lightning flickered across the river in Oklahoma. Grandpa glanced toward the north. "It's coming up a storm. The rain will wash away any tracks before we get a good look at them."

He stood slowly and exchanged words with Judge Rains. As they walked across the grassless yard, Grandpa slipped the pistol back into his holster. The two men looked much older to me in the firelight. For the first time in my life, I realized Grandpa would die some day.

Mr. O.C. and Grandpa stopped beside a second smaller bundle, and then continued on to a third. The flames roared even higher. The bright orange light made everyone there look evil. But I knew Evil had already left.

The heat became even stronger, and Uncle Cody started the engine and backed it up some. Other men did the same, moving their trucks back toward the highway. Grandpa didn't notice it, though he was closer than the rest of us. I guess shock and duty took over his mind.

The rising wind fanned the flames and

brought their voices toward us. Judge O.C. kept his back turned toward the intense heat and protected his face with his hat. "My god, what's this world coming to when people take chopping axes to kids?"

Grandpa shook his head and walked slowly back toward us from the burning shack. "All right then. You men check those bodies closest to the house there and drag them away before they catch fire. Their clothes are already smoking."

Grim-faced men hurried toward the shack. Thunder rumbled in the distance while several more tenderhearted men and women wept beside the cars and trucks. Highway patrol cars with their lights flashing shrieked down the hill toward the creek, slowing to pass over the narrow bridge before speeding up again toward the flames rising into the cloudy night sky.

Grandpa motioned the rest of the onlookers back with his hands. "Make a way for the sheriff. I can't do anything here and neither can y'all. There's nothing we can do for these poor folks." He caught my eye and then looked over my shoulder at Mark. He always felt bad news should be delivered quickly for everyone's sake. "I'm sorry son, but your mama's gone and everybody with her."

I felt a lump in my throat and fought back the urge to cry along with Mark, who wilted into deep, racking sobs. Pepper jumped over the tailgate, put her arms around him and cried just as hard. I got out too, to get away from the hog blood, and retched again.

Cody didn't know what else to do for him, so he stood there and patted his shoulder. I realized I'd been hearing a high, sharp sound and was surprised to find it was coming from Pepper.

Grandpa rubbed the back of his neck and frowned at me in the dim light. Cody caught the look and squinted at my face. "What happened to your eye?"

"Bumped it when I jumped into the truck."

I could tell he didn't believe me, but there was too much else to worry about. "Well, nobody ever died from a black eye. Y'all get back in. I'm taking you to Miss Becky's. We'll have to finish this camping trip some other time. Uncle Ned, you need me here?"

Grandpa shook his head and went to meet the sheriff, who was threading his way through all the cars. "Naw. Go on and take them younguns home. I'll be along directly." He looked so sad for a long moment. "I swear, Top, I'm sorry y'all had to see this. It ain't right."

None of us knew what to say. Mark allowed Pepper to pull him to the lowered tailgate and the three of us climbed in and sat against the cab.

Pepper quit making that noise, but kept wiping tears off her cheeks. Neither of us knew what to say to Mark.

Brady Caldwell started his truck and pulled farther into the pasture so Cody could turn around. After a couple of other men did the same, we had room to get out. Mark still hadn't said a word, but he finally wiped the tears away and I watched the house burn as we turned onto the highway toward home.

It was then I realized there hadn't been any night sounds around the burning house, nothing but the roar of the flames that almost touched the low ceiling of clouds.

Chapter Fourteen

Ned stared into the darkness, talking quietly to himself. O.C. watched Cody take the kids home. He was sorry the young people saw the carnage in the yard. "Bad business."

A two-man team led by Justice of the Peace Buck Johnson worked their way across the yard, checking each body. As a twenty-year veteran of the job, Buck hated this part the most. He was always being called out in the middle of the night to pronounce someone dead so the ambulance drivers from the funeral home could take them away.

Ned turned toward O.C. and the helpless deputies watching the fire, glad the foul odor of burning bodes had lessened. "I'm gonna find out who did this and he'll be lucky to see the pen after I get through with him. I bet it was Lightfoot and if he's not in Oklahoma already, he'll be there by morning and I'll know about it. And mark my words, I'll shoot the son-of-a-bitch myself when I find him."

"Now you don't lose your head over this, Ned. These kinds of things can get personal in a hurry, and it clouds your judgment. Just because he killed these folks close to your house don't mean it's all on you."

"Don't give me any static about this, O.C. I'll hear about it pretty quick if it's Lightfoot and I'll bet you he's the one who done it."

"You know you can't go into Oklahoma after him." The old constable had never let the river act as a boundary when he was after a fleeing criminal or looking for information.

"I know one thing. If I'm over there and run into him, I'll bring back what's left."

"I ain't coming over there to get you out of trouble and I mean it."

"Don't raise your voice to me, O.C."

"Then listen to what I say, you hardheaded old bastard."

The ambulance drivers placed Mrs. Lightfoot on the stretcher. Buck Johnson held the murder weapon as if he intended to chop a cord of wood. He brought it to O.C. "You want to put this in your car?"

O.C. took the double-bit ax by the handle and studied the bloody head in the firelight. "I'll take it to the courthouse. Y'all find anything?"

"Naw. There's footprints everywhere and the state boys will stay till daylight, but I doubt there's much around here to help us."

Ned watched O.C. hold the ax. "There won't be. Lightfoot probably just walked up to the porch and started chopping at them people."

"I'm gonna go when we get 'em all loaded up, if that's all right." Buck rubbed his hands, as if they were dirty.

"Go ahead on."

"I'll be back at daylight."

O.C. scuffed the toe of his highly polished shoe in the dirt.

"Pure dee meanness."

"Mean or crazy. As far as I'm concerned, anyone who'd kill little kids and babies has to be crazy."

"Don't say that. I don't even want to consider an insanity plea if he ever comes into my courtroom."

The house finally collapsed in a giant spray of sparks. The heat increased, forcing everyone back even farther. Ned and O.C. turned their backs on the flames and stared across the pasture toward the lights in Ned's windows. Becky had every light in the house on and Ned knew the party line was smoking.

"Well, he must have been pretty sure of himself to kill these folks so close to your place."

"He knew we were at the dance. Nearly everybody in town was there. It wasn't much for him to waltz in here and butcher these folks without worrying."

"You think he was there for a while, too, watching us?"

"Naw. I reckon he was right 'chere, getting his nerve up."

"His boy was lucky, then, to be at the schoolhouse. He could be laying here too, with the rest of his kinfolk."

Ned jerked his head toward the fire. "I bet he killed the man inside the house. That's how I'd do it. Open the door and walk in and whack him first, figuring he'd be the one to put up the most fight. Then it wouldn't take much to chop up the mama and them poor little kids."

Killings were nothing new to Ned. On a cold October morning ten years earlier, a woman was murdered in a little frame house in Arthur City. Ned was appalled at the blood covering the linoleum floor. So much was splashed on the walls it looked as if someone threw buckets of blood around the room.

As terrible as the scene was in that slaughterhouse, this one in the light of the burning house turned his stomach. Ned was always partial to kids.

He and O.C. sat on the tailgate of a truck

to wait for the fire to burn down. More locals arrived, hearing about the killings and wanting to see firsthand what the whole community was talking about.

Constable Raymond Chase parked his car behind the line of vehicles on the shoulder of the highway, a hundred yards from the gate. He threaded his way through the traffic jam toward the fire while two highway patrol officers reluctantly stayed on the road to direct traffic.

John Washington stopped behind Raymond's car. He didn't have any business there, but he thought Ned or O.C. might need him. There was always a chance the story he'd heard in town was wrong and maybe colored folks had done the killing. Several sets of eyes watched him with suspicion as he passed, thinking there was no reason for the black deputy to be there.

The looks were nothing new. John had been ignoring them his whole life. He walked slowly past the line of cars until Ned waved him over. He joined the gathering at the truck. O.C. stuck out his hand and the watchful eyes shifted away from the deputy.

"Mr. O.C., Mr. Ned. Y'all got any suspicions?"

Ned shrugged. "Naw, we don't know for sure, but I imagine it was Frank Lightfoot."

Trying not to show his relief, John nodded and looked toward the fire. "We going after him?"

"Not 'til we know more."

"Y'ont me to go over to your house and set with Miss Becky and the kids?"

Ned considered the idea for a long moment. "Naw, with all of us around here, she's all right. I bet she has a six-shooter in her pocket right now."

John wasn't sure. "I'll go if it'll make you feel better."

"No. Thanks just the same."

Thunder rumbled again and lightning struck somewhere down by the river. John closed his eyes and saw the afterglow on his lids. Inside that dark place, lit with ghostly lightning, he wondered at human meanness. After a lifetime of dealing with the dark side of people, he tended to study a lot on how some folks could do such things to the innocent.

Opening his eyes, he turned slightly and looked at those gathered around the smoking house, knowing it could be any one of them. He also knew that at least half a dozen of the men near him would easily believe it was one of John's people, because suspicion came easily.

"I'll be ready when you are." His offer was there, if anyone wanted to take him up on it.

Rain finally caught up with the thunder and the bottom fell out. They were soaked in no time. Most of the onlookers gave up, started their engines and went home to wait out the storm. Ned, O.C., Big John and Raymond retreated to Ned's car. They talked quietly about the murders and pondered whether the world would go to hell before all the cotton was in.

Conversation dried up after a while. Ned wondered where it would all end. He'd taken the job years ago to supplement his earnings as a farmer and to give something back to the people in Lamar County. There was no way he could ride a tractor from dawn to dusk and still find out who'd killed these people.

The heavy rain finally drowned the conflagration. The volunteer fire department did all they could with the pump truck, but without the assistance of the storm, the house might have burned all night. As it was, there wasn't much left except for the brick chimney and a few blackened studs jutting toward the low clouds, and the charred human remains.

The storm finally settled into a constant drizzle and the cool front dropped the temperature. Daylight, gray and somber, lit the scene with a flat, shadowless light.

The lawmen still waiting in the car watched through the slapping windshield wipers as Buck and his assistants returned. He picked his way through the smoldering charcoal, pointing and talking, rain dripping from the brim of his pinch-crown hat. With an iron crowbar, he poked through the ruins, peering underneath large pieces and kicking smaller chunks to the side.

Finally, he ordered his men to make one last sweep and waved his arm toward Ned's sedan. "Y'all, c'mere, would ya?"

Ned, John and O.C. emerged into gloomy light, stepping lightly through the mud. Buck indicated the remains of the house. "We have enough bodies here to get a good start on a new cemetery, but I believe we're missing one. Didn't y'all say there was a baby?"

Ned thought back to the day in the yard when he'd brought the groceries, clothes and candy. He remembered a toddler in the tired woman's arms. "Yeah. It was a little girl I believe. She looked like she was barely walking. Why?"

"She ain't here."

"She's probably in the house."

"Nope. We've looked at everything there and we'll look again in a little while, but unless I'm completely wrong there ain't no baby's body burned or otherwise around here. I have men searching the pasture. I even have one looking under all the cars, thinking we may have driven on top of her, but I believe the little thing is gone."

They exchanged glances.

"He took her," O.C. suggested.

"Yep." Ned chewed on his lip. "And I hope she's still alive."

"The man wouldn't kill his baby."

Big John looked toward the smoke and burnt timbers. "I don't know, Mister O.C. He killed most of his other young 'uns. Why wouldn't he kill the baby, too?"

"He probably stole her to take back to his folks somewheres."

Ned thought about the mutilated animals he'd been finding for the past few months. He had no reason to believe Lightfoot was the one doing it, but then again, he didn't have any proof otherwise.

"John, let's you and me sashay across the tracks tomorrow and see if we can stir something up."

"What makes you think he's there?"

"What makes you think he isn't?"

"He's Indian. He'll go back to his own people across the river, not down amongst my folks."

"Or he might hide somewheres else. I don't know what else to do. All my ideas have done played out. I'm going across to Juarez and on to Hugo and look around, but I want to cover all the bases."

Uneasy because the investigation was going to begin on his own doorstep, John wanted to argue with Ned a little more, but with the men around him listening, he showed his respect and waited for the proper time.

The sun finally broke through to melt the clouds away. Quail called in the cool early morning dampness. Ned desperately wanted to go home and sleep, but he knew the rain could delay his cotton harvest and he needed to talk to Ivory. They wouldn't be able to resume picking until the lint dried. It was the perfect time to poke around.

O.C. was anxious to get back home and see to Catherine. Neither had expected him to be gone all night. He scratched at the morning stubble on his normally smooth shaven face. "It's an awful way to end a dance. Just awful."

Chapter Fifteen

My black eye was only a pale yellow smear when I woke up two weeks later with Mark's elbow digging into the small of my back. He was living with us because no one could find any of his kinfolk.

I raised my head, peeked at the bed on the other side of the room and saw Pepper's hair spread out across the pillow. She spent the night staying up late watching *The Blob* on television and being scared to death.

The windows ran with condensation and the smell of frying bacon filled the house. A norther blew through during the night, but I could tell it'd warm up and be fairly nice by noon.

I lay there for a while, my familiar dream fading away. Last night's version of drowning in the Rock Hole wasn't much. Water, overhanging trees and the steep ledge with people walking around, but the sheer regularity of the dream made me wonder if I was going crazy.

I threw off the covers, dressed quickly in the chilly bedroom and hurried into the kitchen. Grandpa stomped in from feeding the cows, cold radiating off his coat, and went into the bathroom to wash his hands.

Miss Becky forked bacon out of the iron skillet. "Mornin', hon."

I speared a hot biscuit from the plate and covered it with cream gravy. "I had that dream again about drowning in the Rock Hole."

Grandpa came in, drying his hands on a towel. They exchanged looks.

I picked up on their worried expressions. "What do you think it means? Do I need to see a doctor or something?"

Grandpa sat down at his place and Miss Becky put a plate in front of him. "Some things happen in this world we can't explain. It could be the work of the ol' Devil, or maybe something's weighting on your mind. I don't know. I'll get Brother Ross to pray for you."

Grandpa didn't say anything for a while. He poured coffee into his saucer, picked it up with his fingertips and blew across the wide surface. He took a careful sip. "It probably means you need to stay away from the Rock Hole. I hear the current changed down deep under there because the flood last year moved some of them big rocks around.

You boys will have to wait for another flood to change 'em back. The Hole may not be as deep as it was and if a knothead boy was to jump headfirst he could break his neck."

"Where else are we going to swim when it gets warm?"

"Well, I don't know yet. Summer is a long way off. Right now I want y'all to promise you won't mess around there anymore until I tell you."

I nodded.

"I mean it."

He needn't have bothered, even though I had my fingers crossed under the table. Swimming was the furthest thing from my mind with the cold north wind moaning under the eaves.

Edgar Weems drove up the driveway and with a sigh Grandpa went out to meet him. He didn't completely close the door and as usual, Miss Becky moved to the far end of the cabinet so she could hear through the screen. I shivered in the cold draft.

Edgar stood on the running board and spoke across the truck cab. "We got trouble down in the field this morning."

"What's wrong?"

"Most of your hands won't pick today. They say they heard about someone committin' sacrifices down in the bottoms, and they're afraid they'll come across one out in the field. Somebody said the Devil is there, and it scared the rest."

Grandpa stood on the porch for a few minutes with his hands in the pockets of his overalls. "All right. I'll be along directly. See who'll work today, and I'll talk to the others when I get there."

"I think Ralston is doing most of the talking."

"I've expected him to show up. And the sorry son-of-a-bitch starts trouble the minute he gets here."

We pretended not to hear Grandpa's explosion, though it really wasn't loud. Miss Becky moved back over to the stove. Edgar turned his truck around and drove away. Grandpa stayed on the porch for a few minutes before coming back inside.

"You kids stick around the house today. I'm still not sure Lightfoot really went to Dallas. I don't want to worry with y'all while I'm trying to get the last of this cotton in."

"Uncle Cody'll be here in a little bit. He's fixin' to carry us to Uncle Arthur's to get Mark a haircut You told me yourself you were about tired of his long hair and you know how Cody is."

"All right, but y'all stay with him or right 'chere until I get back."

I piddled around after he left, until Pepper and Mark finally stumbled into the kitchen, rubbing their eyes. Miss Becky fed them and was washing dishes in a dishpan on the cabinet when she heard a car crunching up the gravel drive.

She looked through the screen door and managed a grin. "Looky yonder who's comin'."

Cody slammed the El Camino's door and stomped the dirt off his shoes on the porch. We hadn't seen him since the night of the murders.

Miss Becky held the screen door open. "Come in this house. How can you look so purty this morning after being up all night?"

"I'm naturally beautiful, I guess. How'd you know I was up all night?"

"Cause you smell like cigarette smoke and whiskey."

"Glad that's all."

Miss Becky gave him a slap on the shoulder and pointed at the table. "You devil, you. Been to breakfast yet?"

"Not yet."

"Well, set down and I'll fix you something to eat."

With his curly hair and tilted back hat, I once again wished I could grow up to look like Cody. Pepper almost danced around the table to hug his neck. He loved on her a minute and took Grandpa Ned's place at the head of the table.

"You want some coffee?" Pepper asked. I

couldn't believe she was serving him. Mark ducked his head and grinned at his plate.

"Sure." Cody slid his cup toward her.

She carefully poured coffee into a thick mug. Miss Becky fried him a couple of eggs. Cody crumbled a biscuit on top of the yolk and mashed the whole mess together.

While he ate, I noticed his eyes kept flicking back to Mark. "You ready to get a civilized haircut?"

Mark shrugged his shoulders. "I've never had short hair. We never had no money for haircuts."

"Well, when it's cut people won't think you're a girl anymore."

"I know a couple of fellers I tangled with can tell you I ain't no girl."

Mark knew he was being kidded, but his long hair was starting to get on people's nerves. Men and boys wore Boy's Regular cuts even though a few of the local outlaws let their hair grow longer to slick back on the sides with H.A. or Brylcreem.

Cody stuffed the last bite into his mouth and stood up. "Come on, kids. Miss Becky, that was the best breakfast I've had all morning."

"That oughta hold you 'til dinner."

"We'll be back pretty quick. I want some of those snap beans I'm smelling."

"Y'all get out of here." She shooed us toward

the door with a dish towel and turned back to her stove. "You kids stay close to your Uncle Cody."

None of us answered. Pepper jumped into the front seat and slammed the lock down with her palm. She stuck her tongue at us through the open window and made us stand outside until Cody unlocked the driver's door with his key. She pulled up on the other latch and I scrunched up against her. Mark got in last and smashed against the door. We couldn't have all fit in the seat if we'd been adults, and as it was, Pepper was almost under Cody's arm.

On Saturdays Uncle Arthur cut hair on the front porch of his house up on the hill not far from the cotton gin. It was funny, him being a barber and all, because he had the worst hair of anybody in Center Springs. Miss Becky always figured he cut it himself by looking into a mirror and I think she may have been right.

The morning chill was almost gone by the time we got there. Half a dozen men were loafing around the sunny porch when we arrived. I was startled to see two waiting customers with guns on their belts. A worn lever action Winchester that belonged to Uncle Arthur leaned against a porch post. Though guns were common, it was a shock to see so many armed men in one place who weren't hunting. It seemed like everyone was nervous about the killings.

Every eye flicked to Mark's long hair the

moment we arrived. They all knew the story behind the Indian boy with us.

Cody shook hands all around. "Mornin', men. This looks like the safest place in town."

They chuckled. Roland Roach, the game warden, waved his hand at the group. "It's a sign of the times, Cody."

Uncle Arthur snipped his scissors in the air behind the hand-me-down barber chair on his porch. He frowned at the unruly head in front of him and changed the subject. "I'll be with y'all in a little while. Howdy, Top, I heard you was living here now."

Uncle Arthur always scared me a little. I could see him snipping off an ear and then saying, "Sorry, boy. Here put this in your pocket and Miss Becky will sew it on when you get back home."

"Yessir."

"You ain't growed much since I last saw you. You need to eat another biscuit."

"I'm trying." For a moment I wished for a regular barbershop with two or three dozen outdoor magazines that I could bury my head in to escape their attention. Instead, I sat on the edge of the high porch and thought about wandering off around the house to find something to do until they quit noticing me. But I didn't want to miss Mark's haircut, so I toughed it out.

He got me off the hook by changing the subject. "Cody, didn't your mama see a ghost once?"

Cody laughed. "What are y'all talking about, Roland? Somebody see a ghost deer?"

The men chuckled. "Naw, we're just sittin' here and got to talking about ghosts and haunted houses and buried treasure and such."

"Well. If you mean the time when Mama was a girl and sitting in bed when a dark woman walked through the window on one side of the room and left through the wall on the other side, then I guess she did. Daddy always said she was asleep and dreamed the whole thing, but Mama vows up and down she was wide awake."

"It wouldn't surprise me." Uncle Arthur snipped his scissors in the air. "Y'all's family has always been able to see or do things no one else can. Top, some of your kinfolk can dream the future, and there's only a couple of other people I've known who can do that."

Cody tilted the hat back on his head. "Great Granddad always told about the time his mama died. He and Granny knew she was bad off and they'd hitched the wagon up to go into town to get the doctor. They hadn't much more than got out of sight of the house when a wooden casket floated across the road, about two feet off the ground. Grandpa reined the mules up and turned them around. He told Granny they didn't need a doctor no more, because his mama was dead, and he was right. And boys, that happened in broad daylight."

A shiver went up my spine. Pepper, Mark and I exchanged glances, and I was proud to see they felt a little spooky, too.

One of the men noticed. "Possum run across your grave, son?"

Pepper poked me in the ribs. "Titty-baby," she whispered in my ear. I gigged her back.

"My granny could put spells on people." I was surprised to hear Mark say anything at all.

Uncle Arthur stopped snipping. "What kinds of spells?"

"Oh, she could make people sick, or make them well, if she wanted to."

The statement wasn't taken lightly. Everyone knew the Indians and Negroes had some secret connection to the other world.

"We're losing a lot when those old witch Indians across the river fade away." Uncle Arthur clicked his scissors. "I bet fifty years from now, when Top there is my age, you won't hear tell of people who can do these things. Hey, Cody, tell them about the time you saw the ghosts in Mr. Hall's house."

Cody showed his white teeth in a smile and leaned his chair against the wall. "Y'all heard it before, but I guess the kids haven't. I slept over with my cousins in Doc Ordway's spooky two-story house right up behind Neal's store. It was built back in the eighteen-hundreds."

I knew the place. The highway forked into a blacktop road behind Neal's store and led past the Ordway place. It had a huge wraparound porch, and giant burr oaks shaded the entire house.

Uncle Arthur forgot he was giving a haircut and stood with the scissors idle over his silent customer's head.

"Well, we'd all stayed up until way in the night. We were sleeping on a pallet in the floor in front of the fireplace, and I woke up and needed to wet real bad. It was cold and I really didn't want to get up to take a leak, but I did. I hadn't much more'n gotten into the hall beside the staircase when something caught my attention and I looked up and saw a man and a woman coming down. They were all dressed up. He had on a top hat and she was wearing one of them long, fancy dresses.

"I about peed on the floor right there because I could see through them, like they were made out of smoke, but the colors were bright. They didn't notice me, though, and floated down the stairs and through the door to a buggy tied to an iron ring driven into one of those big ol' oaks. He untied the horse from the tree and they drove away."

Mark's eyes sparkled bright and shiny and he

kept looking at Cody like there was more. "What did you do then?"

"Well, I ran to the bathroom and peed and got my little ass under the covers as fast as I could."

The men roared and Pepper blushed. I guess she didn't like to think about Cody having to pee in the middle of the night, even when he was a little kid in the story.

"Tell the rest of it." Uncle Arthur snipped his scissors.

"Well, about ten years ago lightning struck the burr oak the ghost buggy was tied to and they had to cut it down. When they sawed it up they hit something made of iron and had to cut around it after it ruined the set in one saw. G.W. Middlebrooks heard about it and went and got that chunk of green oak and chiseled on it for about a month and you know what he found?"

No one offered a thought.

"He found one of them iron hitching rings had grown into the tree. They counted the rings and figured it was there in about the late eighteen-hundreds, right when I dreamed about a horse hitched to the tree."

I almost couldn't stand it. I could feel the hair rise on the back on my neck once again as if one of the morning's cold breezes was left over.

Uncle Arthur finished the haircut and called

next. No one moved, because they wanted to see Mark get his haircut. He finally gave up and climbed up in the chair. Uncle Arthur held his scissors over Mark's head. "I've wanted to do this since I first saw you."

Pepper jumped up, whispered in Uncle Arthur's ear, and he nodded gravely. He grabbed a hank of black hair, snipped, and handed the long tail to Pepper. She sat on the porch, took a long piece of red thread out of her pocket, and wrapped it round and round one end to hold the hair together.

Mark had his eyes closed from the time he sat down, so he didn't see what she was doing. I've read of Indians being "stoic" and never knew what it meant, but I learned that day. His face didn't change as the rest of his black hair drifted down to the rough boards. The men didn't say a thing as they watched.

Hap Scurry even forgot he had a chew in his mouth and dang near drowned before he thought to spit.

In no time at all Uncle Arthur was finished and I was surprised to find that he hadn't given Mark a Boys' Regular. I'd say his was more like one of them Beatles cuts. He nodded when he was finished. "I been wanting to try one of those."

Pepper ran her fingers through his hair when

Mark climbed down. I could see a light in her eyes that went well beyond a haircut. "That looks cute on you."

He looked at his reflection in a broken piece of mirror hung on a post so customers could see what their quarter had bought. He turned his head one way and the other and shrugged. "Feels lighter."

"First time I ever scalped an Indian."

Uncle Cody patted Mark on the shoulder. "You got you a good haircut. Let's go and get us a Coke."

A cold drink sounded good. The next customer was already in the chair, so we told everyone goodbye and drove to the store. Pepper and Mark jogged up the steps and went on inside. They kept eyeing each other and whispering and it was making me sick. Cody hung back as they went in.

I was at the screen door when Calvin Williams drove up in his hay truck with a heavy load. He was shirtless and sweaty because they'd been hauling hay all morning and it had warmed up considerable. Straw and chaff stuck to his skin and was caught in the shaggy hair sticking out from under his dirty cap.

I suddenly felt scared and sick inside seeing Calvin there, because Cody had been around Calvin's wife a little too much lately.

Calvin jumped down from the cab when he

saw Cody. I could tell he was mad from the glassy look in his eyes. The loafers stopped talking, anticipating trouble.

Cody just stood there without being nervous or anything. "Howdy, Calvin."

Calvin pulled off his work gloves. "Wait up there, Parker. I know you been messin' with my woman."

A couple of men on the porch stood up, like they do in a football stadium when someone makes a good play.

"Well, Calvin, I heard y'all weren't living together anymore. She's moved out to Powderly."

"It don't make no difference. We're still married."

Cody shrugged. "You'll have to take it up with her. She says she's done with you. I ain't dragging her out of the house to go with me."

"You're a-lyin'. She'd be home with me if you'd leave her alone."

"I ain't telling no stories, and you know it. She's been done with you for a long time now. Let it go, Calvin."

"You stay away from her!" He stalked across the bottle cap parking lot one slow step at a time, but it was like watching a fuse burn toward a stick of dynamite. He took a big crescent wrench out of his back pocket and held it like a hammer. "I know you was with her at the rodeo a while back and y'all was dancing up at the school house. Everybody's knows it."

Cody sighed. Calvin was working himself up to a fighting mad and there was nothing Cody could do take the fire out of it. "Calvin, let's talk about this somewhere else. It ain't nobody's business but our own, and there's a young boy standing here."

"I don't care if he is Ned's grandkid, and I ain't talking about him. I'm talking about you fooling around with my wife."

"I'm not fooling." The men around them snickered at the crack.

"How about I whip your ass right here and now? I'm not afraid of any shit they taught you in the army."

Cody acted like he was having a normal conversation. "I'm not afraid of you, neither. Now, how about forgetting this right now, and you go cool off somewhere. We can talk later."

I started feeling even more scared when two of Calvin's hired hands came into view from around the hay truck behind him. I knew Tully Joe and Donny were a couple of no-account river rats from up around Kiomatia. Mentally, Tully Joe wasn't all there, but he was a good hand and stayed busy all the time. He had his hands in the pockets of his overalls.

His brother Donny was downright mean. He shook a cigarette from the soft pack in his shirt pocket, bit one out with his buckteeth and lit it with a wooden match. Folks knew he'd drive off the road into a ditch to run over a dog or cat. He was known to go across to Juarez to pick a fight, usually from someone too drunk to defend themselves.

Now it was three to one, and I remembered when I was faced with similar numbers. I thought one of the men in the parking lot might step in and help Cody, but they simply stood there watching.

Pepper and Mark came back outside because Cody hadn't given us any money. Mark was rubbing at the back of his neck, still feeling his new haircut. Pepper started to say something about why I was still outside when she caught on to what was happening. Her eyes got real wide and she made a soft moaning sound in the back of her throat.

Mark stepped up beside me. "What are we gonna do?"

"Nothing. They're grown men."

"Get on out of here." Cody jerked his head back toward us. "Or let me take the kids home. You and I can talk about this some other time."

"Nope. We're gonna settle it right now."

Cody sighed, like he was tired. "You ignorant bastard. Give it up."

The whole incident spun out of control. It

reminded me of one time when me and Pepper thought it'd be a good idea to turn over a new 55-gallon barrel and climb inside to ride it to the bottom of the hill in front of the barn. Neither of us figured what might happen next. I tucked myself in the barrel and Pepper gave me a push to get started.

Gravity took over and I spun over and over as the barrel picked up speed. I was crying and puking by the time I rolled through the barbed wire fence and slammed to a sharp stop against one of Miss Becky's sycamore trees.

Everything picked up the same speed in front of Uncle Neal's store, and there was nothing anyone could do but watch it happen.

Tully Joe and Donny fanned out and started forward.

"You men quit it." Uncle Neal let the screen door slam loudly when he joined us on the porch.

Calvin stopped a couple of feet away from Cody and held the big wrench like a hammer. "This ain't none of your damn business, Neal."

I could see Calvin was mad at the whole world and knew if he could, he'd fight until he got rid of all the rage inside him. Everything started moving fast then, but at the same time, it felt like time had shifted into slow motion. Pepper started down the porch steps toward the two men and I grabbed the back of her shirt to stop her.

When Calvin took another step and Tully Joe started to move in, Cody apparently figured the dance had started. He settled down a couple of inches and threw a right punch so fast I never even saw it. It had most of Cody's weight behind it and Calvin's head snapped back. He landed flat on his back, blood spurting from his squashed nose.

The other two men moved in.

Cody did something I'd never seen on television or in the movies. Tully Joe was on the right. Cody stepped forward, twisted sideways to get all his weight on his left leg and kicked Tully Joe in the chest so hard he banged into the dusty side of a truck. It addled him and he slid down on his bottom for a minute.

Donny swung at him. Cody caught the right cross in his left hand, turned his body to put his shoulder in Donny's armpit, and flipped him over his hip. He landed with a thud on the bottle cap parking lot and then Cody he did the second thing I'd never seen anyone do on television. Still holding Donny's wrist while he had him down, Cody twisted the man's arm until his shoulder popped loud enough for us to hear up on the porch. Face down, Donny screamed into the dirt.

Pepper made a shocked squeak behind me.

Calvin was back on his feet, and the way Cody was turned, Calvin had a clear shot at hitting him in the back of the head with the wrench. Cody sensed the blow, because he jerked his head back and instead of caving in his skull, the wrench glanced off and only addled him. He staggered forward, but not for long. He threw one of those kicks again and caught Calvin in the stomach. His breath went out in a whoosh and he took a step back.

I believe Cody intended to hit him again, but a fellow in a slouch hat I hadn't seen before jumped down from the top of the stacked hay and knocked Cody off his feet. By then Tully Joe had recovered his breath from the kick against the truck and he waded back into the fight. They swarmed Cody like wild dogs. Slouch Hat had him in a stranglehold from behind and Tully Joe started hitting Cody in the ribs.

Pepper screamed again, mad this time. I held on tighter so she wouldn't get hurt.

"No, Pepper!"

Mark was off the porch and into the fight like a bottle rocket, but he didn't last long in amongst grown men. He hit Slouch Hat in the ear with his fist and Tully Joe caught Mark a backhand lick flush against the jaw. Mark was down in the bottle caps and he looked to be dead to me.

Donny was screaming about his shoulder and thrashing around next to him while Tully Joe and the other feller worked Cody over. For a minute there I thought someone was stabbing at him with a knife.

I hollered and ran down the steps with Pepper right beside me. A couple of the men watching the fight grabbed ahold of my arm to keep me from getting in the middle of things and I couldn't get away.

They had Pepper by her arms, too. She kicked and screamed so loud I could barely think. "Let go of me you, sonsabitches!"

All the commotion wasn't loud enough I didn't hear the crack of the punch though, and Tully Joe fell back, holding his jaw and spitting teeth. I didn't see that punch or the one that caused Slouch Hat to hunker up and go rolling the other way, holding himself between his legs and gagging.

Cody stood up, bloody from the wrench blow to the head, and grinned. I swear it. He was grinning like he was back at the dance while blood ran from his eyebrow and covered half of his face. It was the most frightening thing I'd ever seen. If it had been anyone but Cody, I'd have run off screaming when he chuckled to himself.

Calvin caught his breath, got back up and took another half-hearted swing, but Cody socked him again in his bloody nose and he went down. Cody got dirty then. He kicked Calvin in the head to make sure he stayed down, and then he went over and deliberately kicked Slouch Hat right in the nose, too. Blood spurted and Slouch Hat flopped over on his side and curled up in a ball. Cody turned to Tully Joe, who was lying on his back and pushing with his feet to get under the hay truck. Cody grabbed him by one foot and pulled him out to finish him off.

A fight was one thing, but this was much, much more. It wasn't a fight anymore and somehow the honor of winning was gone. I started to turn my face away, sick to my stomach.

"What's going on here?" I looked up to see Grandpa getting out of his car with a sap in his hand. I don't think anyone else in town could have stopped Cody because he was finally mad, but Grandpa did it without even raising his voice.

The fight was over. Cody quit dragging Tully Joe and straightened up like he'd finished hoeing a row and was waiting for Grandpa to pay him. The ring of men surrounding us parted and Grandpa walked through.

When he heard Donny hollering in pain and saw two of his grandkids held in the parking lot and Mark's nose bleeding, he looked scared for a minute, but then his eyes went cold. "That's enough. Y'all better turn my kids aloose."

The men holding us let us go real quick and

Pepper hurried over to check on Mark who was sitting up. He shook his head, dazed.

"Shitfire. I think his nose is broke."

Cody knelt down and held Mark's chin gently in his hand. "It ain't broke, and you watch your language." He blinked the blood out of his eye.

Grandpa looked around the parking lot. "Somebody tell me what's going on here."

Since it was the parking lot of his store, Neal Box stepped forward. "Calvin and these three fellers jumped on Cody and he cleaned their plows for 'em with what he learned overseas."

The explanation satisfied Grandpa. He squinted at Cody's face. "Get your point made?"

"Yessir."

"You do this all by yourself?"

"Yessir."

"I'd give a purty to have seen that." Grandpa grinned for a minute once he was over his shock of seeing us kids in the middle of everything. "You boys got hold of a snapping turtle, didn't you?" Growing up, we'd always heard a snapping turtles bite and won't turn loose until it thunders. "Any of y'all need another dose?"

Tulley Joe was spitting blood and pinching his nose closed. "Naw, we're done."

Grandpa's eyes darted around the crowd to see if there was going to be any argument to the story. He walked over to Calvin and nudged him with the toe of his shoe. "You still breathing?" Calvin grunted a response and Grandpa did the same with Donny. "Quit your crying or I'll give you something to cry about. Tully, who is this feller here in the hat?"

He coughed and spat. "Name's Donald Adams. He's from up on Boggy Bend. Calvin hired him to help haul today."

"Good." Grandpa dug his cuffs from his back pocket. He knelt and snapped them on Slouch Hat's wrists with an oily clicking sound. "I recognize the name. You have a flyer out on you, boy. You're under arrest and so are the rest of you, so just lay there until I can get somebody out here to help haul all y'all in. Now, which one of you sonsabitches hit this young boy here?"

Pepper answered for them. "Tully Joe hit him with his fist."

"Um hum." Grandpa looked hard at Tully Joe. "I'll deal with you later." Then he took a hard look at Mark. "What happened to his head?"

"Haircut," I said. Grandpa gave me a quick once-over. "Y'all all right?"

"Yessir."

He turned to Cody. "What's all this about? Can't you take them kids anywheres without someone getting hurt or killed? Y'all get off from the house apiece and get in trouble every time. I ain't forgot about Top's fight at the dance."

"Norma Faye."

"What?

"You asked me what it was about. It's about Norma Faye."

Grandpa grunted and walked back to the car and his Motorola.

Cody checked us kids again and waved toward his car. "Y'all get in. I'll take you home."

Pepper started toward Tully Joe, intending to give him a kick, but Mark took hold of her sleeve and she went with him. They got in the back of the El Camino. I got into the passenger seat and Cody pulled out on the highway.

I didn't say anything, and he looked across the cab. "What's wrong with you?"

"You won, but you kept kicking them fellers. You didn't fight fair."

"Well, there ain't no such a thing as a fair fight. Even if it had just been me and Calvin, one of us would have been better, so it wouldn't have been fair to the other. A fight is never even. When the rest of them joined in, then it had to go to a different level."

I kept looking at my feet, wondering why Cody felt he had to explain himself.

"I could have quit when they were down, Top,

but the truth is they'd have gotten up and come after me again and then maybe I'd have gotten the worst of it. Men have to defend ourselves or family any way we can. I didn't know if Uncle Ned was coming or not. No one else was helping. So it was all up to me. Do you see?"

I raised my eyes and looked at Uncle Cody. He looked ahead through the windshield, driving with one hand on top of the wheel and his elbow out the window. "But you kept hitting and kicking them while they were down."

"Yep. I was keeping them down. They had to know, I mean *know*, what they'd tangled with so I wouldn't have to do it again some time down the road."

Feeling a little better, I nodded. "Would you have killed them?"

"Nope. They're not worth going to jail for. But there ain't nothing wrong with being in the right and killing a man who's trying to kill you first. But we were just fighting and I intended to win. Do you see the difference?"

"Kind of."

"Look at it this way. I know you got in a fight at the dance a while back."

I gave him a shocked look, but he grinned and kept talking.

"You didn't have to go outside. You could have

stayed in the gym and waited for me, and we'd have left without a problem down the road. But you knew the trouble would still be there somewhere. So you went out and faced it. With a little more experience, you'd have won and it would have been over. That's what I knew a few minutes ago. It had to end right there, and that's what I was doing."

"All right."

My mind was reeling with the discussion when Cody slowed to turn in Grandpa Ned's drive. Constable Raymond Chase passed the highway from the other direction, so I knew some people were going to jail.

I hoped he wouldn't come to the house and get Cody, too.

Chapter Sixteen

Ned was so frustrated he felt like throwing his badge out the window and going home. Cody was running with a married woman and there was sure to be a killing over it pretty soon. Someone was torturing and killing animals and leaving threats toward children. Ralston was causing problems in the field, and even with everyone in Lamar County looking, no one could find Lightfoot.

It didn't make sense. How could they expect him to locate a wraith that appeared one night to slaughter eight people in a shack out in the middle of a pasture and then vanish into thin air?

It was almost too much for a man who just wanted to get his crop in.

Ralston was already gone from the bottoms when he arrived from the mess at the store. Most of the hands were bent over the cotton plants in the field. A few idled near the high-sided cotton wagon in the shade of a nearby red oak. Ned stopped in the dirt road and got out.

"What's the matter?"

The group by the wagon looked undecided for a moment, until one of the younger men stepped forward. He spoke in a halting, nervous voice. "Mister Ned, we're kindly afraid to be around here. We hear the Devil is working these fields and we don't want to be messin' 'round with him."

"The only thing working around here are them." Ned pointed to the hands in the field. They'd stopped picking to stand in the rows, shading their eyes to watch the meeting under the tree. "Or they was."

"You know what I mean Mr. Ned. Somebody's been sacrificing animals down here."

"You're Sheffield Roosevelt's boy Gilbert, aren't you?"

"Yessir."

"He doing all right?"

Gilbert didn't want to talk about his daddy. It made him uncomfortable because he and Ned had known each other all their lives. He wanted to settle the matter of the animal mutilations instead of talking like they were in the church yard.

"Well, since he's quit working, he's stove up. He sets on the porch and dips snuff these days, complaining about his back."

Ned nodded at the answer and toed the dirt, thinking. "Naw, Gilbert, that sacrificing thing ain't entirely true as far as I know. Somebody is torturing and killing animals, that's a fact, but I don't believe there's any booger-bear or devil involved in it. I didn't want to tell anybody because I didn't know enough to talk about. Still don't."

The hands shuffled uneasily and gazed across the shimmering field. "You ain't caught him yet?" Gilbert stated the obvious more for himself than for an answer.

"Not yet."

They waited some more.

"Mr. Ned, we got that to worry about and now Ralston thinks you might need to do something for us since all these killin's have started around here. You know, y'all ain't got aholt of the man who killed all them poor Indian folks, either. Maybe if you, uh, paid us a little more for bein' afraid and all..."

"Do for you? Where's Ralston now?"

"Him and three others left to go back to town."

"Did them others used to work for me?"

Gilbert analyzed the question. The past tense was obvious. "Naw sir."

"Well, it's a good thing. Ralston ain't nothin' but trouble and you know it. He's down here stirring things up so's I'll give y'all more money, but I ain't agonna do it. Y'all agreed to the wages you're getting, or will get when you get to working."

"Ralston and his friends says we oughta strike. He says you ain't paying us even colored wages, and we can get more money in Dallas." His voice trailed away.

Ned started to walk away and stopped. "I didn't know there were crops to pick in Dallas. You can go to the city if you want to, but you'll come home empty-handed and hungry. And besides, Gilbert, you *can't* strike. Y'all don't have a union, and if you do think you want to quit, I'll hire some folks hungrier than you are to pick the rest of this cotton. I'm liable to pay them a little more for not aggravating me."

"But the killings," said a young lady Ned recognized as Olivia, one of Ivory's daughters-in-law.

"Look, the fact is animals have been killed, but they aren't just here in these fields, and it's only been *animals* as far as I know. The Lightfoot folks were killed at night by their daddy hisself, leastways that's how I figure it, and I doubt he had anything to do with these animals. It wasn't the Devil, and we're gonna catch Lightfoot sure enough.

"Now, I done told you I'm not raising any wages, and if you don't want to work then you can ride the wagon back to the gin and I'll hire somebody else. You see Ivory and his woman out there, they've been working for me for over twenty years and I've always treated them right and I'll keep on doing so. Y'all do what you want, but I'm through talking."

Ned left the group and joined Edgar Weems, who had quit weighing cotton sacks to listen to the conversation. Ignoring the little cluster of hands still milling around, Ned finished his business with Edgar a few minutes later. When he passed them again on the way to his car, Gilbert and his friends had picked up their sacks and were headed slowly into the field.

Ned left the bottoms and drove back to the store. He was thankful he didn't have to drive Adams and Tully Joe to the Chisum jail. Young Raymond Chase had hauled them in after getting over the awe of one man beating four others all by himself.

Ned arranged for one of the men at the store to drive Calvin's uncovered hay truck and park it in his barn. No matter that Calvin was no-account, it wasn't right to let hay sit outside and ruin if it was to rain.

He went home to check on Cody and the kids. Miss Becky had everything under control there. He found them gathered around the table, eating cornbread crumbled into tall glasses of sweet milk.

The snack looked good to him, but Ned didn't have time to eat. "Y'all all right?"

"We're fine." Cody looked around the table and spooned cornbread into his mouth.

Neither Pepper or Mark spoke. Top simply concentrated on his eating. Miss Becky indicated everything was all right with a slight nod, but there was no reason to question them right then. They'd communicated the same way through decades of marriage.

Ned left, and when he got on the highway, he called Big John on the radio to tell him about Ralston's actions in the field.

"He's been acting pretty sorry all right."

"Have you seen him in town?"

The radio was silent while John thought for a moment. "I might have seen him at his mama's house. I'll go by there directly after I get through here."

"Where are you?"

"In Arthur City. Some of my people who sell catfish up here on the river had trouble today, so it might be a while before I get away."

"You talking about the place on the right coming out of Oklahoma?"

"Yep. They say some colored folks came in and took a lot more fish than they paid for."

"I'm already across the creek bridge and headed your way. I'll be there in a minute."

"Come on."

Still angry at Ralston's stunt in the field, Ned drove over a small hill and saw Ralston's '32 Ford parked nearly in the bar ditch. He recognized it as and stopped behind the vehicle.

He keyed the Motorola. "John?"

"Yessir."

"Ralston and his bunch are here beside Jimmy Lee Collier's pasture. Why don't you come over here real quick. You can talk about catfish later."

"On my way."

Ned replaced the microphone on the dash bracket and stepped out of the car. The windows were down and the four black men inside watched Ned get out. He hesitated beside the left front fender of his car. "Ralston, get out of the car."

There was a moment's pause before the four doors simultaneously opened and the men stepped out. All four wore dark sunglasses. The two from the back seat were dressed in khakis and white tee shirts. Both had pistols in their hands. Ralston slipped out from behind the steering wheel. He reached into the floorboard by his feet and picked up a jack handle. The fourth man in a neatly pressed red checkered shirt exited the front passenger side with a butcher knife.

In all his years as constable, Ned had only drawn his pistol once during an altercation. He was surprised to suddenly find the little Colt pointed before he even knew it was in his hand.

The frustrated mad he'd been working on for weeks rolled over him in a great, red rage.

"Y'all stop!"

The men continued to advance. A covey of quail exploded from the tall grass beside the car and flew into the nearby tree line. At the sound, Ned thumb-cocked the pistol and almost pulled the trigger of the double action. His stomach knotted in fear. Ned aimed at the center of the man nearest him. "Goddammit, I said stop or I'll shoot you right there."

Something in the tone of his voice stopped them. The men holding pistols appeared undecided as to their next step. Behind the plastic shades their faces were without emotion, as if they were merely going about some common daily duty. Only Ralston was scared.

Ned held the Colt with a steady hand on the man in front of him. "You'll be first, you son-of-a-bitch. And when I go to work with this six-shooter, you'll all be dead by the time you hit the ground. Now put the pistols down!"

The cry of a jay was the only sound on the empty two-lane highway. All five men stood motionless. No one wanted to make the first move in the dangerously explosive situation.

Ned looked over the front sight at the big man holding the pistol. He focused on the plain white tee shirt, keeping an eye on Ralston standing slightly behind him. Watching the other two men near the bumper on the passenger's side, he had everyone accounted for.

If he raises that pistol I'll shoot both of them with the guns first, Ned thought. He watched the man's face. *I wish I could see his eyes. He'll let me know what he's gonna do with his eyes.*

The jay called again, an oddly familiar and comforting sound accompanying the potential tragedy playing out on the highway. The man's pistol raised a fraction of an inch.

Ned spoke conversationally, though his finger tightened on the trigger. "Don't." He realized he'd been hearing the whining of distant tires on pavement for a long moment.

Big John's car roared around the bend in the road and squalled to a white, tire-smoking stop in the middle of the highway. The big deputy stepped out of the car with his own handgun drawn. "Whoa! Put 'em down boys!"

The gunman on Ralston's side of the car flinched at the shrieking tires, but he kept the revolver in his hand. Startled, the other two looked over the sedan as the giant deputy charged across the highway.

Seeing Ned in danger was almost too much for John. Always a man of action, he didn't hesitate.

Reaching into his back pocket with his free hand, he gripped the leather handle of his sap, and before anyone could respond to the new player in the dangerous scenario, he knocked Ralston senseless with a backhanded slap behind his ear. Without changing momentum, he took a forward swing to the back of White Shirt's head. He also collapsed beside the car, and the pistol landed in the road.

With the first threat gone, Ned shifted his aim toward the second gunman and the man behind. Neither of them made a move from the time Big John stepped out of the car until Ned's pistol was pointed at them. Shocked at the suddenness of John's actions, they dropped their weapons, threw up their hands, and it was over.

Ned motioned with his pistol to get them started. "Y'all lay down over there in the ditch."

John's rage was over as quickly as it had arrived. He slipped the sap back in his pocket. "Can you believe it?"

"Believe what?"

"Smell."

"What?"

"Smell."

Ned sniffed. "Fish."

"Yep. These boys are the ones who stole the fish in Arthur City. I heard they were headed this way but I didn't expect you to have them already."

"Nearly didn't." Ned 's voice suddenly shook. He wanted to sit down, but steadied himself on the fender instead. "I'm not sure why they were sitting here beside the highway. What the hell were y'all thinking?"

Checkered Shirt raised his head. "We's waiting on you."

"Waiting on me?" Ned suddenly realized why they simply sat there when he rolled up. Stealing the catfish was a ruse to get him alone on the highway, but he'd stumbled onto them almost without hearing about the theft. He was lucky they didn't have sense enough to hide in the brush beside the road and ambush him then. "What fer?"

"You been giving Ralston a hard time. We told him we'd take care of you and make everyone here in this sorry one-horse-town show him some respect. Then maybe our people here will see they got rights just like white folks. They don't want to work for the white man no more."

"What's you name, boy?" Big John asked, moving around and cuffing the men.

"I ain't your boy, Tom!"

"You ain't *nothin'* layin' in a ditch. Now I'll ast you again. What's your name?"

"Bubba Walls."

"Bubba, I don't know any Walls. Who's your daddy?"

"I ain't from around here."

"Figures. You're a little confused about a few things. You don't want 'no one' to work for the white man, but at the same time you're stealing from your own people. I think you're sorry and no 'count."

Ned finally regained his composure. "I never asked anyone to work for me for nothing. I *hired* Ralston's people."

The other man piped up. "But you're paying them nigger wages. They have a right to make white man's money."

"Who're you?" Ned leaned against the hood of his car to steady himself.

"Tyrel Johnson."

"Tyrel, I pay a good wage for a good day's work. It's what I can afford, and no one has to work for me. I don't care what color a man is when I hire him. What have you done to change things besides start trouble with your city ways? Well, now you got you a good job for a long time. Pullin' a gun on the Law done got you a place on the chain gang."

"Figures. Put colored folks to work cleanin' the ditches."

Ned shook his head in frustration.

John's voice rumbled deep as he finished checking Ralston's pockets and moved to the other man beside the rear tire. "You're trying to draw us into something we don't have any control over. You talking about changing the world, and there ain't a thing me or Mister Ned can do about it. We're trying to get along up here on the river, and I'm getting tired of talking to fools like you. Mister Ned, let's get them to jail so I don't have to look at 'em no more."

"But you don't know what it's like to be different from white folks." Bubba ignored John's presence.

Ralston's head quit spinning, though it hurt like the devil. "Yes, he does," he surprised himself by defending Ned, a man they'd planned to murder. "He's married to an Indian."

"Indians are as bad as white people."

Ned flushed. "Leave Miss Becky out of it."

Ralston considered the fix they were in. The fog of pain in his head caused him to question his association with the other men. He blamed himself for getting into this mess by stringing off down to Dallas and hooking up with the trio on the ground around him. He didn't know anything about them, except their booze-soaked ideas sounded good in the dark, smoky Dallas club. Now he was lying on the ground, cuffed and bleeding.

Pulling Bubba to his feet, Ned was wondering to himself why he was even in a conversation with his prisoners. "I'm trying to make a living, same's you."

"By knocking people in the head."

Big John's newfound patience was coming to an end. He tightened the cuffs around Bubba's wrists harder than necessary. The man hissed in pain when John pushed him toward his car. "He didn't hit anybody, fool. I did. I'll jerk a knot in anybody's head if they point a gun at a lawman, especially Mister Ned. You're lucky. If we was on our side of the tracks, I'd-a shot you. And I haven't made up my mind not to shoot you yet!"

Bubba had already seen how the Deputy Washington handled things. He sighed in relief when John slammed the door of his car. John returned with Tyrel and put him into the back seat without saying a word and walked back to nudge the unconscious man with his toe. Getting no response, he knelt to tie the man's hands with a length of cord since they were fresh out of handcuffs.

Finished, John left him on the ground and rummaged in the sedan's floorboard under the steering wheel. After a moment he stood up holding a knife wrapped in newspaper. "Looky here."

Ned joined him beside the open door and peeled the knife from the damp paper, feeling the knot return to his gut. With growing excitement Big John again searched the dirty floorboard under the driver's seat and found another knife and two large screwdrivers that looked familiar. "We may have found your man."

Ralston grunted in an effort to see over his shoulder. "What are y'all talkin' 'bout?"

"Cutting up animals," Ned answered. "You want to tell us about that?"

Tyrel stuck his head through the open car window. "We don't know nothing' about no cut-up animals. That's something you're trying to get up so you can put us in jail."

Big John laughed at his convoluted way of thinking. "Aw, hell, I don't need to get anything up to throw you in jail. You're already there, boy, you just ain't in the cell yet."

Ned knelt beside Ralston. "Tell me about this knife."

"Nothin' to tell."

John held the second knife and screwdrivers. His greatest fear was realized. One of his people was terrorizing the countryside. "What have you been doing with this knife?"

"Nothin'." I always keep a knife handy, same as you."

"You cut anything up lately? Dogs or such?"

"Aw, naw. You ain't blaming none of that on me. I heard about all that stuff a little while ago, but I didn't have nothing to do with it."

Ned pondered the young man at his feet.

"Somebody killed Cody Parker's bird dog. Maybe it was you."

Ralston didn't like it one little bit. "I wouldn't mess with Cody's dogs. He'd kill you for that."

"Hey, Law, you gonna leave us sitting here all day?"

"Shut up, Tyrel, or I'm liable to leave you in there 'til the mornin'. What about this knife wrapped up in the paper here, Ralston?"

"It ain't mine. I thought you was talking about that watermelon knife in the floorboard. I found the one in your hand out in the woods not far from your cotton patch, Mr. Ned." He turned his head to see. "I had to go outdoors this morning while I was talking to Ivory and the others and I went out behind some bushes. While I was squatting there I found that knife laying on that little ol' piece of paper and picked it up. It looked like a good knife and it was dirty so I left it stuck on the paper till I could worsh it off. There was a wore-out old screwdriver there, too, but I didn't pick it up."

Ned felt deflated. Somehow he knew Ralston was telling the truth. "What else did you find?"

"Nothin' else."

"Was there anything dead close by? A dog, a coon or maybe a possum?"

"I'm having trouble thinking. Damn, John, you almost caved my head in."

"Answer my question."

"Aw, there was something stinkin' not far away, but I didn't go try and find out what it was. We can go look if y'ont to."

"I'll go all right, but after I take you to jail."

"Why don't you turn me loose?"

John stared downward at Ralston. "You're full of bull. You're going to the pen for what y'all were fixin' to do to Ned. If you're real lucky you'll be on one of them Huntsville chain gangs with Tyrel there."

"But we really didn't *do* nothin'."

"I don't want to hear it." Ned put the knife in the floorboard of his car.

"You want to hear where Lightfoot is hiding?"

"Shut up, Ralston," Tyrel's scared voice came from the car. "That damned Indian will kill us all for talking about him."

Ralston wouldn't quit, knowing his chances were slipping away. "I know where he's hiding. You let me go, and I'll tell you."

Ned was tired of talking. "You're worrying the piss out of me. Here's how it is. You tell me and I'll let Judge Rains know how you helped us find Lightfoot, and it might make it easier on you. But I'm not foolin' with you no more."

Ralston didn't have to consider the offer. "Done. He's hiding with kinfolk over in Chisum.

They live in a little ol' shack at the end of the dirt road that cuts back behind the Mt. Holiness Church. It's the only house down in there. You'll know it when you see it."

Ned and Big John exchanged glances. Things were going their way.

"Let's get these boys to jail, John. I'm tired of standin' on this highway."

O.C. was happy to see Ralston in handcuffs and even happier to hear he'd been involved in a threat to a peace officer. The charges were solid. Within an hour of getting the information regarding Lightfoot, Sheriff Griffin's deputies drove to the house in Chisum and took him into custody without incident. Everyone in Lamar County breathed easier.

Three hours later, Ned and John were back in the river bottoms. The sun rested in the treetops by the time they returned to the empty field where Ralston found the knife. They scratched around the general area until they found where he'd done his business.

Ned kicked through the tall dry grass between the field and the woods. Big yellow grasshoppers whizzed away in all directions. It was Big John who first got the whiff of death that led him to the corpse.

"My lord, Ned."

"Didja find something?"

"I reckon."

Ned joined him. "Whew, it's…" he trailed off as he got a good look at the tiny, unmolested body of the Lightfoot baby lying in the grass in front of them. "Oh, hell."

Chapter Seventeen

What Grandpa and Mr. John found near the field stayed with folks for a long time. Everything was there, the body, the knife and the newspaper clipping. The baby hadn't been touched, though it looked like someone was interrupted before they got started. Grandpa figured Ralston or one of the other hands scared the killer off.

Or he just wanted to send a message. The talk at the store and at church was about the goings-on in the bottoms. They wanted to say it was Frank Lightfoot, but Grandpa kept saying the timing didn't work out. Even so, the newspaper said Lightfoot confessed. Grandpa learned the truth about what happened at the shack, but the part about the baby's disappearance kept bothering him.

The front page story in *The Chisum News* said Lightfoot snuck up on the house after a week of hard drinking to find his wife living with another man. When he looked through the open window and saw them all sitting around the table like a family, he lost his mind and grabbed the first thing at hand, which was a double bit chopping ax leaning against the wall beside the back door.

The family didn't know what to do when he kicked the flimsy screen door open. He killed the man who had taken his place with the first whack, before he could get up from the table. Willie, the young man I'd seen leaning on the porch post, was no match for his crazy daddy and went down before the rest of the shocked family could respond.

By then Lightfoot was in a blind frenzy and said he didn't clearly remember what happened afterwards, but he was sure the coal oil lamp got knocked over. The dry wood quickly caught fire. Some of the kids didn't have a chance to get out of the house.

Lightfoot chased his screaming wife out into the yard and killed her there, leaving the ax buried in her body. When he turned around, Willie had crawled from the burning house, trying to pull the baby with him.

Lightfoot finished him off with his knife, but came back to himself when he saw the coughing baby on the porch, so he grabbed her up.

Miss Becky clipped the story from the paper and read it to us. "The rest of the kids were hers but the least one took up with me," Frank Lightfoot told the courtroom. "Two or three of them older kids crawled out of the house, but I could tell they were already burned pretty bad and they quit moving before y'all got there. I hid in the woods while y'all were millin' around the fire like a bunch of cows. The baby had quit crying and was acting funny. I squatted there and held it and then it went limp and was dead. I guess the smoke or them culoil fumes killed it.

"While y'all were still waiting for the fire to die down I set there in the dark holding it until it got cold. After a while I laid it down by a stump to come give myself up, but I changed my mind. Then, when I went back to pick it up, it was gone. I thought I was wrong about it being dead and maybe it had crawled off, but then I seen someone ducking through the brush toward the cars on the highway, so I went the other way."

Miss Becky shook her head at the table and said, "Ummmm ummmm." Then she read some more.

"I was just drunk, that's all. I don't know why I did those things. But besides, I don't think them kids was all mine. Mark is, because I can see myself in him, but the rest was nothing but mouths to feed."

He swore to Mr. O.C. he was telling the truth. Mr. O.C. was furious, though, the way Lightfoot referred to the baby, calling her an "it" and not getting help when every man in town was standing there in the yard. Lightfoot's last words as they took him out of the courtroom were about his murdered wife. "That gal weren't much to look at, but she sure could cook if she had something to put on the stove."

The trial was scheduled for the spring and things quieted down, except for what happened to the baby. The coroner said it died from the smoke. When Grandpa and Mr. John found it a full two weeks after the fire, the little thing looked almost normal, not like it would have if the body had been in that field for the whole time.

Grandpa said he figured someone had kept it in an icebox for a while, before taking it to the field. He thought Ralston had scared him off before he could do anything to the little body.

Everybody was glad Lightfoot was in jail, and they thought the animal mutilations were over. But Grandpa kept telling folks that the baby couldn't have been laying there that long and Lightfoot couldn't be the man people had started calling the Skinner. Even so, they just looked the other way when details came up that didn't fit.

Miss Becky said it was like them ostriches in the cartoons on television. They just wanted to bury their heads in the sand instead of dealing with the truth. We were ordered to stay near the house or have someone with us if we went anywhere.

"There's still a lot we don't know about this crazy bastard," I heard Grandpa say to Mr. O.C. on the phone one day when he thought I was outside, instead of listening from the bedroom. "He could be watching the house right now, and I'm about half-afraid Becky'll shoot the first person who comes up to the house at night while I'm gone."

After they arrested Frank Lightfoot at his relative's house in Chisum, those same kinfolk that hid him found out Mark was living with us. Frank at first told his family that everyone in the house was dead, so they were excited to hear Mark was alive. In some sort of strange way they wanted to take him into the same house that hid his murdering daddy.

Mark didn't want to go, but he had to. They drove up to get him one afternoon after school in a wore-out Pontiac that smoked and rattled on only seven cylinders.

Mark didn't say much when they stopped in the yard. He recognized his uncle and sort of withdrew inside himself. Without a word to anyone he went in the house.

The Indian man who was driving didn't get out. He spat tobacco juice out the door until Grandpa went over and leaned on the roof and talked a good long time to him. The man never said a word, but I figure he couldn't because he wouldn't spit past Grandpa, so he was probably drowning while Grandpa talked. I got a sense Grandpa laid down the law about Mark and what he'd do if he heard he was being mistreated.

Miss Becky was hanging clothes on the line with her mouth full of wooden pins. Mark's aunt was dark and we could see the Choctaw in her face through the open car window. Miss Becky finished pinning the sheet on the line and when the woman got out, they spoke for quite a while next to the clothes line. Miss Becky planted her feet and gave the woman what for. In fact, she did most of the talking and finger pointing.

I went inside where Mark was packing. He didn't have anything when he came to live with us but the cast-off clothes he wore on the night of the murders. Miss Becky's cooking put some weight on him, and a growth spurt kindly put him into a bind. She sewed him a few shirts during the following weeks and Grandpa brought home some britches from one of his trips to town.

Instead of picking up the new clothes, Mark laid his outgrown shirt and pants on the bed and started to unbuckle his belt.

"What are you doing?" I asked.

"Changing clothes." He wouldn't make eye contact with me. "I'll leave these here and you can have 'em."

"Them clothes are yours. Miss Becky will have a fit if you don't take them with you."

"You think it'll be okay?"

I felt a lump in my throat, and my eyes started burning. "Sure, gather everything up while I get you something to carry them in." I left so he couldn't see the water in my eyes. Mark's eyes were watering, too, when I came back and gave him two paper grocery sacks. We choked it down and put his clothes into the sacks and went outside.

Miss Becky met us on the porch, sniffling. Mark hugged her neck and she whispered in his ear for a long time. He listened, nodded, and then kissed her cheek. She kissed him back, ran her fingers through his black hair and then let him go. I followed him out to the car, not knowing what to do or say. He shook Grandpa's hand and put his sacks of clothes in the car.

Grandpa raised his eyebrows toward the man behind the wheel and gave a little half-nod to drive his point home.

Mark stood with me beside the door for a long minute. "Pepper's going to throw a fit," I said.

"I'll write her a letter."

I raised my right hand. "How?"

"Paleface." With a quick grin, he punched me in the shoulder and climbed in with what looked like about twenty other Indian kids in the back seat.

I watched them drive off in a cloud of blue exhaust.

During the next few weeks neither Miss Becky nor Grandpa talked about Mark when I was around. I could tell they missed him pretty bad, and I did, too, because it was fun to have a boy around.

Pepper sure acted funny when she heard Mark was gone, and she didn't stay with us for quite a while.

Grandpa finally got all his cotton in. One morning it was nearly seventy degrees at sunup.

The next morning there was a frost.

Chapter Eighteen

Top and his grandparents sat on the porch, enjoying the long shadows of the evening and the mourning dove calling from the woods across the highway.

The phone rang in the living room. Miss Becky grunted out of her rocker and went inside. She called through the screen door. "It's for you, Daddy."

"Who is it?"

"Neal Box."

"What's he want?"

"You know Neal isn't going to tell me. He's wantin' you."

Ned sighed and went inside. "Hello."

"Ned, this is Neal. You better get up here to the store. Bill Stevens is up here."

"Ain't no law against Bill being at the store."

"I know, but he's been drinking and he's getting loud and poking people with his nub."

Bill Stevens lost his right hand in a hay baler

accident back during the War. Never one to be held back due to such a minor thing like the loss of an appendage, Bill continued to work as hard as ever, using the stump as if a hand were still attached.

The calloused stump was hard as stone. Whenever Bill was drinking he tended to poke his listeners with the blunt end of his wrist.

It was like being rammed with a baseball bat, and if the conversation turned heated, the poking became almost violent. Men could usually take it up to a point, but ladies found themselves frightened and angry, almost violated, by being poked with his nub.

"All right. I'll be there directly." He hung up the phone and spoke through the screen door. "Mama, I've got to go up to the store and stop Bill Stevens from poking people again."

"When will that man ever learn?"

Not bothering to change his clothes, Ned pinned his badge to his overalls, slipped the 32.20 into his front pocket and the sap into a back one and drove to the store.

Bill was out in front of Neal's store, talking loudly to a group of men. When Ned got out of his car, Bill drove home a point by poking some fellow Ned didn't know in the chest.

The man took a step back from the force and

then moved forward, his hands doubled into white-knuckled fists.

Ned slammed his car door. "Hold it, mister. Bill, come here."

The stranger turned his anger toward the man in overalls until he caught a glimpse of the badge. His eyes immediately shifted to the bulge in Ned's pocket and then slipped to the ground at his own feet. Ned watched him fade back toward the porch before directing his attention to Bill.

"Bill Stevens, you old son of a gun, how you doing?"

Bill frowned at Ned and rocked slightly on his unsteady feet. "Hidy, Ned. I'm doing good. I been drinkin'. What are you up to?"

"Aw, I heard you was here, and I wanted to see you."

"Well, I been meaning to talk to you." Bill started to jab at him with his stump.

Ned batted the arm away as if swatting at an annoying fly. "Now don't be poking people with your nub, Bill. I've done told you nobody likes it and it hurts."

"Well, they don't like it 'cause I ain't got a hand."

Ned sighed. "People don't care about your hand, but they don't like being jabbed with a nub. Especially when you're drunk."

"I ain't completely drunk, and I'll poke who I want to."

"No, you won't. You're on your way to being mean drunk, and you know I won't tolerate it. And if you jab anybody else I'll lay a sap upside your head. Now, get in the back seat of my car here and let me take you home. You don't need to be driving in the shape you're in right now."

"I ain't in bad shape."

"You will be if you don't get in the car. Now, go ahead on and let me talk to that feller over there while you rest." Ned opened the car door and walked away from Bill as if he'd forgotten the man. The tactic was perfect, because without anyone to argue with, Bill simply sat in the back seat with one foot on the ground to wait.

The man started an old Ford pickup but was unable to leave because of the haphazard parking of the other men. Ned's own car plugged the last remaining bit of space in the lot. The stranger looked annoyed and scared.

Ned walked over to the stranger's truck and laid his hand on the edge of the open window. "How you doing?"

"Fine." The driver glanced around nervously, as if looking for escape.

"You know Bill there?"

"Naw, he was just poking me when I disagreed with him about something."

"You're not from around here. You from Chisum?"

"Hugo."

"I've never seen you here."

"Well, I'm not really from Hugo, but I moved there about a year ago. Had a job with the circus 'til lately."

"Oh, you one of them clowns?"

The man suddenly became angry. "Mister, I weren't no clown. Not everybody in a circus is a clown. I shoveled elephant shit and put up and took down tents 'til I couldn't stand them people no more. They put more stock in their animals and canvas than they do with people, so I left."

The quick display of anger was a surprise. Ned slipped both his hands into the back pockets of his overalls. The leather sap felt good. A tickle in the back of his mind made him wonder if a man with such quick anger could be the type of person to channel his feelings into mutilations. He'd already shown his aggravation toward animals.

He wrapped his fingers around the sap. "Now don't get mad. I was just asking."

"I'm not wanted for anything, sheriff."

"Aw, I ain't no sheriff. I'm just constable

around here and I never meant you was wanted. I only wanted to visit for a minute. You got a name?"

"Babe."

Ned brightened. "Babe? Like in Babe Ruth?"

"Yeah, my daddy liked baseball."

"Well, Babe, you play ball?"

"Never cared for it."

"I used to play a little pasture ball. You didn't get Bill to start talking about baseball did you? He gets carried away when he's talking about the Houston Colt Forty-fives."

Babe shrugged. "We were talking about a lot of things."

Ned nodded and looked the truck over. "This your truck?"

"It belongs to a friend of mine."

"He loan it to you?"

Babe looked toward the store. "I just come up here to get some bread and baloney."

Ned looked into the empty seat. "You're leaving without it?"

"Well, I guess I better. I never did get inside."

"No need to leave. I ain't runnin' you off. What did you say your last name was?"

"I didn't."

Ned nodded. "But if you was to say, what would it be?"

"Carter."

"All right, Babe Carter. You sit right here in the truck, or go inside for your bread and baloney and I'll be right back. Now, don't you leave before we say goodbye."

Ned turned and started back to his car. He glanced over his shoulder after a couple of steps, but Babe sat behind the wheel staring straight ahead.

Bill was stretched out asleep in the back seat. Ned folded his legs inside and closed the door, then went around and called in on his radio, giving the dispatcher Babe's name and the license of the truck.

While he kept a wary eye on the stranger, two locals wandered over from the domino hall. They mostly ignored Nub, asleep in the car, but Babe was a different story. Already anxious and fearful due to the Skinner in the river bottoms, they asked Ned a dozen questions before the radio finally squawked back. He picked up the microphone. "Did you find anything out?"

"Yep. Babe Carter did five years in the McAlester prison for armed robbery. He liked to rob stores, but there aren't any warrants out on him right now."

"What about the truck?"

"Belongs to Larry Dockery over in Idabel, but it isn't reported stolen."

"All right, thanks, Frankie." Ned replaced the microphone on the holder. *Well, at least he can't be the man I'm after,* he thought.

"You gonna arrest that man?" one of the farmers asked.

"No reason to." Ned told him and returned to the truck. "All right, Babe Carter. I reckon you can go when you're ready, or when these boys move their trucks. Now, don't forget your bread and baloney."

For the first time Babe looked Ned directly in the eye. "That's all?"

"No reason to bother you anymore."

"I haven't had much luck with lawmen."

"I imagine not, but maybe you ain't run into the right kind. Now, you make sure you stay out of trouble."

"You know about me now, don't you?"

"I know you done your time and paid your debt and now you're a free man. You be careful around here, because all these boys are carrying guns these days."

"What for?"

"Some meanness, and we don't know yet who's doing it. Walk soft on this side of the river."

"Well, thanks, I guess."

"You take care now, Babe Carter."

When Ned started his car and turned around on the highway toward Bill's house, the ex-con was still sitting behind the wheel, staring at the store. Driving off, Ned worried that he was considering every encounter as a potential lead to the killer.

If he didn't get control of the situation and his own suspicions, he'd be looking for the crazy man every time he answered a call for a family fight, or whenever he pulled over a drunk.

It was no way to operate as a lawman.

He glanced in his rearview mirror at the sleeping man. *Could it be Bill? Is he the one? Nah, it ain't like that* Fugitive *television show where the one-armed man did the killing. Bill couldn't be the man I'm looking for. It'd be hard to do all those things with just one hand and a nub.*

Chapter Nineteen

It finally cooled off for good in October. Skeins of honking geese flew over the bottoms, on their way south toward the Gulf Coast.

The mornings were frosty and the cold settled in the low places, making steam rise from the streams and branches crisscrossing the fields. The leaves began to change; the persimmons to yellows, the oaks to reds, and the sycamores and sweet gums turned red, yellow and orange.

Grandpa took me squirrel hunting while leaves fell around us. He let me carry the target gun and taught me to shoot fox squirrels in the eye to avoid ruining the meat. I learned to stand still with the rifle while Grandpa walked around to the other side of the tree and made noise to get the squirrel to turn on the limb to give me a clear shot.

One Saturday morning we loaded half a dozen bales of alfalfa into the back of the truck along with a sack of range cubes and went to feed his cows in the Whitman pasture.

It was my job to climb up in the back of the truck with a pair of wire cutters and break up the bales of hay and scatter the sections. Then he made a u-turn and drove slowly back past the cows while I shook range cubes off the tailgate.

Finished, he let me drive around the pasture for a while in low gear. I wove through the trees and around the pool. Sometimes I followed my own tracks back through the frost. Tiring of dodging cattle, I drove through the gate and he rewired it behind us.

I slid back over to the passenger side, and he took the wheel. "Let's go by Myrt Howard's place. I need to talk to him."

Myrt and his wife lived in a leaning shack in a pasture of cow pies. They had a grown son, Clayton, who spent his day sitting on a pallet in the middle of the wooden living room floor, playing with beat up pots and pans.

Clayton was just one member of the large family and he didn't get much special treatment. He was mentally about two years old and always laughed when we dropped by. I made it a point to talk to him when we visited Myrt and he'd grin and drool at me. I wasn't ever afraid of Clayton, but I kept a distance between us because he was a big man like his daddy and could have hurt me without ever intending to.

He was asleep on the floor like a little baby in front of the wood-burning stove when Grandpa knocked softly and Myrt's little wife opened the door. "Hidy, Ned," she whispered.

"Florence."

"Myrt's in the barn with his bird dogs."

"Sorry to bother you."

She gave him a sad smile and closed the door.

I was excited at the news, because Myrt was the only man I knew who raised Brittany spaniels. Most quail hunters used rawboned English pointers, and they ranged way off from the hunters. The smaller, loving Brittanys stayed close.

We walked down to the chicken-wire dog pen under a wide red oak beside the barn, but Myrt wasn't there. A mama dog stuck her head out of the tipped-over 55-gallon barrel and looked at us with sad eyes. I could tell she had pups because her bag was swollen. Dogs in other pens barked and jumped up with their feet on the chicken wire.

"Myrt?" Grandpa hollered over the din.

A gruff watery voice called through the closed barn door. "In here."

Grandpa lifted the latch and we stopped inside the dim interior so our eyes could adjust to the light. Myrt met us in the long hall that stretched the dusty length of the barn. Feed cribs on either side gave way to stalls. Dust glittered in the beams of sunlight slanting through wide gaps in the barn's walls. The air smelled like sweet feed, alfalfa, and manure.

Myrt probably weighed three hundred and fifty pounds. He kept his gray hair sheared close to his bullet head. His eyes were tiny and close together, and his jowls hung down like a bulldog's.

"Hidy, Ned." His voice was thick and juicy from a mouthful of chewing tobacco. Myrt was a nasty chewer, content to spit anywhere and on anything. The floor of his truck was brown and thick with dried tobacco spit.

His eyes flicked past Grandpa to me. "Hidy, Top." He held a claw hammer in his left hand and a puppy in the other that looked as if he were almost weaned.

"Hidy." I looked with interest at the puppy and the hammer. Myrt wasn't holding him like I would have. He held it like a can of peaches. The pup kept whimpering for his mama.

The men stood for an uncomfortable minute while the pup tuned up loud and long. The mama dog in the pen outside heard him and let loose with a howl of her own. Myrt shrugged and spat into the dirt at our feet. "Daisy out there got stuck with a litter and here it is hunting season."

Grandpa cleared his throat. "I saw her."

"I don't know who the daddy is."

The puppy wailed again. Myrt started to turn away, back toward the one open stall door, and then stopped and looked at us again. My eyes slipped off the wiggling puppy and into the stall behind them. I went numb and took a step back, suddenly realizing why Myrt held a hammer. Still bodies cooled on top of a 'toe sack lying in the dirt.

"I don't believe the daddy was a Brit. Some stray climbed over the pen and got at her. Daisy won't hunt as long as these puppies are on her."

Without thinking, I took a little step forward and then another. Myrt jogged the hammer up and down in his fat hand like he was tapping tacks. The little one wailed again. Myrt suddenly held it out to me without a word.

Grandpa looked at the pup and then me. "Take that little feller outside for a minute."

"I don't need a bunch of mongrel dogs to feed." Myrt kept tapping at the air with the hammer.

I hurried outside, trying to breathe and not cry at the same time. Tears ran down my cheeks as I trembled, held the little puppy, and sniffed his hair. I knew I shouldn't have, but I opened the pen's gate and slipped inside with his mama. He wiggled even harder and I sat him on the ground. He ran to her and almost immediately went to nursing when she laid down.

The morning chill didn't matter. I squatted

there in the pen for a long time, watching them and talking softly to Daisy. After a long while Grandpa left the barn and stopped outside the dog pen.

"You ready to go?"

I didn't say anything. It took a long time to raise my eyes to Grandpa. Knowing what would happen as soon as we left, I slowly stood and bit my lip to keep from crying.

"Well." Grandpa pointed downward. "Grab Hootie there and let's get."

Relief washed over me. I picked up my new puppy and we got.

Miss Becky discovered a footprint in the soft soil under my bedroom window a few days later. She liked to put cut flowers on her table and she raised everything from black-eyed Susans to daffodils and irises in the beds around the house. Frost had killed everything, however, and the freshly turned dirt had only one track in it.

We knew the print under the window didn't belong to any one of us because the sole and size didn't match up to anyone. Grandpa Ned frowned for most of the day and kept returning to the print to stare at it and then slowly scan the pasture and trees at the back of the house, talking quietly to himself.

I could tell Miss Becky was concerned, and the pocket on one side of her house dress sagged with the weight of something heavy. I suspicioned she had a pistol in there, because once when she leaned over to get something out of the chest freezer, I heard a distinct bump. To see if I was right, I climbed up on the china cabinet to see if her little .22 automatic was still there on the top shelf where she always kept it. It was gone.

I'd heard stories about how the pioneers and Indians had fought all along the Red River back in the olden days, and with Miss Becky now carrying a gun like Grandpa, the tales became clear. I felt proud of her.

At dinner Grandpa also noticed the shotgun beside the back door and looked thoughtful for a moment. Then we both knew Miss Becky wasn't taking any chances and the whole thing really began to scare me.

"Y'all make sure the winders are locked up tight," Grandpa said after we'd eaten. "Hootie can sleep in there with you from now on, too."

Miss Becky got up to wash the dishes. "He didn't say in the bed with you, though."

"Yes, ma'am." I fed Hootie a fried potato under the table, knowing he'd sneak under the covers after dark.

Chapter Twenty

Ned's eighty-eight-year-old brother died after Thanksgiving. Arnold Rob Parker had been a character all his life, and his adventures kept the community talking. Even his funeral on an unusually warm November day provided folks with enough fodder to keep the busybodies happy for years.

When Ned arrived at the church, he realized they'd forgotten to name the pallbearers. After a quick parlay, Cody and Raymond Chase were selected to join four other early arrivals to carry Arnold's remains.

Ned then waited under a wide shade tree with the young men to watch the mourners as they arrived. Though the coroner said Arnold died from a heart attack, Ned wasn't convinced the service was not for a murder victim. Even there, he couldn't get the killer off his mind, and he wanted to study on every man that passed. It was probably wrong, but he found his entire life was consumed with finding the man responsible for the atrocities in his community.

Men in slacks and limp white shirts joined the group of pall bears to stand or hunker in the bare dirt under wide shade trees. Others observed the solemn occasion by wearing a blue sport coat over faded overalls. The gathering crowd talked of Arnold's exploits and dimly remembered hunting trips and events best left unspoken so close to a church.

Some younger husbands almost stopped for a moment, knowing the conversation was bound to be good, but an impatient tug on the coat by an irritated wife persuaded them it was safer to continue inside.

Miss Becky and Aunt Ida Belle drug Pepper inside when they arrived, but Top joined his Grandpa Ned to hear Isaac Reader talk about one night long ago.

"Listen, remember the night Arnold Rob went to sleep under his '34 Ford truck when him and Carl Dibner and all of us were camping out down at the creek?" Several nodded at the right time, having heard the story several times. "Carl pulled a rope across Arnold's chest to make him think it was a snake. The first time he did it Arnold raised up so fast he dented his head on the muffler. Listen, when he laid back down Carl did it again. He nearly scared him to death that second time, too. But the third time Arnold Rob got mad.

"Listen, listen, he grabbed it and threw the rope toward the fire, threatening to kill the next one if he did it again. The only thing was, the third time it really was a big ol' chicken snake. You should have seen the bunch of us scrambling to get away from a flying snake!"

Everyone laughed quietly. Ned's eyes flicked from man to man, looking for a clue, any kind of an indication that someone in the group was the person he needed so badly to find. Even though the coroner said Arnold died of a heart attack, Ned was sure the killer would be at the funeral. Ned could feel him there.

Stories came thick and fast, causing the men to chuckle quietly in guilty pleasure. Twenty minutes later the funeral director waved them inside, and they reluctantly tore themselves away and filed in.

The dry autumn air warmed rapidly and quickly became stuffy, so every window gaped open to capture any available breeze. The ladies fanned with the McGinnis Brother's Funeral Home fans. The Last Supper on one side and Jesus and the Lambs on the other fluttered so fast they ran together and looked like little lambs were standing around the supper table.

Arnold had the most pleasant expression on

his face of anyone they'd ever seen in a casket. He looked positively pleased with himself. Most figured it was because he had passed on while sitting up in his deer stand the first morning of deer season. His buddies were proud Arnold took The Last Walk while in his stand. It was a good place to go for two reasons.

One was because Arnold loved to hunt deer. He went while doing something he looked forward to each year.

The other was because his large bulk would have been too much to bear if he had died while on a quail outing, because his friends would have been forced to carry him out of the field.

Even then they had to wait until Buck Johnson arrived to pronounce Arnold dead. Ned thought it was ridiculous, because rigor mortis had already set in and it was obvious to anyone with enough sense to tie his own shoes that Arnold had gone on to his reward.

Once he was pronounced, it took five grown men who responded to the news to lift him out of the stand and maneuver the corpse into the back seat of Sheriff Donald Griffin's car for the ride to the funeral home.

Because he was so stiff and already in a sitting position to begin with, the men simply put Arnold upright in the back seat. Sheriff Griffin wasn't happy about this turn of events, but there was nothing he could do about it.

Ty Cobb Foxx slapped Arnold's hat back on his head, because he didn't know what else to do with it. When they shut the door he noticed Arnold's right hand was still in the raised position because, when they pried the rifle out of his fingers, the arm remained upright.

Isaac Reader almost waved back before he caught himself.

Sheriff Griffin drove and at every stoplight in town folks saw Arnold's upraised hand and waved in return. Later, it was a shock to realize they'd waved at a dead man. Others confidently said Arnold was alive when they saw him.

"I swanny, he looked so natural in that police car."

The pallbearers filed down the aisle after everyone had settled in. They took their seats on the first row, directly in front of Ned and the family. The service began in the tiny church when Harvey Willoughby, the Methodist preacher, stepped forward and placed his worn Bible on the pulpit. "Arnold Robert Parker. Born November seventh…."

They suffered through the litany of dates, survivors and accomplishments as the heavy atmosphere began to take its toll on the congregation.

Accompanied by an out-of-tune piano, Arnold's

lifelong friend, Minnie Delores, stood and butchered *The Old Rugged Cross* with a caterwauling rendition that dried up a nearby milk cow for a week.

By the third verse Ned could stand her trembling voice no longer. For the first time in a long while he gave up thinking about the killer and once again began talking to himself. "After hearing that, I believe we're burying the wrong one today."

Miss Becky poked him the ribs for being disrespectful.

The out-of-character wisecrack hit six funny bones at the same time. Cody ground his teeth and tears trickled down his cheeks.

Eyes closed in musical ecstasy, Minnie Delores raised her chin for a high note. Her quavering voice and quivering neck wattles were too much. The pallbearers ducked their heads. "Think she made that sound with Arnold?" Cody nudged Raymond. The congregation thought the young men up front were shuddering with unrestrained grief.

"Bless their hearts."

"God love those boys."

Henrietta Lewis, whose hug led to the fight between Top and Cale Westlake, shifted her massive bulk forward in the pew and placed a meaty hand on Cody's shoulder. "It's all right, hon. He's in a better place. He didn't have too much fun in this old world anyway."

Mary Lou Skaggs missed the last couple of notes on her piano but made up for it in volume. Minnie hadn't heard it thunder in years and it wasn't surprising to anyone when the singer and pianist failed to end together. Minnie suddenly found herself out of music and hurried through the last sentence to end alone, suffering Mary Lou's glare.

The boys were on dangerous ground when Minnie finally tottered to her chair and plopped down. Since she was so deaf, she had no idea anyone could hear any better. She leaned to the side and loudly broke wind. The sound carried with clarity of Gabriel's Horn.

"Praise the lord!" she said primly and gazed over the congregation of mourners.

"My lands," Miss Becky sighed.

Cody and Raymond leaned against each other, hiccupping and wiping their eyes, desperate to get a grip on the laughter that rocked their pew.

"Bless their hearts."

"Praise the Lord!" Willoughby temporarily forgot he was presiding over a funeral.

Ned snorted. "Praise the Lord's right. We couldn't have gotten through that song alone."

Minister Willoughby mercifully wrapped up the service. Since the adjacent cemetery was only a few steps away, it was traditional to carry the deceased through the door, down the wooden steps, across the patchy lawn to the gravesite.

Hands folded in front, the minister closed his eyes and nodded solemnly. Tortured grunts erupted from three throats as they lifted the heavy casket. When they pivoted to walk down the narrow aisle, Cody's knee popped like a firecracker.

Tears leaped into his eyes. He bowed his head in pain and took a step. "Oh, lord."

"Yes lord! Please help those poor suffering souls!"

"Y'all look like you need help," Ned said as the boys passed.

"Amen!"

More wails erupted from mourning women who simply loved funerals and were having a *helluva* time. The service was getting dangerously close to breaking out into a revival.

Six heads ducked toward the floor as the young men lock-stepped down the narrow aisle and squeezed through the open double doors to navigate the tricky wooden steps.

When they came through the doors, Arnold's hunting buddies honored their friend with a ragged twenty-one shotgun salute. The startled pallbearers almost dropped the casket, thinking someone was taking one last shot at Arnold to settle a grudge.

The final act of the day unfolded at the

gravesite. When they attempted to lower Arnold's casket into the hole dug by several of Arnold's closest friends and relatives, and Mr. Jack Daniels, Cody and the boys realized the casket was a good six inches longer than the grave.

"My lord," Ned said to O.C. as the young men nearly dropped the casket head-first into the hole. Muffled four-letter-words wafted across the crowd of rapidly departing mourners. "What a send-off."

It was the last time anyone laughed in Center Springs for a good long time, and they wouldn't have laughed then, had they known the man known as The Skinner was right there the funeral the whole time.

Chapter Twenty-one

A week of freezing weather finally killed off the last remaining leaves. Deer season was in full swing and trucks went past the house with antlers poking over the sides of the bed. I wanted to hunt deer, but there was no one to take me since Grandpa wasn't a big game hunter.

Pepper and I were reading comic books in the house when Raymond Chase pulled up in the drive and honked the horn. Miss Becky stomped from the bedroom to look out the window. "I swanny. Ned, when is he going to learn some manners?"

He picked up his hat and was pulling on his coat when we heard footsteps on the wooden porch. Raymond opened the kitchen door and burst inside without knocking. Miss Becky was about to light into him, when she saw a look on his face.

Grandpa did too. "What's wrong?"

Chase hadn't even taken off his hat in the house. "Ned, I got bad news. This morning some boys out deer hunting found your cousin Joseph in the woods out toward Slate Shoals, while you were gone to Dallas. He'd been cut up pretty bad. I don't have a lot of the story yet, because Sheriff Griffin saw me over by the truck with the witnesses and threw a wall-eyed fit saying I had no business getting involved in the investigation."

"Let's go."

"It's already took care of." Chase finally took off his hat and laid it on the television, beside Grandpa's pistol. "They're already gone."

Grandpa settled back into his rocker by the space heater, angry because no one had called him. "Tell me."

"You kids go in the kitchen." Miss Becky shooed us toward the door.

It didn't make any difference, because we could hear from in there, but we went.

Raymond turned his back on us. "It was pretty bad. Somebody spent a while killing him. He was broke down a little at a time, shot in both knees and both arms. I reckon it was to keep him from fighting or getting away. Then they field dressed him and skinned him like a rabbit, mostly likely while he was still alive."

Horrified, Miss Becky covered her mouth. I could see Grandpa through the door, barely rocking and shaking his head. "Oh, lordy."

Pepper couldn't contain herself. "Shit." We

exchanged looks and I felt the hair rise on the back of my neck. I noticed she had goose bumps on her arms.

"Those boys who found him are in bad shape, too. They was hunting out there and came across his truck. He was in the bed, like you'd do with a dead deer."

Joseph had been close to Grandpa when they were kids, but they drifted apart over the years. I even remembered hearing he took a notion to get into law work. For two or three months, Joseph rode with Grandpa at night on a few calls, but when he lost the bid for constable in Precinct 2 against Raymond Chase, it took the wind out of his sails and he went back to Slate Shoals to raise cattle.

"We don't know how long he'd been dead. Could have been days, since he lived alone. The cold kept him…fresh, so the whole thing looked like it just happened."

Miss Becky stood up. "That's enough." She came into the kitchen with us. Neither Pepper or I knew what to do or say, so we stayed at the table with our comics, not even pretending to read.

Grandpa stopped rocking and leaned forward with his hands on his knees, as if trying to get his breath. "Who found him?"

"Them twins, Ty Cobb and Jimmy Foxx. You know they run the woods all the time, but this one messed them up. Both of them were white as sheets when I saw 'em. I doubt they'll be hunting around Slate Shoals any more for a while."

Tears filled Grandpa's eyes and ran down his cheeks. He wiped them away and rocked again. "Ty Cobb and Jimmy Foxx. Them two keep turning up in all this."

"I've been thinking the same thing."

Grandpa stood and gave Raymond a sad pat on the shoulder. "Thanks, son, for bringing me the news."

"I'll be around if you need me." Raymond left, ruffling my hair as he passed. I shivered again as Miss Becky went into the living room to hold Grandpa for a while. He didn't cry, but I could hear him blowing his nose in the bandana he always carried in his back pocket. Miss Becky prayed long and soft while Pepper cussed under her breath and told me what she'd do if she ever laid eyes on the Skinner.

We attended Joseph's funeral, but it was a closed casket. Ty Cobb and Jimmy Foxx were there, and Grandpa kept watching them, mumbling to himself from time to time. It didn't seem like he was all there to me. His eyes kept flicking around, even during the prayers. I know, because I peeked when everyone else's head was down. It looked like he was busy watching instead of thinking about his cousin Joseph.

After that day, Grandpa spent more and more time away from the house, looking for Skinner. It seemed like he didn't think about anything else.

Christmas was usually a big event with a tree, presents and a lot of fireworks, but I'd gotten my present early when Hootie came home with me. The puppy was my constant companion, and even Santa's gift of a new Daisy BB gun on Christmas morning didn't overshadow my little buddy.

We didn't see Uncle Cody for quite a while. He worked nights at his joint across the river and slept through the day. I heard Calvin Williams' wife Norma filed for divorce and from time to time someone ran across her and Cody out somewhere. The busybodies stuck their noses in the air about it, but Miss Becky never let on she cared at all.

The only time I heard the men talk about it was outside of the church house one Wednesday night. Grandpa always carried Miss Becky when it was dark and waited in the parking lot with several other heathens until the service was over. Sometimes I went in with her and other times I stayed outside with the men, if it wasn't too cold or Miss Becky didn't fuss too much.

Cody and Norma popped up in conversation while I was there with them, but the men changed their tone and talked in some a code only they understood. I heard the words "red firecracker" and "wish I was young and stupid enough," but I didn't get anything else and finally gave up trying to figure out what was going on.

Enough snow fell on New Year's Day to turn everything white and Grandpa found fresh footprints leading from the burned-out shack in the pasture to my window and back again. It was obvious the tracks were made by an adult.

I was in the barn with him and Uncle James while they loaded feed sacks and hay into the truck, and worried over what the new tracks meant.

Uncle James held out his hand. "Top, hand me them dikes from over there." He turned to Grandpa while I climbed down off the hay to get the wire cutters where they lay on the lid of a barrel. "I'm scared to death about whoever made these tracks. I don't believe I want Pepper staying over until this thing is over. You ought to think about letting Top come stay with us, too."

Grandpa took off his felt hat and rubbed his bald head, a sure sign he was thinking or worrying. "I don't believe a mile will make much difference, but it wouldn't hurt to keep Pepper home."

"Ain't you afraid of what might happen?"

"Sure am. That's why I try to stay ready." Grandpa gave the pocket of his overalls a pat. I was surprised to think he was carrying a pistol now, even while we fed the cows.

"That'll only help if you're close by the house." Uncle James took the wire cutters from me and broke open a bale.

"Miss Becky knows what to do."

"It might not be enough."

I could see Grandpa's neck and face redden. He studied on it a good long while. "I know it, James. But I'm doing all I know to do."

I believe Uncle James realized he was goading his dad and backed off. "Well, I'm scared to death about this feller."

"I am, too."

They nailed the wooden casement windows shut after we got back from feeding.

January was cold and icy. We fed the cows, gathered the eggs and stayed inside to keep warm. One ice storm took down the power lines, and we had to use coal oil lanterns for a couple of days, but it wasn't any big deal. We stayed warm because the Dearborne space heater operated on propane.

We got out of class for three days because the buses couldn't run, but it wasn't much fun since we couldn't go outside. The bottom dropped out a couple of times and the thermometer on the porch read zero at least twice. We fed the cows each day and broke the ice off the stock pond for them to drink. Mostly I stayed inside and read or smoked up the house with the Wood-Burning set Pepper gave me for Christmas.

The weather kept meanness down, too. Grandpa went out on a few calls, but they were mostly troubles between men and their wives, trapped inside by the weather. The Skinner must have stayed in during the cold spell and everyone breathed a little easier for a while.

In February, Miss Becky had us hang her quilt rack so she could go to sewing on the wedding ring quilt she pieced together in December. When she wasn't sewing, she kept the rack raised up against the living room ceiling with pulleys Great Grandpa installed years before. It lowered easily to lap level whenever she wanted to sew. The rack was wide enough to stretch the quilt completely out while they worked on it. I liked to crawl underneath the tight material while the ladies sat around and stitched.

Women from all over came to the house with their sewing kits to help out and visit. Sometimes after they left, Miss Becky had to pick out some other lady's stitches.

"Bless her heart, Doneen is sweet as she can be, but she can't stitch worth a flip."

I lay on the couch with a book one day while nearly a dozen ladies chattered and stitched up a storm. The conversation followed the usual lines of kids, farming life, and husbands, until Miss Becky brought up some interesting news.

"Y'all, I need to tell you something. Ned found where somebody left tracks under the back bedroom window a while back. He thinks that feller who is doing so much meanness around here made them."

Miss Ethelda Fay made a sound like she'd stuck her finger with a needle. "Did he try to get in?'

"No, Ned and James nailed the windows shut just the same. Have y'all seen anything around your houses?"

I looked up at the silence and saw they were shaking their heads no.

"Well, I swanny." I recognized Miss Sara Hemphill's voice.

I glanced over and noticed something I'd never seen before. About half of the farm wives wore knee hose, some wore stretched out wool socks and a couple had nothing but pasty white calves held together by varicose veins. I stifled a giggle and turned back to my book.

"Are you scared?" Miss Sara wanted to know.

"I'm not afraid." Miss Becky stopped and took a pin from between her lips. "But I think we all need to be more careful than keeping the latch on the screen. A little metal on a wood frame won't make much difference if a man tries to get in."

"We keep a shotgun by the door." I didn't recognize the woman. "But I hear he's after kids, and we're fresh out at my house. They're all growed and gone."

Miss Becky took a couple of stitches. "Well, we all better keep an eye out. I don't know if anything has happened in the daylight, but when the men are out of the house, we all need to be ready for anything."

Miss Estelle glanced toward the hall at the .22 standing in the corner. "A little target gun ain't gonna be much."

"Ned's pistol there on the TV is enough. Besides, I have anothern' nearby. Y'all need to be ready." She nodded at the women around the quilt. "Ned, Gilbert, Arthur and the rest of them aren't much use to us when they're down in the field. It's up to us to take care of ourselves, if need be."

A chill went down my spine at the thought of those ladies dealing with a killer, if one wanted to get in the house. But at the same time, I knew being with them was safe.

◇◇◇

At breakfast the second weekend in February, a car pulled up the drive and I looked through the window to see Uncle Cody opening the dog box in back of his El Camino. His big pointers hit the frosty ground and ran around the yard, poking their noses into everything. Hootie heard them outside and barked like there was a bear trying to get in.

Grandpa opened the door to let Hootie out. "That's why I wanted him in the bedroom with you. He can hear me open the icebox from up at the barn. If this dog's nose is anything like his hearing, he'll be a hunting son of a gun."

Hootie hit the porch at a floppy run and slid to a stop when Cody's three bird dogs gathered around to sniff him from end to end. He stood there and took it until he decided he'd had enough, then gave them a growl. The grown dogs were so surprised they backed off.

Uncle Cody whooped and tilted his hat back. "That little feller's gonna be tough. C'mon Top, you and Ned get your guns and lets see if we can kick up a covey or two this mornin'."

"Can Hootie go?" I was excited about a hunting trip.

"Sure, but he won't be able to keep up. He's still too young. You'll have to carry him before long."

We stepped off the porch and into Grandpa's pasture beside the house. While we loaded our shotguns, the pointers locked up on the day's first covey in the dried up remnants of Miss Becky's vegetable garden. The birds flushed forty yards away.

Cody moaned and cussed the dogs while Grandpa laughed. The pointers looked embarrassed and slipped under the barbed wire fence between our pasture and Mr. Barker's, and hunted even harder.

Hootie couldn't keep up with the bigger, long-legged dogs, but it only made him work harder. He buried his nose in the tangle of briars along the fence and I had to drag him away from the recent bird smell before he'd give up the scent. He didn't have the experience to know they were gone, but it must have smelled pretty good to him. As soon as we crossed the fence, he struck off behind the big dogs with his nose on the ground.

Uncle Cody watched him closely. "He has something else in him but danged if I can tell what it is. But I allow the spaniel took over, because his nose is so good."

The dogs pointed the second covey not fifty yards from the first. The bobwhites held and Hootie had time to catch up. Instead of charging past the older dogs, he slowed down when he winded the birds and sort of crept up slow and easy. He didn't know what was going on up there, but he sure liked the smell.

May was the oldest, and she held a point with the other two honoring from behind. The closer Hootie got to May, the slower he moved until he'd crept up beside her. She knew he was coming and kept rolling one eye in his direction, knowing the youngster was showing some promise, but not caring much for his lack of manners.

"Whoa," Uncle Cody held his free hand out to stop us also. "Whoooa."

Hootie cut his eyes back at Cody, but he didn't really understand the command. One more step forward and May gave him a deep, low growl. Quivering with excitement, Hootie stopped, but his tail was up in the prettiest little point I'd ever seen. He shook even harder and waited to see what would happen next.

Uncle Cody held his hand out to me. "Stay back, Top. All three of us don't need to shoot over your pup. This little .410 won't be too loud and it'd be best for someone to hit a bird so he can see what this is all about."

I wanted so badly to shoot over Hootie's first point, but I knew Cody was right. Grandpa Ned waited a few feet back, with his shotgun lying in the crook of his arm.

Cody stepped up closer. The dogs kept their

eyes fixed on the grass in front of them. Hootie turned his head to see what was going on. Cody took another step and the covey exploded from almost under the dog's noses.

Cody waited until the birds leveled off and dusted one. The bob fell in open ground and bounced once. The dogs ran for the retrieve. May already had the bird in her mouth and was bringing it back to Cody. She slowed only long enough to growl again at Hootie, who jumped up to lick at her face and smell the bird. When Cody knelt down, May placed the quail in his hand.

"C'mere Hootie." Cody roughed him up some, letting him get a good nose-full of bird. "Good pup. Good dog." He stood and put the quail in his vest. "Top, Hootie there is gonna make a fine bird dog. He didn't even flinch, and I know for a fact he's never heard a shotgun go off."

We hunted a wide circle around the house. Uncle Cody was right, Hootie finally gave out from trying to keep up with the big dogs and Cody slipped him into the game bag at the back of his hunting vest. He wiggled around some for a while, sniffing at the birds in there, and finally fell asleep with his head hanging out, not even waking up when we shot.

Chapter Twenty-two

As another cold month rolled by, there wasn't much to do around the house. One chilly Saturday Grandpa took me to visit Judge Rains at the courthouse. While I drank my strawberry soda in a corner of Mr. O.C.'s cluttered office, Grandpa complained about Lightfoot and Doak Looney. Doak was back in jail again, and they were in adjoining cells.

"'I god, O.C., couldn't you separate them sonsabitches a little bit more? We don't need them getting together and thinking up meanness to do when they get out."

"Well, I guess I could take one of them home with me at night, if that'd satisfy you."

I'd never heard them act like that before. They jawed at each other like Pepper and I did when no one else was around. It made me feel proud to know Grandpa was talking like I was a grown man and not a little kid listening in.

"They'll get their stories together."

"They don't have one to patch up, and neither one of them has the sense God give a goose. Besides, I told Griffin to put them there. I considered sticking both of them in the same cell in the hopes one of them will kill the other'n, but I changed my mind because I can't sit in here all day waiting for it to happen."

"Well, I don't like 'em together."

"I don't like 'em apart, neither. Lightfoot spent most of his time hollering out of his window at people on the street down below. It got so bad I had him moved into an interior cell."

"Sonofabitch can scream till he turns blue in the face and I don't care. I hope he gets to liking fried baloney, 'cause that's all he's gonna get until June." Grandpa gave me a startled look when he remembered I was there.

"You gonna go up there and see him?" Mr. O.C. swiveled back and forth with his hands folded across his middle.

"Naw, I ain't got no business up there with him. I just hope the jury finds him guilty of murder and they send him to the chair."

"We won't be so lucky."

"Give him some extra sheets. Maybe he'll hang himself and save the county some time and money. C'mon, boy, finish your strawberry and let's get."

Mr. O.C. winked at me. “Y’all don’t run off. Stay and visit a while longer.”

“Naw, we gotta go. Come go with us. We’re going to Frenchie’s for a burger.”

“Better not.” Mr. O.C. perched his glasses back on his nose and turned to his work. “I have a Dallas lawyer coming to see me here in a minute.”

As we went out the door I realized they enjoyed arguing with each other as much as Pepper and I did. It wasn’t long before Doak was sent down to Huntsville again. I heard his boy that Grandpa arrested at the still back in August had long since been released to live with his mother not far from Blossom.

◇◇◇

Grandpa and I leaned on the gate after supper one evening, watching the early season flies pester the cows.

“Grandpa?”

“Hum?”

“Why do people hang dead animals or fish heads on bobwire fences? Like the coyote we found across the creek bridge.”

“Well, I reckon they’re proud of what they shot, or caught. It also scares off other predators.”

“Oh.”

We stood there for a while longer, watching

his old plowhorse, Jake, crop the new green grass shooting up through the dead stubble. "Grandpa?"

"Hum?"

"Can me and Pepper start getting away from the house some now that it's warmed up?"

Grandpa didn't say anything for a minute. "Well, not for a while longer. I think finding Joseph dead like they did means it ain't over yet. I doubt he's done with his meanness toward our family." He leaned heavier on the gate. "You still having those dreams of drowning?"

"Yessir, every now and then."

"Well, those dreams worry me. You know how our family is. One or two of our kinfolk have a second sight, but none of us have ever been able to understand how to use it. You dreaming of drowning in the Rock Hole could mean anything."

"Nothing has happened, and I've been having that dream for months." I felt like I was making some headway.

"I understand. Maybe the good Lord is telling us something through you. Someone is after our family. Maybe it's somebody I've arrested before, or it could be some crazy feller from Dallas, but it don't make no difference. Y'all can stay around the house in the daylight and that's all. You're lucky James even started letting Pepper come back over.

I'll beat the whey out of you if either of you goes anywheres near the bottoms."

"We've been wanting to hunt arrowheads on the Center Spring branch."

Grandpa sighed. "Naw, not yet. Y'all can stay around the pasture and barn here, but let one of us know when you leave the house and don't you ever let me catch you out after dark."

Jake suddenly had a spell. Maybe it was because winter was over, or the annoying insects overcame him, but he lifted his tail, farted and loped across the pasture like a colt, ducking his head and kicking up his heels.

Grandpa chuckled. "Blamed old fool. If he runs much more, he'll be so stove up tomorrow he won't be able to move."

Chapter Twenty-three

Ned thought he had a break in the murder case late one Sunday evening when he dropped Miss Becky, Top, and an angry Pepper off for evening services. He joined a dozen husbands and sons, mostly dressed in bib overalls and blue dress jackets, leaning on the sides of their trucks while they waited for the visiting lay preacher from Oklahoma to finish. The men outside weren't usually known for attending services, but not knowing the preacher, they didn't feel bad about waiting outside.

Brother Ross was usually pretty good at watching the clock, but he was ill and the visiting preacher was wound up in the Spirit and showed no indication of slowing down. His squeaky voice ripped through the open doors.

"Y'all are going straight to Hell!"

Ned walked into the light spilling from the open door. "Who's that?"

Isaac Parker, Neal Box and James chuckled.

"It's Irwin Jackson." James nodded toward the small porch and the girls bike leaning on the peeling wooden post. "Brother Ross is down in his back so Irwin showed up tonight to take his place. He rode that there bicycle all the way from Grant."

"That's 'cause he's crazy as a Bessie bug," Ned opined, thinking about the distance from Grant, Oklahoma. "I believe I'll go in and listen for a spell."

Removing his Stetson, Ned stepped through the open door and quietly took a seat at the end of the empty rear pew.

"It's a world of sin!" Irwin shouted, his oiled hair springing up with a mind of its own. His dingy white shirt was wet with sweat and he jumped up and down like a jack-in-the-box. "This whole county is full of sin, and you're all sinners! Hallelujah!"

Ned looked around. Nearly thirty of the most devout citizens in Lamar County sat upright in shock. Miss Becky and the kids perched together on the third row on the right with Miss Whitney.

"There's no hope, no hope a-tall!" Irwin bounced on his toes, slapping the well-worn open bible in his left hand. "Look around you! Leviticus seventeen tells us that nothing but a blood sacrifice will cleanse the soul! Amen-uh!"

Ned leaned forward, listening intently.

Irwin read from the bible. "And the Lord spoke to Moses, saying bring forth him that cursed throughout the camp, and let all who heard him lay their hands upon his head, and let all the congregation stone him. Hallelujah!" Irwin slapped his bible closed for emphasis. "He wouldn't have been brought to trial if his crime had been secretly committed within the walls of his own house. There, no one knew of his sorrowful sins."

Is he trying to tell us something, Ned wondered. *Is this the man I've been looking for, delivered right here to me?*

"But we're all outside our own walls brothers and sisters. Amen-uh. We are all naked and ashamed in the eyes of the Lord! That's why I'm here tonight, to tell you the truth. And the truth will set you free!"

His voice lowered.

"You have no hope, because we are all sinners. Yes, I'm a sinner too! You'd be dumbfounded by the sins I've committed, yet tonight I stand here before you washed in the Blood. I'll sin again, but the Lord will cleanse my soul, if I just ask him. No matter how badly I sin, I'll be forgiven and you, Robert Barley, you're a sinner too, both in public and behind the walls of your house." Irwin raised his voice for emphasis. "You're going to Hell if you don't accept Jesus into your heart!"

Never one to argue, Tom stared down at his new shoes, which quite honestly pinched his feet.

Is he telling us he's the one I've been chasing? That's a pretty clear statement. Ned changed his mind. *No, this want-to-be preacher in baggy black trousers was nothing but a possessed zealot. But then again, who else would have the time to wander the country on both sides of the river? Preachers didn't watch the clock, and their comings and goings would be familiar as they visited the houses of the old folks and shut-ins.*

"You, Joyce Etta Foster, you know your sins!"

Too bad, Ned thought. Joyce's husband Willard wasn't there to hear his wife's name called in public.

Irwin jumped the short six inches off the stage and pointed his finger toward the back of the church. "Ned Parker! You are a sinful person! The good Lord is about done with you!"

The entire congregation turned to look at the constable on the back row. Ned didn't change expression, but he felt his neck began to redden. Although he had a lot to be sorry for, this little banty rooster was irritating him. The frustration and worry of the past few months was beginning to fuel his anger.

Maybe I'll just take him in and let O.C. have a go at questioning him.

Missing the dangerous spark in Ned's blue eyes, Irwin turned his verbal attack to his next target. "Sister Jean Whitney, y'ain't safe! You're going straight to Hell!"

Then, as if Ned possessed Top's insight into coming events, he knew without a doubt what Irwin was going to say next. The stress of the past few months washed over Ned like a tidal wave. The old constable saw red. He rose and charged up the hardwood aisle like a mad bull.

Caught up in the rapture of his belief, Irwin had turned his attention to the second pew on the left where Miss Becky sat with the children. He danced a little jig and leaned over, pointing his finger directly at Miss Becky's nose.

Frightened, Pepper heard heavy footsteps on the hard floorboards and looked over her shoulder at the wrath roaring down the aisle behind them. Top stared at the preacher with open-mouthed shock.

"And you, Sister Ruby Becky! You may believe you live the Life of Christ, but unless you dig down deep in the dark places of your soul and confess the festering secret we all know is in there, you're going straight to …"

Irwin's words suddenly choked off when Ned's fist grabbed the lay-preacher's soiled white collar and drew it tight around his neck like a roped calf.

Miss Becky had lived a good Christian life since the day Ned met her and no one, especially not some scrawny little weasel from Oklahoma, was going to speak out against her.

Irwin's soft hands grasped the strong wrist as Ned nearly yanked him off his feet. Giving the skinny preacher a good shake, he headed for the door, Irwin stumbling along behind, choking and gagging.

The congregation was shocked to their feet at Ned's actions in the house of the Lord. They exploded through the open double doors like a bullet shot from a gun, startling the men outside. Ned took two steps to the edge of the porch and like cracking a whip, yanked Irwin forward and into the darkness. He landed on his knees in the dirt coughing and gagging, trying to get air past his damaged throat.

Ned couldn't resist the sight of Irwin's butt up in the air and in his anger stepped forward and gave him a good kick in the seat of his shiny pants, sending the man scooting forward on his chest. "Now, you can go straight back across the river before I work you over with this here sap in my back pocket!"

Shaken, Irwin showed some sense and without a word, stumbled toward his bicycle to pedal away in the darkness as fast as his legs could pump, away from irritable constables.

James worked at his teeth with a toothpick. "Disagree with Irwin's sermon, Ned?"

The group of real sinners hanging around the cars laughed at the show. No one knew what had gone on inside, but to a man they knew if Ned threw someone out of the church house, he deserved what he got.

Isaac Parker was clearly surprised to see someone ejected from a place of worship. "Listen, I never heard of such a thing."

Breathing hard, Ned was planted on the porch, solid as an oak tree. Miss Becky left the kids at the door and watched Irwin pedal away from the circle of light for a moment, then took her husband's arm. She knew what had happened and why he'd lost his temper. It wasn't all about Irwin's verbal attack, though Ned had taken care of her all their adult lives. "Ned?"

Her soft voice took the anger from her husband, as it had countless times throughout their marriage. He took a deep breath, looked at his strong Choctaw bride, and nodded toward her as if she'd said something profound. "Y'all get in the car."

Showing uncommon sense, Pepper hurried off the steps without a word. Top followed. Ned started to apologize to the pale faces around him in the yellow light, but he changed his mind and turned toward the car to go home.

Isaac Parker mouthed a home-rolled cigarette and lit it as if nothing had occurred. “Ned, listen, I intended to tell you before you went inside. I heard a nigger boy was killed tonight down on the river.”

Shocked, Ned stiffened. He hadn’t heard anything. “What happened? Did he drown?”

“Nope. Walt Simms was down there trapping and found him. Listen, he was all cut up and it scared Walt so bad he drove straight to Chisum and got Sheriff Griffin. I’m surprised you didn’t hear anything about it.”

Ned was surprised also, and angry. He glanced down the oil road, hoping to see Irwin and maybe kick him a little more to make himself feel better, but the preacher was already gone.

Ned started to ream Isaac about why the hell he’d waited to tell him, but he realized it wouldn’t do any good. “You sure it was Walt Simms who found him?”

“Yep, sure as shootin’.”

“James, take them home. I imagine I’ll be gone a right long spell tonight.”

James walked over and leaned into Ned’s open passenger window. “Y’all need to come with me.” Not surprised by his announcement, Miss Becky and the kids changed cars.

It didn’t help Pepper’s disposition any when she stepped into a puddle of fresh tobacco juice and got it all over her shoes, but it beat walking home across the pasture and dodging cow pies in the moonlight. "Shit."

Miss Becky obviously heard her for once and cracked her in the back of the head with her big hand. Top grinned at the sight, glad she'd finally gotten caught.

"Y'all be sure and lock the doors," Ned told her. He shifted his weight from side to side until they left. It was almost as if he wasn't sure what to do, whether to go home and protect his family, or pursue the lead.

He left the group of men and settled into the front seat of his car. He keyed the Motorola's microphone and called for Big John. He had to repeat the process several times before John answered.

"Ned, something wrong? I was in the church house and one of the kids outside heard you calling on the radio. I believe I might need to wear him out for not being inside listening to the preachin'."

"Yeah, something's bad wrong." He swallowed the bile rising in his throat. "I just got word Walt Simms found one of your young people dead down on the river. You know anything about it?"

There was a long, silent pause on the other end. "No. Gimme a few minutes."

Ned stayed behind the wheel as he waited.

Fifteen minutes later Big John was back on the radio. "Ned?"

"Go ahead."

"It happened all right. Sheriff Griffin took the report and sent the state law out there. I'm not sure right now why he didn't tell me, but I intend to find out."

"Meet me at the river bridge."

"On my way. I'll call Raymond, too."

They met Raymond Chase in the darkness on the Texas side, near the stone welcome marker. While cars whizzed past on the highway, he related the story, what he could get out of Sheriff Griffin. "According to Walt Simms who was running his traps not far from the river dump, he came across a little nig…" He flicked his eyes toward John, who seemed impassive. "Uh, colored kid who had been skinned and hung over a fence not far from here. He said in his sixty years on the Red, Walt helped find the bodies of more than two dozen people who had drowned in the river, but he vowed this one was the worst he'd ever seen."

John kept shaking his head at the news. His hands trembled and he fiddled with some change from his pockets to give them something to do.

Ned knew the party lines in town would buzz

for a week with the horrible news about a boy draped over the top wire of a five-strand barbed-wire fence. The killer had finally graduated to children. "Was there an advertisement or a picture this time?"

"The sheriff didn't say. According to what I found out, though, someone who likes to hurt took his time. They found a knife, several big screwdrivers and a fire. Looks like he enjoys poking people with hot screwdrivers in places you don't want to think about, before he field dressed him."

John looked as if he could barely contain his emotions. "That poor little baby." He sniffed and wiped at his eyes. "Ned, this stinks to high heaven, and Sheriff Griffin ain't talking much to any of us about this. It's like he's trying to keep us away from something or another. He's as sorry as Poole ever was."

"Careful talkin' 'bout folks." Raymond leaned against Ned's car and crossed his arms. "Everybody seems to be kin to everybody else around here."

"Well, you know how Ned and I feel about Poole. He weren't much punkin' as a sheriff and as far as I'm concerned, him and Griffin are both just alike. You reckon this one is connected to Mr. Ned's troubles and all them animal killings?"

Raymond shrugged. "It looks like it to me. I believe he's been gigging Ned for some reason or the other, and I bet this one is either for fun, or because he wants to scare the whole damn county."

"They're scared all right, and this might cause someone to get shot." Ned rubbed the back of his neck where it ached from tension.

People were still carrying guns wherever they went. There wasn't a man in the little community who didn't have a pistol on his belt, or one in his pocket. Doors that hadn't ever been locked were fitted with bright new brass hardware, and no one traveled late at night. The horrific display on the fence was sure to cause a panic throughout the community. It was only a matter of time until vigilante talk was sure to come up at the store.

"He's scaring *me* for sure." Ned stared at the moon rising from the river. It bathed the bottoms in a thin, pale light. "Think there are any tracks we can compare to the one under Top's window?"

"Probably were." Raymond toed the dirt as if to demonstrate. "But all these yahoos walking around here have trampled most of the evidence."

"We may need some more help," John finally admitted to the two law officers with him. "Looks like this ox is still in the ditch. All this time, and we ain't named it yet."

Once again Ned wondered if he shouldn't give O.C. his badge and stay at home. Ned wished he could talk to his old great-granddaddy, John

Parker, one of the first Texas Rangers who chased the Comanches through these same bottoms. The old man would know what to do, but Ned was at a complete loss.

"Well, I know who it wasn't." He picked up the microphone and woke the Motorola up. "I'll call O.C. and tell him Ralston's off the hook."

Constable Raymond Chase studied the muddy river glittering in the moonlight below them. "This time."

Chapter Twenty-four

June roared in with a vengeance. Grandpa always said the meanest storms blew in at night. Those scared him worse than anything. Daytime storms didn't faze him. Once we watched a cyclone touch down west of us, throwing up dirt, trees and pieces of barns. At the same time, Grandpa stepped off the porch to get a better look and happened to glance toward the east where another tornado traveled parallel to the first. Bracketed by two twisters, we had perfect seats to watch them pass, but he only stood there, holding his hat and feeling the wind.

As I said, darkness was a different story. Lightning woke me up one night and I saw him moving anxiously from window to window to see what the clouds looked like. Lightning told him more than he wanted to know.

Grandpa rushed through the house. "You and Pepper get up. It's a bad cloud and we've gotta go before the cyclone gets us."

He turned on the bedroom light and didn't wait for an answer.

It was the first time Pepper had spent the night in over a month. She woke up slow. "What?"

I heard Miss Becky's bare footsteps on the linoleum in the hall. Lightning filled the bedroom in stark, white light and damp wind blew the loose screens. Hootie sat at the end of the bed with his ears perked forward, looking out the window. He growled softly, more to himself than aloud.

Thunder rattled the loose panes and the wind moaned around the eaves. The lights flickered and went out, making the darkness even more sinister. By the time we rubbed the sleep out of our eyes and dressed, Grandpa was back in the hallway with a flashlight in his hand.

"Y'all come on, we have to get to the storm cellar!"

Uncle Henry's cellar, the closest protection from a cyclone, was about a mile away. Grandpa never had any intention of digging his own cellar, as long as Uncle Henry was alive. The only drawback was the amount of time it took to drive the short distance in a storm.

Pepper groaned. "It's only a damn thunderstorm. He wouldn't care if it was daylight."

I hurried to pull on a jacket to turn the rain. Hootie barked in excitement. Pepper wanted to complain some more as the electricity came back on, and then went out again, plunging the house back into darkness.

"Shitfire."

"Shhh. Miss Becky is gonna hear you again."

"No, she won't, and I don't care anyway." Lightning flashed and the stark light made Pepper's face even whiter. She never woke up in a good mood.

"Y'all ready?" a voice from right beside us made my heart stop. Lightning struck close by, and Miss Becky handed me a flashlight. Either she chose to ignore Pepper's language or the thunder muffled our conversation.

"Let's go!" Grandpa shouted anxiously. I could see his flashlight beam between lightning strikes.

Hackles raised, Hootie followed Grandpa as he rushed through the house. "What's wrong with him?"

"Guess he don't like storms." Miss Becky held the screen door open for us with her foot and tied a bonnet under her chin at the same time. "Y'all hurry."

Pepper ducked her head and we plunged into the stormy night.

"Get in!" At the sound of Grandpa's voice, the yard dog Carlo slipped out from under the car.

Miss Becky's bonnet blew off her head and

only the chinstrap kept it from flying into the night. Pepper's hair whipped in the wind and flew in her face. Hootie shot off the porch when something moving beside the back corner of the house caught his attention. He roared a challenge at a dark figure disappearing behind the smokehouse. Carlo joined the chase and their barking was almost drowned by the thunder and wind.

I cupped both hands around my mouth. "Grandpa! Someone's out there!"

Lightning again slashed the sky with a ripping sound, this time revealing a man dressed in dark, wet clothes running across the pasture away from the house. A metallic glint in his hand caught the light.

Hootie jumped at the figure.

Darkness.

Thunder boomed and I shouted for Hootie to come back.

Grandpa jumped out of the car and started toward the pasture when a deep rumble like a freight train filled the air around us. He stopped as if reaching the end of a rope and looked at the sky.

Miss Becky held the car door open. "Ned! The cyclone's coming, and we got to get these kids under the ground. He's a runnin' already and we don't have time."

"Hootie!" I doubted he could hear me over the storm.

Pepper joined me. "Hootie, get back here!"

"All right. We don't have time to fool with him!" Grandpa started the car. "Get in!"

Miss Becky grabbed my shirt with surprising strength and shoved me into the back seat, sparing me the decision to abandon my dog. But Hootie ran back around the smokehouse and jumped in, tracking muddy water on the dusty cloth upholstery. Pepper dived in behind me. Grandpa had the car in reverse before Miss Becky slammed her door and we hit the wet highway in a slide.

I turned to look out the back window. "Somebody was fooling around the house, Grandpa."

"I saw him." Lightning struck a tree across the road in a shower of flame and sparks. The tree would have burned had it not been for sheets of rain slashing out of the sky.

"My lands." Miss Becky turned to look out the back window. "That feller was back."

Grandpa gripped the wheel with both hands and looked through the windshield at the black clouds roiling overhead. "It don't matter right now. The cyclone's gonna catch us."

"Not till it quits raining. That twister ain't here yet." Miss Becky didn't look overly sure of her comment.

Thinking about a cyclone scared me, and I could see Pepper's mouth was open with fright. I unconsciously rubbed Hootie's wet head while we hissed down the highway in a spray of water. His hair was sticky. In another burst of lightning I saw blood on my hand. It scared me and in the next flash I saw a shallow cut seeping blood. I wiped it on my wet jeans.

"It's gonna catch us," Grandpa repeated.

The wipers barely kept up with the volume of water. It didn't take long to reach Uncle Henry's house. Grandpa turned left up the red clay and gravel drive toward the top of the hill. In the headlights I could see other cars scattered near the storm cellar, thirty yards from the house.

He shut off the engine and we jumped out into the driving rain. Lightning picked out the cellar's wood and metal door. Rain carrying red mud in great streams washed around and over the tops of our shoes.

Pepper was scared. I could tell she wanted nothing more than to get underground. She'd never acted afraid of storms before, but all of Grandpa's fear rubbed off on her. A nearby thunderclap made her scream. We jumped over the narrowest streams and splashed through the wide ones as we raced through the rain. The roar was even louder and the wind whipped our clothes. Hootie splashed along behind us.

Grandpa held his hat with one hand, bent over

and hammered on the slanted cellar door with his fist. I saw his lips move and knew he was shouting, but the wind whipped the words away. The wooden door opened to reveal two men sitting on the plank steps leading downward to safety. A sliver of yellow light split the darkness and the odor of burning coal oil was sucked out into our faces.

The storm nearly tore the door from their hands and they strained on rope handles to keep it from flying off. Grandpa grabbed the door's edge. "Hurry up!"

Pepper raced down the narrow steps. Miss Becky followed quickly, trying to hold her cotton dress down and keep a hold on a canvas bag. Hootie hesitated, frightened of the kerosene and damp dirt smells, but I kicked him in the rear and he went down the steps on two front legs like a circus dog.

"There it is!" someone shouted from below ground. I turned in the doorway to see the tornado heading straight for our shelter. I dove in and heard Grandpa's shout to close the door and he jumped down the first three steps. Only a moment later a gust of wind yanked all the men off their feet.

Then the door slammed down and Grandpa threw the enormous iron bolt to lock us in with the smell of damp clay. The men exchanged glances, and everyone spoke in hushed tones. Sounding like a freight train on tracks of lightning, the cyclone roared overhead.

Dim yellow light from coal oil lamps lit the long, narrow interior barely high enough for a grown man to stand upright. Splintery oak benches lined both sides of the cellar. Rough shelves on the back wall sagged under hundreds of canned goods in glass jars.

Nearly a dozen other adults made room for us on the benches. Pepper and I were the only kids. We sat beside each other and I pulled Hootie close to keep him out of trouble. He trembled on the dirt floor beside me, his head still leaking blood. With shaking hands I reached for my puffer, shocked to find my pocket empty.

Miss Becky noticed my look and opened her bag. "I knew you'd forget."

"It almost got us," Pepper told Aunt Mamie as I sucked medicine into my lungs.

"The good Lord made sure it didn't." She held something in her lap. I looked closely and saw it was a pink baby pig. "Seems like I always have baby pigs around, Top. That 'un you brought a few months back is growing like a weed. We'll have bacon next winter if the cyclone don't carry him off tonight."

The moaning wind squeezed through the cracks in the door. Uncle Henry glanced fearfully toward the vibrating cellar door. "I hope the house is still standing when we get out of here. Then I'll worry about bacon."

The talk of food made Pepper hungry. "I'd like some bacon right about now."

Miss Becky reached into her bag again and unwrapped a dozen cold biscuits from a dishcloth. "I knew y'all'd be hollerin' you were hungry, so I brought these. Maime, can the little 'uns open a jar of them preserves or some of that plum jelly we put up last year?"

"Lands yes. Right after we thank the Lord for leading us all safely down here tonight."

"Shit," Pepper said under her breath as everyone bowed their heads.

◇◇◇

We stayed in the cellar for nearly an hour until the cloud moved on toward Chisum. The men sitting on the steps talked quietly about the dark man outside of our house.

"You think he was trying to get in, Ned?" Uncle Henry asked.

"I sure do."

"You've got The Skinner after you."

I didn't know the man who spoke, but the words sent a shiver up my spine. Grandpa looked shocked, and then glanced back toward us to get them to shut up.

"That's what the *Chisum News* called him," the man defended.

Grandpa shook his head. "I don't like that talk. He's nothing more than a man. Giving him a name makes him something more than he is."

They got quiet for a while and we waited. Someone occasionally peeked outside to let in some fresh air and watch the roiling sky until they decided it was safe.

"It's lightened up some." Grandpa stood up to stretch his legs. "I reckon we can go."

We stepped out into the dim morning light like refugees emerging from a bomb shelter. The gray clouds continued to spit rain, and lightning flickered in the distance, but it wasn't anything like what chased us into the hole in the ground.

Grandpa used his flashlight to check for damage. Uncle Henry's house wasn't much worse for wear except for a few shingles. The tornado jumped over the house and then touched down again to take the barn before chewing up the trees in its path. In the pasture beyond, the barn and low built pig shed were gone. The pigs rooted in the mud as if nothing had happened.

In one of the last flickers of lightning we could see the trees were a sorry sight down toward Center Spring Branch to the southeast. All in all, we were lucky.

The older folks thanked Aunt Maime and Uncle Henry for letting us stay with them again. The house looked the same when we got home, but both the barn and the chicken house were missing long pieces of sheet-iron roofing. Some of the iron was wrapped around the highest limbs of a chinaberry tree growing up along the fencerow.

I opened the car door and Hootie remembered the excitement of our rapid departure. He ran back to the smokehouse and made several circles trying to pick up a scent, but the heavy rain washed the ground clean. Carlo was nowhere to be found.

Miss Becky and Pepper started into the house, and then paused. "Ned, you want to go in and turn on the lights?"

He hesitated, then looked at her on the porch with her hand deep in the pocket of her house dress. I knew she was holding the butt of her pistol. "All right." He checked the house and turned the lights on in each room while we waited on the porch.

When he was satisfied it was safe, Miss Becky and Pepper went in while Grandpa and I stayed in the yard for a few minutes.

He stared off toward the pasture for a long moment, talking quietly to himself.

I couldn't stand it any longer. "Did you see him?"

"I saw *someone*." Grandpa came back to himself and walked over to my bedroom window.

"It was a man wearing a Sunday coat and hat. I think the storm surprised him."

"It surprised us all." He rubbed his fingers against the wooden sill bearing the marks where someone tried to pry it open.

"What do you think he was doing hanging around here last night?"

"You don't want to know, son."

All of a sudden we heard a commotion in the house and Pepper started crying. Grandpa started to run, but Miss Becky called out to us. "It's all right. Me and Pepper are just washing something out."

Grandpa peered through the window saw Pepper standing in the hall with a bar of Dove soap in her mouth. He chuckled. "Somebody's getting her mouth washed out."

It tickled me. "I guess Miss Becky heard what she said before we left the house tonight."

"She hears more than you think. Keep that in mind."

"I will."

I heard banging and saw Miss Becky through the window, driving nails once again into the wooden casements. They exchanged looks through the glass and she disappeared to hammer nails into another window before she let Pepper spit.

Chapter Twenty-five

Ned blew across a mug of steaming coffee. "The son of a bitch killed my dog the night of the storm."

He and O.C. Rains were huddled in deep concentration in the back booth of Frenchie's café. A wooden screen door on Main Street opened onto the long, narrow cave with booths along the left and a long mahogany counter running along the right. The only illumination came from a dozen large droplights suspended four feet below the high hammered tin ceiling. It smelled of grease, coffee, and fresh baked pies.

The cascade of chilly rain missing the downspout and splashing on the concrete sidewalk outside didn't register with Ned. "Carlo chased him off just as we left for the cellar and this morning when I went to feed the cows I found what was left of him on the porch. Somebody quartered that dog and left him either for a warning or to scare us. It pretty much did both."

O.C. stuck his index finger through the thick handle of the mug and sipped his scalding coffee, staring at the black look on his friend's face. "The Skinner wasn't after your dog though, was he? He wanted them kids."

"Now *you're* calling him that." Ned shivered.

"Well, it's as good a name as any." O.C. studied his coffee.

"I believe you're right about him figuring to use the storm to get them kids out of the bedroom. At any rate, he wasn't expecting the winders to be nailed shut or for us to get up and leave, so we surprised him and he run off. I reckon James was right. Pepper don't need to be around so he can get both kids at the same time."

O.C.'s eyes snapped across the table. "You know how that sounds?"

"I know having them in two different places keeps at least one of them safe for the time being." His shoulders slumped. "I'm gonna have to get a new dog. I can't be gone from the house without a dog in the yard to bark if anyone comes up."

"What about the little pup of Top's?"

"Well, Hootie is half-growed, and he's inside. I need a nose and ears outside. This is getting bigger."

O.C. blew across the coffee's surface. "The bodies are starting to pile up." He took a cautious sip.

"Yeah. John Washington says the colored boy

was to throw us off the track, but he's dealing with his people now, too. They're as scared as we are, even though he thinks this guy intends to use my family to pay me back for something. I swear. You can't go up to the store without people wanting to know what was done to that little colored boy. They all think someone they know will be next. Men are afraid to go to the field and crops ain't getting in, because they think someone will come to the house while they're gone.

"You should see it. Everybody is afraid. Whenever folks come to the store, they bring the whole family now. It reminds me of Saturdays when we was kids. You remember how our daddies would wait all week and then everybody went to town for groceries and shopping?

"I get calls every night because people think someone is sneaking around their house. Folks are fighting more at home because they're scared. Some people are even keeping their kids at home instead of sending them to school. I feel the same way. We don't let Top or Pepper hardly get out of our sight. What kind of person goes after your family if he's mad at you?"

"Crazy people." O.C. took another sip. "Maybe he killed the colored kid when he couldn't catch any of your kinfolk out and around. I asked Donald Griffin about what he found around the fence, but he didn't say anything about a piece of newspaper."

Ned rubbed his bald head in frustration. "Griffin probably didn't pay attention to any evidence. It galls me to think he wanted to wrap everything up and get out of there without letting any of us know. He don't care about colored folks."

"Well, we're in bad shape here. I hate to bring it up, but do you think he might have had something to do with Arnold Rob?"

"Naw. The coroner told me it was his heart."

"But we don't know for sure."

"No, we don't know for sure, but I ain't digging my brother up right now!" Ned's voice rose.

"All right." O.C.'s eyes lifted from his own coffee mug and he put out a pacifying hand. "More bad news is an Oklahoma feller driving on highway 271 north of the river saw something hanging on the fence early this morning and he stopped to see. It was a young white girl, cut up like all the others and folded over the top strand of bob-wire like a dead wolf...and that colored boy. That makes three on fences."

"Why didn't you tell me?"

"I just did, and it was in Oklahoma. They're working on it now, but nobody knows who she is yet, neither. I called in the FBI right after I heard about it. They'll be here tomorrow."

Ned glared at him.

"Now don't take this wrong, Ned. I had to, because neither you nor Donald Griffin has any business dealing with these murders by yourselves, because they're happening in two different states. This thing is getting bigger than any of us can handle, it's growing fast, and it's getting partly personal. The Bureau has a whole department dedicated to these kinds of murders. When I talked to them this mornin' on the telephone the agent told me they have a name for them now. They're called psychopath killers."

"I'm not turning my back on what's going on in my precinct. Psychopath killer or not."

"I'm not asking you to turn your back on anything. You need to understand that these boys do this for a livin'. Go about your business on this side of the river, but let 'em alone and don't you get in their way."

Ned felt his ears getting hot. He shared the same territorial traits as O.C. felt toward visiting judges in his courtroom. "They better not go to messing with my people. I have several more folks to talk to and I'll find out who's doing these killings. I don't want them in my way."

"Goddammit, Ned!" O.C. heated up just as quickly.

Frenchie looked up from her newspaper

behind the counter and sighed. Ned and O.C. Rains had been arguing in her café since she first opened the doors in 1945, and it was always the same thing. They'd yell a while and then leave together to go on about their business.

"I told you these boys are professionals. They'll get to the bottom of this pretty quick. If you're gonna find them before the FBI boys get here, you better get busy."

"I been busy."

"Then get busier."

Ned felt his face swell with frustration. "Hell, O.C. They're federal and they won't get to the bottom of a goddamn thing." He pointed a finger across the table and jabbed it at the judge for emphasis. "Think about two men in suits driving up in their new cars to my people's houses. If they don't get run off with the business end of a shotgun, the best they're gonna do is stand in the yard and hope the dog don't bite 'em."

O.C.'s voice raised in response. "They're *trained* in this sort of work."

Other customers turned to look at the two arguing lawmen.

"They're *city* people. They don't know nothin' about the country. Some folks out there haven't talked to anyone but kinfolk since the *War*. All your FBI people are gonna do is scare this psychopath killer, and the sonofabitch'll lay low until they're gone."

"*You* ain't making any headway!"

The accusation stung because it was true. The deaths were coming thick and fast with no suspects in sight. Ned felt he was no closer to finding the killer than when the monster first started to cut up animals. He sank inward and fiddled with the badge on his shirt. His stomach rolled, and he could see himself throwing the gold-plated star on the scarred table and walking out of the café. "My lord, O.C. We're lost."

"Not yet."

He rubbed his bald head and rested his chin on his big hand. "I'll find him somehow."

A rumble of thunder rattled the windows, and conversation stopped as everyone in the cafe glanced out the flyspecked window.

They sipped for a few minutes while the storm moved on. Ned held up his mug. Frenchie folded her paper and brought a fresh pot to refill their cups.

He blew across the surface. "You finding anything out from Ralston or that bunch of outlaws he's running with?"

"They don't know nothing. Somebody put the fear of God into Ralston, and I think it was Big John out on the highway that day. He fell off his high horse pretty quick after y'all brought them in.

without slowing. He slid to a stop on the gravel drive and he was out of the truck, pulling a shotgun out one-handed. "Any word?" The fright in his voice said he was one step below an all-out panic.

"Not yet. I don't know where to start looking, but they walked to wherever they went." Ned pointed to the north and the blue anvil-shaped thunderstorms rising over the barn. "James, you start up and work the gully, cutting through Joe Daniels' pasture to where it ends at the spring. You'll be able to see their footprints in the sand if they went that way. If they didn't, come back here to the house."

Without a word, James grabbed a flashlight and took off past the barn at a run.

"James!"

He turned and Ned pointed toward the north. "It's coming up a cloud. You're gonna have to move fast, and so are we."

With a flip of his hand, James disappeared around the barn. Ned watched his son and realized he wasn't sure which way to go. He first looked eastward toward the creek and the bridge, but he dismissed it as being too far away. Westward put the kids either on the highway or near any one of several houses on a little oil road leading to the bottoms, so he didn't think they went that direction either.

I had warrants on one of his friends and he's going back to Dallas."

They sat together without talking. O.C. could tell Ned had something on his mind. He waited for his old partner to speak.

Ned finally reached a decision. "I been at this a long time."

"If you're talking about law, we both have."

"That's what I'm talking about. I'm afraid it's all passing me by."

O.C. watched Ned's face and for the first time noticed the deep lines at the corners of his eyes and on his forehead. The creases were a revealing map on the face that had aged twenty years in the past few months.

"I don't know nothing. I don't believe I'm able to do my job anymore." Ned rubbed his head again, a sure sign he was worried, and sighed.

O.C. looked up in surprise. "I thought you were planning to catch this man."

"I know it, but I was mad about them FBI boys. Back when I started we used to break up stills and family fights and arrest drunks, and I knew what I was doing. But the other day I found a bunch of bales of something hid out under the creek bridge and found out it was mary-wana. Some mary-wana addicts, I guess, have decided to grow or sell dope around here. I don't know nothing about that stuff. Shitfire, it could be growing in the ditches and I wouldn't know what it was if it stung me."

"You know it's illegal. Same as shine."

"I know I can't even catch whoever put it under the bridge. Now I have something the FBI calls a psychopathic killer and I can't figure out what he's doing. Who'da thought we'd have somebody running around chopping up animals and hanging people over fences like dead coyotes. What's next? You think all the young people in town are going to get together and riot during an Elvis Presley picture show like they do when them Beatles play? You think the coloreds here in town are gonna start doing like them people in the cities and have them civil rights protests?"

O.C. cleared his throat. "Ned, we're both getting old, but it don't mean we can't do our jobs."

"Maybe not for you. Everything you do is in your head. You know the law and know what to do when we drag people into court. Me, I have to get out and look around and talk to people on this deal. In between I have crops to raise and stock to feed. It may be time for a younger man." He held out his shaking hand. "Look at this."

"Younger men have more energy and their hands are steady, but they don't have much in the sense department."

"Neither did we when we first started."

As he stared glumly at his coffee, sadness and the futility of a lawman in a changing society swamped the man who only wanted to do the right thing. His elbow on the table, Ned ran a hand over his bare head.

Frenchie saw their mood and brought another warm-up. "You boys look like somebody died."

"Not somebody, something. Ned's enthusiasm."

Frenchie snorted. They'd been a couple of curmudgeons all their lives, and she didn't see anything different. She returned to the counter and brought them each a slice of peach pie. "Y'all eat these and you'll feel better."

Ned smiled up at her. "Thanks." She left and he sipped the strong brew. "I think I'll even quit farming. I might keep a few head of cattle and some chickens and be done with it."

"You'll sit on the porch and waste away if you do that." O.C. reddened again because he'd seen it happen to several of his friends.

"I'd like to sit on the porch for a while without worrying about whether it's gonna rain, or if it's raining too much, or if there's somebody out there breaking the law. O.C., I'm tired."

The judge paused and looked down at the table. The conversation was going nowhere and he needed to change the subject right then. "Oh, say, I got some more news for you. "Delbert Poole died last night."

"Well." Ned carefully examined his laced fingers, remembering the man and his hard ways. He wasn't sorry to hear the news. "He was a rough old cob, but I didn't know he was in bad health. What killed him?"

"Heart quit beating, I guess."

"You know he used to carry a machine gun?" Ned moved his shoulders to ease the tension in his neck.

"Yep. I have it locked up at the courthouse. He showed up one day last year and asked for it like he wanted to borrow a shotgun to go quail hunting, but I wouldn't give it to him. I knew he'd lost his mind by then."

"I never trusted him much farther than I could kick him."

"Me neither. He did things his own way, because he felt he was right. I never trusted him after I got back from Germany. I'll always have a sneakin' suspicion he killed One-Arm George, but there was no way to prove it."

"I know."

"He took that little bit of news with him, but I'm sure he done it and even worse meanness. I heard tell he messed with that boy of his. They say his wife ran off with the boy the first time she found out, when he was about four, but somehow Poole talked her into coming back home.

"The second time, though, when the boy was about five or six, she caught him again and left for good, changed her name and was through with him. I tried to get her to file charges against the son-of-a-bitch, but she wouldn't because she was scared. Then she moved up to northeast Oklahoma and nobody has heard from her since. Now that Poole has gone, though, it makes me feel a lot older somehow. I reckon you're right. Our kind is dying off, but you still have one more outlaw to catch, and then you can quit if y'ont to."

"You won't let anyone rest, will you?"

"Nope." O.C. thought for a moment. "Now, who were your suspects?"

"All of them?"

"All of them."

"Well hell, I studied on half a dozen, but the killings never stopped, not even when one or two of my best guesses were in jail."

"List them anyway."

"Doak Looney's boy, Lightfoot, Ralston… those were the ones I brought in."

They discussed each man without bringing any new details to light.

"Then there's Calvin Williams and those hired hands of his, Donny and Tully Joe. In my mind I've accused might near everybody in town. I thought about that mean little shit Cale Westlake at one time."

"Well, he may be a wild kid, but he ain't no killer."

"I know it, but you see how it's got my mind going in circles? I've been suspicioning Ty Cobb and Jimmy Foxx, because they've been around at least three times, finding dead animals and people, but I don't think they have enough sense to play this kind of game.

"Hell, I can't even clear Cody in my mind. How's that for a man to think of such about his family? And I can't tell you how close I watched Mark Lightfoot when he was living with us, even though I think the world of that boy."

O.C. found a rough spot on the handle of his coffee cup and worried at it with his thumbnail. "What about somebody else in town?"

"That could be the problem. It could be anybody, and I don't have any suspicions that single out any one person. I've talked to Neal, and he's keeping an eye out in the store. Cody watches the people in his bar over in Juarez, and Big John knows what's going on across the tracks. Hell, everybody I know is carrying a gun, or has one close by, and they're all watching each other like nobody trusts anybody anymore. I just hope they don't take to shooting one another over the least little thing. All in all, it ain't like we ain't doing nothing, but we're spinning our wheels."

"Then go back and start spinning them from the start."

"It was pretty general at first, just people finding the animals. I guess the first time it became personal was when Cody's bird dog was stole, though if I recollect, there was six carved-up animals before that. Remember me telling you about the burnt squirrel, the gutted coon and that coyote?

"Now listen to this." Ned held up an index finger. "Add two more coyotes gutted, skinned and hung on fences, a gutted calf in Oklahoma left to die on its feet in misery, another skinned dog Ty Cobb and Jimmy Foxx brought in, a cut up goat in a culvert, and my dog Carlo that was butchered like a deer."

"I hadn't added all that up."

"Well, then cipher in the Lightfoot baby. It wasn't cut up thank god, but somebody had kept it in an icebox for some reason. Then Joseph was quartered like a beef while he was hunting. It all led to tortured and skinned kids on fences and somebody trying to get into my house."

"My lord."

"See? There's been a lot of blood, and I don't have any idea who it is, and maybe this is just the beginning. I've also had several people come by the house to tell me they think it's a field hand. They don't have any proof. They're just naturally suspicious of colored folks."

"Do you think it's one of John's people?"

"I think it could be anyone big enough to rear up on their hind legs. Big John talked to everyone down there and he don't have any suspicions at all. I've never heard of a field hand doing something like this. Hell, they'll cut one another over some gal, or when they get drunk and mean, but it's over pretty quick. I think this is a white man."

"I heard tell them circus people could be involved."

Ned snickered, feeling a little better at the thought. "Yep, Isaac Reader thinks so and he's still scared to death about it. He's been sleeping with a shotgun in his bed ever since he found Cody's bird dog. I don't think it's them. Everyone suspicions circus people when things are stole or when there's trouble, but I've not had much trouble with them myself, outside of a little drunk driving. I know some of 'em are running from something, but they've acted right most of the time."

The rain slacked off to a light shower. O.C. drained his mug. "Well, I gotta go. You keep at it. Whyn't you go by and see Cody. He might have an idea."

"All right." Ned's knees cracked when he stood up. "I told you I was getting old."

They huffed out of the booth, and it took a minute for O.C. to straighten up. Putting on their Stetsons, the two old men each left Frenchie a nickel and limped toward the door.

Chapter Twenty-six

Ned pulled into Cody's gravel drive as rainbow formed behind the departing storm. A howling pack of dogs met his car.

For once Cody was home. He stepped out on the porch at the commotion and motioned Ned inside. "Hush up! Ned, don't let them pups get you muddy. Get down, Silky!"

The dogs settled down and Ned rubbed each of them once, so they'd remember who he was. He dodged the puddles and climbed the steps of Cody's neat little frame house. The porch was big enough to sit on, but not like Ned's.

Buckets holding a scattering of tools and screwdrivers lined up against the house, the result of some job left unfinished. Ned shook his head and grunted. Now he was looking for evidence at his own nephew's house. He couldn't shake the bad feeling, though, as he wiped his feet and stepped inside.

"Have a seat, Uncle Ned." Cody pulled a

chair out from the chrome and Formica table. Ned could smell beer in the house and on Cody's breath. "What brings you out here? I don't think I've seen you out this way since I got back from overseas."

"I oughta be ashamed of myself for not coming by sooner." Ned pitched his hat on the afternoon's edition of *The Chisum News* spread out on the table. The paper fluttered, revealing a pair of scissors before the page fell back into place.

"I'm still working on this case, looking for someone who can help me find who's doing all these killings."

"I read about the latest one in the paper. It's awful what people do to one other."

"You've seen it firsthand, I reckon, over there in Viet Nam."

"Yeah, and it'll be worse in the next few years. This is quicksand we're getting into over there."

"You're like O.C. You don't talk about war much."

"No one ever asked me, but there ain't much to tell." Cody opened the icebox. He hooked another beer for himself and a Dr Pepper for Ned. He popped both caps with the opener hanging from the cord around his neck and handed the bottle to Ned. "On Monday I was standing in a rice paddy with a rifle across my shoulder and Friday night I was getting off the bus down from the Grand

Theater. No one knew what I saw, or what I'd been through. Hell, half of them still don't know where Vietnam is,and they don't care. For the others, it was like they don't know enough to ask or care."

"Well, maybe they thought you didn't want to talk about it."

"I usually don't."

"You better not let Miss Becky look in that icebox."

Cody winked. "Don't you bring her over here without calling first."

They drank in silence for a few minutes. Ned looked around the kitchen, almost bare without curtains and knickknacks on the walls. Cody quickly drained his beer and opened still another bottle. The alcohol soon loosened him up. Cody started talking and it was like he'd been waiting for someone to ask him the right trigger question to get started.

"Ned, I saw a lot of things over there I need to forget. That's why I don't talk much about it, and it's probably why O.C. keeps his war to himself, too.

"My squad was working with the NVA, that's the North Vietnamese Army. Our job was to teach them how to fight. I guess they're like us, our army. But they *weren't* like us. Those little people over there are brutal. It wasn't the killing I minded much, that's what war is. And I saw my part of killin'."

Ned didn't say a word. He listened and stared through the open screen door at the dogs sprawled on the porch.

"There was one guy they shot. They call them Viet Cong or VC for short. He was wounded, laying there on the ground with his guts sticking through a hole in his stomach, and those people stomped him for the fun of it. They didn't even change expressions, and the VC never made a sound while they tortured him. He couldn't have run off or fight, he was too shot up, but they stomped and stomped."

"Maybe he'd done something to them."

"Naw. They didn't know him from a hole in the ground. They're mean. They look at an enemy different than we do. I bet they broke every bone in that feller's body before he finally died. That's how they got information out of prisoners.

"They were god-awful. The first thing they'd do is accuse the village chief of being VC. Then they'd beat him up or kill him, after they raped his wife and daughters while he watched. That would scare the rest, and they might talk. It was nothing for them to shoot half the livestock in the village just for the fun of it. I remember one guy, he liked to kill their dogs and pigs and he always stuck their heads on a pole for a warning.

"It gives me bad dreams. I have nightmares every night about that little country. The only time

I sleep good is when Norma is holding onto me. I don't know what I'd do without her, though I know the trouble we're causing."

The outpouring of information soaked into Ned like a cold rain and made him feel miserable. Each time Cody became agitated, he moved the newspapers around, unconsciously lining them up with the edges of the table while he talked. Ned couldn't help but notice two or three clipped ads beside the scissors he saw earlier.

Cody got up and opened another beer. They were going down quick. "All that will mess a man up inside. It happened to several of my friends over there. But if you were raised tough, you had a better chance to leave it all behind."

His voice trembled with emotion. "I feel a rage inside. Like when those boys started in with me at the store, I felt good. Lord amighty. I wanted it to keep going for a while."

"I'm glad you stopped. I didn't want to arrest you for killing somebody, even if it was Calvin and that worthless Tully Joe and his addled brother."

"Aw, I wouldn't have killed them, Uncle Ned. But they deserved what they got. I know the three of them ganged up on some feller a few nights before over in Juarez and they worked him over good. He wasn't any good at fighting back so they took advantage of him. A little jail time or a fine wouldn't have been enough. I paid them back in what they understood. They deserved it."

"They did at that." Ned reached out and placed the empty Dr Pepper bottle on the table beside advertisements featuring young boys about Top's age. Another hawked a sale on young girl's dresses. Ice crept up Ned's spine. "What are these?"

Cody was surprised to find them in Ned's hand. "Uh, they're ads for kids' clothes. Remember, Top's birthday is coming up and I wanted to get him something he'd like. You know how he's growing. The other day he mentioned how much he liked a shirt I had on, so I was trying to find him one like it."

"Pepper too?"

"Well, you know how kids are. If you buy something for one, you have to get the other'n something, too."

Ned looked at Cody for a long time, feeling heavy and sad inside. "Do you know anything about these killings son? Something you need to tell me, or something you don't think is even related? I feel like I'm grasping at straws here."

"I wish I could help you." Cody opened the icebox once again and pulled a bottle across the aluminum shelf with a rasping sound. "I've asked and asked, and no one over in Juarez knows a thing."

"You have any ideas?"

"Yeah. I think it's someone who's young and maybe been in the army."

The answer surprised the old law man. A sick, empty feeling spread across his ample stomach. "What makes you think that?"

"Well, Griffin dropped by to see me this morning. There are some FBI men expected to be in town tomorrow, and since I own the club across the river they'll most likely be talking to me. They have something they called a profile that they're following. According to the profiles, young folks who like to torture animals grow up to do the same to people, because they had something done to them when they was kids, probably. It got me to thinking about torture and how easy it is for the guy to get away, like somebody was raised here and knew the country, and then I thought about a veteran."

"Did Griffin say who they're going to talk to tomorrow?"

"Nossir. I guess they're gonna poke around some."

"Humm," Ned stood on shaky knees, picked up his hat.

Cody put the fresh bottle on the table amid the empties. "Don't run off. Stay and I'll fry us some taters or something for supper. I'd appreciate the company."

"Aw, I reckon I need to go. Come go with me."

"Nope. I gotta stay here and feed the dogs. I'm fixin' to go to the club. I need to be there before six tonight. By the way, did you come by here for anything else in particular?"

"Naw. I've dropped by a few times at night when I didn't think you'd be at work and missed you. You were probably with Norma."

"I guess I was. Hey, I need to get them kids again soon. I still owe them a camping trip."

"Not 'til I find out who's killing folks around here." Ned looked Cody squarely in the eye and was startled to find he'd forgotten they were blue, like his. "I want to keep them close to home."

"I know what you mean. Let me know what else I can do."

"I will." Ned put his hat on and left.

Chapter Twenty-seven

I still don't like to talk about it much, but the last week of spring brought bad news from Dallas. The Highway Patrol came to the house and told Grandpa it looked like Mama completely lost her senses near Terrell, where Daddy was taking her to the hospital.

Mama started to slip a little after I was born. Until I was seven or eight, she acted funny sometimes. There were times she'd stay in bed all day. The days stretched into a week or two at a time as I got older. Dad took her to the hospital in Terrell, where they helped people with mental problems.

After I got older and knew what was going on, Dad talked with me about living with Miss Becky and Grandpa Ned. I didn't mind, because everything was usually tense at the house in Dallas, and I liked being in Center Springs. Then one day Dad told me I'd be living with them until Mama got all right.

I reckon she never did, because one day she opened the car door at seventy miles an hour. In the struggle to keep her in the seat, Dad lost control of the Galaxy and went into the ditch, flipping over several times before coming to rest upside down.

There was nothing for the rescuers to do to save them when they arrived. Grandpa brought them back to be buried beside kinfolk.

I can't remember much of what I did during those few days. I think my mind shut down. I was sad, but there were no tears, and that made a lot of people wonder about me. They visited with Miss Becky or Grandpa, talking in soft tones in the living room.

It was a hot spell and everyone was wet from sweating. I remember being hugged a lot while other people wanted me to eat. I barely remember the funeral, except the same little church was packed full and cars lined the highway once again.

Back at the house, I lay down on my bed to look out the window while the adults visited. As the sun went down, the older folks went outside under the sycamores and talked until well after dark. The skeeters must have finally run them in, and I heard talking inside.

Pepper came in to lay beside me. We listened to the whippoorwills in the pasture.

Mr. O.C. joined the adults still sitting in the

living room. I recognized his voice. After a spell they reached some sort of decision. Miss Becky brought two pieces of coconut pie to the bedroom and put them on the dresser. She sat on the edge of the bed and stroked my hair. Grandpa Ned and Mr. O.C. shifted uncomfortably from foot to foot in the hall.

Grandpa cleared his throat. "Top, do you like it here?"

The question sounded strange, but adults often did things that didn't make sense to kids. Pepper listened without saying anything for once.

"Sure."

"Well, I believe we'd like for you to stay here with us."

Miss Becky nodded and nervously picked at a stray thread on the bedspread.

Of course I planned to stay with them. I couldn't go back to Dallas. I had no intention of living anywhere else. "That'll be all right."

Miss Becky started sniffling, and she rubbed my head some more.

"Good." Grandpa stood a little straighter. Mr. O.C. grunted from the hall and left. Grandpa looked around the bedroom. "All right, then." He shuffled from one foot to the other for a few seconds like he didn't know what to do, then he left the room and Miss Becky fluffed a pillow for a minute before following him.

Pepper grinned at me and scratched my back. After a while we sat cross-legged on the bed and ate the pie. I heard Grandpa and Mr. O.C. in the yard as they walked to the cars.

"Looks like you and Becky have a grandboy to raise."

"I reckon."

"I'll have the papers ready for you tomorrow morning. Y'all can come by the courthouse, and we'll get everything signed."

"Thanks. Thanks for everything you've done."

"Aw, you know I'd do anything for y'all."

"I know it. Come back and see us." I recognized Grandpa's footsteps on the porch, and he and Miss Becky went back to visiting with the folks who were still there.

I learned about custody papers much later. The next day I became a permanent citizen of Center Springs. As the days passed, my pain eased a little at a time until it faded into the past.

Chapter Twenty-eight

The warm spell continued and us kids began to get jittery. The only way to scratch the itch was to get out from underfoot.

Grandpa would have taken a belt and worn our butts to a frazzle had he known Pepper and I planned to go stringing off on the day of the Incident. I don't think we really snuck out, more like we decided to get out of the house for a while before we went nuts.

He was up at the store, watching the fun as Neal Box cleaned out half his stock and burned it in a big bonfire in the pasture beside the store. The night before, Ty Cobb's dogs spotted a skunk slipping under the store as Jimmy Foxx pulled into the parking lot between it and the domino hall. Being hunting dogs, they jumped over the side when the pickup stopped and dived in after it. When the battle under those floorboards was over, the skunk was dead, but not before he gave both dogs a good healthy spray.

Everybody loafing around the domino hall whooped it up at the fight and had even more fun when the gagging dogs jumped back into the pickup, trying to rub the yellow skunk spray off on anything they could find. Doing what was right, Ty Cobb crawled up under the store and drug out the dead skunk, getting dosed pretty good himself in the spray sticking to the ground and the floor joists. The smell broke up the game, and everyone left the domino hall before ten o'clock.

They left to get rid of the skunk and wash the dogs, but no one thought much about the inside of the store until the next morning when Neal opened the doors and the smell hit him. Anything not in cans was ruined, so while most of the Spit and Whittle club watched, Neal burned everything from bread to the candy from the oak cases to brand new shirts and jeans. It took several months for the smell to finally go away, and whenever the humidity went up, the store smelled skunky.

Pepper spent the night with us and planned to stay all day. With Grandpa gone, Miss Becky took advantage of the good weather, and as soon as we got up, she had me pry the nails out of the frames and open the windows to air out the house.

I fetched the hammer like she said, but I

wasn't convinced opening the windows was a good idea. "What about the Skinner?"

"It's bright daylight and I doubt if a crazy person is gonna come up here to get us while the sun is shining. We'll nail them back up tonight, after the house breathes for a while. Now, y'all help me move this mattress."

She stripped the beds, and we helped move the floppy cotton mattresses through the front room and out into the yard to sun. It was like moving a dead calf through the house.

Neither of us had any intention of being drafted into housework, so when Miss Becky grabbed a broom to start cleaning, we made other plans. Pepper stuffed two sticks of crackers and some rat cheese into a muslin bag, and I locked Hootie in the corncrib so he couldn't follow us.

I knew it would be snaky where we were going, and I didn't want him to get bit by no moccasin while we looked for arrowheads. I'd seen snake-bit dogs, and knew it was a horrible way to die. Going to a vet was out of the question, because it cost too much money.

I grabbed my BB gun, though, in case we did see a snake.

Daddy told me Indians once camped and hunted along Center Spring Branch not far from Grandpa's house. They traded with the settlers and hunted up and down the clear, cold stream that never dried up in the summertime. When he was our age, he and his cousins found enough arrowheads along the banks to use in their slingshots. He said they were second only to smooth, round rocks for shooting targets.

It didn't take us long to cut south through the pasture to the branch. It was good to be free of the farm, and we felt like a couple of colts kicking up our heels. When we got there, Pepper hung the bag of snacks from a nearby shady limb.

"We'll get a whipping if they find us gone."

I shot at a frog. "They won't catch us. They'll think we're down at the pool. We'll get back before they holler."

We found a rusty can, so I set it up against the bank and we shot up half my BBs. I showed Pepper how to adjust for distance, and she did pretty good for a girl.

She had her slingshot, and when we tired of the gun we practiced flinging the smoothest rocks we could find. While she was looking for pebbles, Pepper saw an arrowhead. "There's one!" She jumped across the narrow stream and picked it up. She was disappointed to find the tip broken off.

I was secretly glad. "Stay over there on the girl side of the branch. You look on yours and I'll look on mine."

"You're just jealous because you're afraid I'll find another one before you do.

"Uh, huh!"

I was walking with my head down, carefully watching the gravel and wishing I could find one.

"Look, another one!" she shouted.

I started wondering if an Indian had lost a bag of arrowheads, if they carried them in bags at all. "There must have shot targets around here like we done." I kicked at a riffle of sand at the edge of the water and stopped. Instead of an arrowhead, I found something most people would give their eyeteeth for…a spear point.

In disbelief, I reached into the wet sand and gravel and pulled out the point. "Look." I could see where a groove was carved to tie it onto a rawhide handle.

Pepper splashed across the stream, not caring if she got her feet wet. "Shitfire. I can't believe you found that."

"Me, neither."

"You want to trade?"

"Not on your life." After examining it for a good while, I put the point in the back pocket of my jeans. "Get back on your side."

We kept going, walking slowly along the edge of the stream. Our luck must have run out, because for the next long while we didn't find anything else. Then Pepper stopped at the edge of a plum thicket and pointed at the gravel. "Hey, look at this footprint. Somebody's been here today."

"Wonder who? Nothing is in season right now, so there shouldn't be anyone hunting." I saw water seeping into the deeper heel print.

"Bet it's Walt Simms or maybe the Wilson twins. Maybe they came through here last night."

"Nope. Somebody made this print a few minutes ago. " I was suddenly scared. Anyone on decent business would have heard us coming and hollered to let us know he was there. The fact that they had gone on was an indication that we needed to get our little butts out of there right then.

"Let's go back. We left the crackers and cheese back there, and now I'm getting hungry."

Pepper looked suddenly scared also. "Good ide…" she began, when an arm shot out of a thick bush behind her and grabbed her around the neck. Before I could say a word, she was yanked out of sight with a gagging sound.

I'd never been so scared in my life, and I didn't know what to do. Everything inside my head screamed run, but my cousin had simply disappeared right before my eyes.

"Pepper?" I could hear thrashing in the leaves behind the bush. I needed to go around to the other side and find out what was going on, but terror held me firm. I suddenly lost my breath. "Pepper?"

The bush before me literally exploded. Limbs and leaves leaped forward. Up to then I'd forgotten the BB gun in my hands, but without a thought I leveled it and pulled the trigger. I heard the crack of air and a sudden painful hissing sound before I landed on my back so hard it knocked the breath out of me. I looked up through the leaves to see mare's tails sweeping across at the blue sky and remembered Grandpa always said those kinds of clouds meant rain.

A bush shaped like a man straddled me. I wondered how a bush could turn into a man, and then everything went black.

Chapter Twenty-nine

After his conversation with Ned, John seriously considered the possibility that the killer could be a black man. He was on his own when it came to investigating the murders of colored people. The white Law sounded good when they talked about catching the killer, but everyone from John's side of the tracks knew it was only lip service. Ned was the only person he knew who worried about coloreds the same as whites.

John needed more information and more eyes helping his investigation. He left the courthouse and drove across the tracks, leaving solid concrete for broken blacktop and the local barbershop. Ragged trees full of broken and dead limbs lined the streets of peeling clapboard houses, a stark contrast to the well manicured streets of nearby Bonham Street.

Some houses were only shacks, while others had porches. Few had grass in the dusty yards. John passed several boarded-up houses, once honky-tonks that One-Arm George shut down. Scattered throughout, though, were neat little homes that defied the neighborhood.

He parked in a shady yard by a "colored only" sign hand lettered in red paint. He grinned. Everything in that part of town was colored only. He joined his friends on the sagging porch.

"Gentlemen." John shook Ed Corley's hand with a loud slap, then worked his way around the group the same way. He took an empty chair beside the porch. He and Ed had been friends since boyhood, when both of their families made a living working the fields. By the time the young men turned eighteen, both John and Ed knew they'd do anything not to spend their lives working for pennies a day in the hot sun.

Ed opened his pocketknife and began shaving a piece of soft red cedar into a toothpick. "Taken anybody to jail today?"

"Naw. Know anybody needs to go?"

"'Bout a dozen, I reckon."

Ed chuckled, finished shaving his toothpick, and began to work on his teeth. "You still on them poor younguns was killed here while back?"

"Yep."

"I think you got your hands full with The Skinner."

John crossed his arms. "You're right, but lordy, I hate that name. None of this makes sense. First somebody cuts up animals for two or three years, they stop for a while and then they start in again before stealing and killing people."

"It's the Devil hisself down in them bottoms," Reverend Sanders boomed from the barber chair Tom Hubbard had moved out of the house and onto the porch to better catch the soft afternoon breeze. He'd already decided to move back inside after he finished with the Reverend, because he smelled rain. "The old Devil comes out to do meanness of his own every now and then. I believe he gets tired of working through other folks and likes to get his hands bloody hisself."

John recalled the advertisement Ned found under Cody's mutilated dog. "Why would he want to kill young people too?"

"'Cause they pure and he don't want no purity on the face of this earth." The Reverend switched to his deep bass sermon voice. "He'll defile what's good and leave the evil to roam at will, spreading hurt, disease and pestilence *throughout* the land."

"Proves why you're still here cutting hair," Ed told Tom, and everyone laughed.

The Reverend frowned. "It ain't no laughing matter Brother Ed. Folks is gettin' away from the church and that leaves more room for the Devil to work. Our troubles are coming home to roost with this skinnin'."

"Be still before I notch your ear." Tom waited for Brother Ed to settle down and then shaved his neck with a well honed straight razor.

"The problem here is there ain't nobody heard nothin'." Big John opened his pocket knife to clean under his fingernails with the largest blade. "This meanness can't be kept completely quiet. Somebody has to know something. I'm wondering if there's people keeping things to themselves because The Skinner is his own kin."

From inside the house, a soft voice quivering with age stopped the discussion as if were a shout. "I believe I know who he is." Jules, the courthouse elevator man, liked to sit by the still warm woodstove.

Even Tom stopped cutting.

After a lifetime of standing in the elevator in relative invisibility to white folks, Jules had become used to listening to everyone's conversations instead of talking. If and when he finally spoke, folks generally took notice.

"What do you know, Mister Jules?" Big John leaned forward so he could see through the door.

"Las' night I heard a racket out behind my house, some'eres around 'leven o'clock I reckon, and I stuck my head outside to see what was the matter. I thought a possum might be after my chickens, but I seen somebody trying to get my back screen off, and I hollered and he run off."

Jules and his wife Lily lived in a brightly trimmed shack at the outskirts of town. Long ago someone had given Jules some leftover watery paint. The window trim was blue and the door red.

"Who was it?" John asked.

"Well, I can't rightly call his name in the open."

"What makes you think it was The Skinner?"

Jules stayed inside by the fire and no one could see his expression. "'Cause it was. He's one of your people."

Tom forgot the scissors in his hand. "You saying he was black?"

"Nope. Y'all ain't listening. You're hearing my words, but not what I'm sayin'. I didn't say one of our people. He's one of John's people…he's a lawman."

John felt cold all of a sudden. Like Ned Parker, he despised a crooked lawman. "Who is it then, Jules? Don't keep pulling on us."

There was a long pause inside the dim room. "It's Sheriff Poole's boy."

After a silence longer than a year, John cleared his throat. The men exchanged glances.

"Who?"

"Poole's boy, that Constable Chase."

"Wait, I'm confused. Raymond Chase is Delbert Poole's son?"

"Yessuh."

"Jules, you sure for a fact?"

"Yessuh. Course the boy never carried his daddy's name, because they never was married. I know because my cousin Corina kept their baby some and found out they was common-law. Everybody thought she'd married him, but she moved in his house 'cause she come up expecting, but she wouldn't marry him. It was all jus' for looks."

"What makes you think it was him? Why would he be trying to get into your window in the middle of the night?"

"'Cause I found out about him one day when Raymond Chase had this young boy in handcuffs, Doak Looney's boy, and he was bringing him up to Mr. O.C.'s office after they arrested him for making whiskey. The boy said he seen what was done out in the woods, and he knew who done it cause he'd watched it. Raymond Chase got that boy in a corner and whispered in his ear like I couldn't hear.

"Y'all knows how it is. Sometimes white folks forget we're standing there, or that we ain't got good sense. I didn't act like I heard, but I know what he whispered to that boy. He said, 'Son, don't you ever say a word about me or I'll shove a hot screwdriver up yo' ass and gut you like a dead coon.' That's what he said. He said 'I've had experience with a knife and I know how to make you last fo' days 'thout givin' you the luxury a'dyin'.' He said that to that poor scared boy."

"Maybe he was trying to scare a confession out of him." John suddenly realized the terrible truth. He could feel the blood drain from his face.

"Maybe you ain't heard tell of that boy since that day." Jules grunted out of his chair to shuffle into the open doorway. "He went to Blossom, but no one has seen him since he left. He's in a shaller grave somewhere and there he'll stay 'til the good Lord comes back. Maybe you think Jules ain't got good sense, either. But I know for sho' he was tryin' to get in my house so's he could kill me and my 'leventh wife, Lily, and he wouldn't have to worry no more then about me tellin' what I know. He told me. Jus' the other day he got on my elevator and when I close the gate he told me to hold on, that he had something to say to me. I reckon he got to thinking back about me hearin' him whispering them things after all.

"He got right in my face and told me he had punishment for Mister Ned and his family and once he was finished with him, if I ever said anything, he'd come and do the same thing to me. He looked at me and said you know how good I am at keeping things alive past when they want to go. He said, 'You heard tell about the bottoms.'

"I don't know what he has against Mister Ned, but I ain't afraid to say I been scared ever since then and I keep my ol' pistol primed and ready."

He pulled his faded shirttail up to expose the butt of a worn revolver stuck in the belt around his skinny waist. The men on the porch exchanged uneasy glances. Now they had suddenly become part of whatever was going on in the bottoms and none of them liked it. The white Law wouldn't take it very well to know folks on the colored side of the tracks was keeping information about The Skinner to themselves.

My god, John thought. *There's he's killed and hidden bodies we don't even know about. How many more could there be?*

"Another thing."

"What Mister Jules?"

"I reckon you got to handle this right."

The yard was completely silent. John felt the hair on his neck tickle with goose bumps. "What are you saying, Mr. Jules."

The old man snorted and held onto the door frame. "I tol' you I lissen. I knew your daddy well, John. One-Arm George was a good friend and one day he came by the courthouse while I was eating my dinner out back there on the retainin' wall and told me he'd learned Sheriff Poole was messin' with his boy like men ought not do. But he was afraid Poole knew what he'd learned. George wanted to let somebody know the truth, in case something happened to him, and something did, and Poole did it."

"So what do you mean handle this right?" John looked around the porch for help in understanding. He'd always known Poole had probably killed his father, and the confirmation was both a burden and a relief.

"So I mean this thing could tear the town apart. You got to deal with them people across the tracks there the right way. Handle it careful like, so none of it gets on us, like it did your daddy, so they knows fo' sho' Raymond Chase is The Skinner and not one of us. It'd be easy to blame on colored folks, so's they won't have to say the real killer is a white lawman. Now, I don't know nothin' else, and I'd not like to say any more." Jules turned around and went back to his warm stove.

"Men, y'all listen to me now," John rumbled in his deepest authoritative voice. "Mister Ned and Mr. O.C. needs to know this, and then they'll tell Sheriff Griffin if they want to. But I won't say for sure it was Jules who told me. Y'all need to keep it quiet, too."

Tom went back to snipping at Reverend

Sander's hair in silence. They agreed without a vote, each man's thoughts sinking in deep and true.

John crossed the yard and called Ned on the Motorola, but there was no answer. He had no idea Ned was breaking up Miss Becky's vegetable patch with the garden plow, getting ready to plant. O.C. wasn't in his office, either, compounding his frustration and sense of urgency. Close to a panic for the first time in his life, Big John drove to Frenchie's café hoping to find O.C. having coffee.

The judge was there all right, straddling a stool at the counter. John saw him through the window when he parked his car in front of the building. Anxious to the point of carelessness, John nearly jerked the screen door off the hinges on his way in. Every white face in the café snapped toward his frantic entrance. Realizing the unwritten law he was breaking, even as a Deputy Sheriff, John stopped in momentary indecision.

He'd been through Frenchie's door only once, as a child. A sharp memory flashed in his mind as he hesitated at the threshhold.

When John was six, he chose to enter the café through the front, instead of taking the longer route into the alley to where the colored folks ate in the back. He barely made it six steps inside when a strong, white hand grabbed his arm.

"What you doin' in here boy? You know better

than to come in the front door of this café." The faceless man spun John around and sent him back through the door with a swift kick to the pants. "Don't you come back in here no more. You take and get your greens in the back."

His early humiliation finally submitted to the urgency of the situation when he saw O.C. Rains' silver hair at the counter. He started toward the judge, knowing clear as day what was coming, when Wilbur Meyers slipped off his counter stool and put John's hand in the middle of his chest to stop him.

"You know better than to come through the front door, Officer Washington."

For the first time in his life Big John's placid patience snapped. He grabbed the hand on his chest and his massive biceps bulged. Wilbur's wrist snapped like a dry stick. He was a mechanic at the Ford house and considered himself the toughest man on the north side of town. He found in an instant that he wasn't a patch on Big John's shirt. His shriek echoed through the café. Clutching his injured wrist and sinking to the oiled wooden floor, Wilbur suddenly realized the raging black man in front of him represented more than skin color.

Big John was already reaching for the sap in his back pocket to deal with two other men rushing from the counter when O.C. slammed down his coffee cup and slid off his stool.

"You men stop! This is one of my deputies, and if anyone lays another finger on him, I'll have y'all working the chain gang down in Huntsville before tomorrow evenin'. Now, y'all sit your asses back down." He snapped his fingers loudly. "John…John, nobody's messin' with you. Settle down, now."

Big John's eyes cleared and his anger dissipated as quickly as it had materialized. He slipped the sap back into his pocket. The men pulled Wilbur from the floor and escorted him outside, giving John a wide berth as they passed.

With an effort, the big deputy focused on O.C.'s concerned face. "We need to talk somewhere, Mr. O.C. Right now."

Realizing John would never consider entering Frenchie's without a serious reason, O.C. grabbed his hat from the counter and took his arm. "Frenchie, put it on my tab. C'mon, let's get outside."

Stunned into silence, Frenchie simply nodded. She watched the two men leave through the front door. Once it slapped closed behind them, the café exploded in outrage.

Seeing John's car parked at the curb, O.C. didn't hesitate to open the door and sit in the front seat. John went around the front and settled behind the wheel. His eyes flicked to Wilbur getting into a nearby truck for a ride to the emergency room.

O.C. saw his glance. "Don't you worry about Wilbur. He assaulted a peace officer and I'll take care of the rest later on. Now, what's wrong? How come you to bust through the door like that?"

John swallowed hard and rubbed his forehead. "I know who the feller is Mister Ned's been chasing. I know who The Skinner is. I just heard for sure."

"Heard from who?"

"Jules." John told him the story he heard at the barber shop.

"Are you sure? You know what you're saying is the truth?"

"Yessir. Jules told it for the truth and I believe him. I'll stake my badge on it."

"That would explain a lot of things. Did you tell Ned yet?" O.C.'s first indication was to call the FBI boys set up in a basement room at the courthouse, but then he changed his mind.

"Can't raise him on the radio. I was gonna call him on the phone, but I wanted to tell you first. I'm about to drive out there now."

"All right. Let's get back to my office and I'll call him from there. Then you light up this car and drive out there, in case I can't get him on the phone. Now, carry me down to the courthouse and then get going."

Half a dozen faces watched them leave through the flyspecked windows in front of Frenchie's café.

John shifted into gear and in seconds O.C. got out of the car at the courthouse steps. John leaned over and spoke through the open passenger window.

"Jules, Mr. O.C."

"Don't worry, John. I won't say where we heard. Now, git!"

Chapter Thirty

Ned had to know what John had discovered. With the big deputy on his way to Center Springs, O.C. hurried up the granite stairs to his office, since no one was there to operate the elevator. He was out of breath and had to sit for a moment after unearthing the black rotary phone from a pile of papers on his desk. He dialed the five numbers for Ned's house.

It rang over eight times before Miss Becky finally picked up the receiver. "Hello?"

"Becky, this is O.C."

"Well, hidy. I was just thinking about you. I'm churning right now and there'll be fresh buttermilk tonight. You and Catherine oughta come out and visit for a while and get you a glass. How is she today?"

"She's fine. Becky, is Ned around the house?"

The terse tone in his voice let her know the judge had something on his mind besides buttermilk. She became serious. "He's up at the garden. You need him?"

"I do. Right quick."

"All right." He heard her put the receiver down on the telephone table. Her footsteps retreated into the distance and he heard her calling Ned from the porch in a shrill voice.

Frustrated and impatient, O.C. could do nothing but chew the inside of his cheek while he waited for Ned to leave the plow and walk the hundred or so yards back to the house. If he was using Jake to plow it would take even longer. O.C. thanked his lucky stars that Becky wasn't the type of woman to come back on the line and try to engage him in small talk until Ned arrived.

When he could no longer stand it, O.C. finally heard the screen door slam and Becky tell Ned who was on the line. The receiver rattled as Ned fumbled with it. "O.C.?"

"Yep. Deputy Washington knows who's been doing killing out there."

Suddenly weak-kneed, Ned sat down on the hard wooden seat of the telephone table and clutched the phone with a white knuckled grip. "Who is it?"

O.C. told him.

"What makes you think Raymond's The Skinner?"

O.C. told him the story he'd heard from John. Ned listened in silence until O.C. finished and then sighed. "It all makes sense then." The pieces had fallen into place. "He started this meanness when he was a kid. Then he joined the army and went overseas to Vietnam. The trouble stopped for a couple of years, and it started again once he got back. I guess being over there finished doing something we can't imagine. It must have swole black inside until he worked hisself up and took to killing people back over here."

"That's what I figger. Them FBI boys say it's how the pattern works. Those newspaper ads were part of a plan, but I can't figure out why he's after your family."

"He's mad at me. There ain't nobody knows it, but I caught him a time or two when he was a kid. Once he was messing with a heifer out at his granddaddy's place, you know what I mean."

"Yeah."

"I chewed on his ass a while and turned him loose with a warning. Then I caught him racing down on the creek with one of them real young Miller girls in the car. I didn't let that one go, and I took him to his mama's house. She lived in a tarpaper shack out near Blossom. We struck a deal where Raymond worked off a kangaroo sentence I cooked up. After that he seemed to straighten up and fly right, so I never expected something like this."

"Well, he's stewed on it quite a while." O.C.

held the receiver and stared at the piles of papers on his desk, but not seeing them at all. "He's been turned like that all his life."

"How come?"

O.C. told him the remainder of the story and Poole's involvement. The final piece was clear as a neon sign.

Ned took a deep breath over the phone. "Oh lord. I didn't know who his mama was, or that he was Poole's boy. By the time I met her life had about used her up. I should have probably done something else, or told you when he got elected, but I thought he'd outgrown all that and maybe he'd make a good lawman. It would have been different if I'd known he was Poole's boy though, and what had been done to him."

"Don't go second-guessing yourself. You've had the opportunity to arrest half the boys in your precinct at one time or another, but you did what was right and either warned them off, or told their daddies. It ain't your fault."

"Well, now we got troubles. Have you told those FBI boys about this?"

"Nope. It's been yours from the git-go. John's on his way out there to your house and we decided not to use the radio, in case somebody heard. Y'all are gonna have to handle it from there. I'll let them know tomorrow, after y'all arrest him."

"I'll find him. He's off today, so there's no tellin' where he is."

"All right, then. Let me know what you find out," O.C. hung up without another word.

Ned replaced the receiver, but he missed the second click as Miss Whitney gently hung up the party line. He wouldn't have heard it anyway, because he was almost shaking with relief to find the suspect wasn't Cody, who'd been at the top of his list for the past couple of weeks.

He turned to find Miss Becky standing beside him. "I'm fixin' to go with John when he gets here."

"You got time for supper?"

"Naw, he'll be here in a few minutes and I need to clean up first. Where are the kids?"

"They're somewhere here abouts. They lit out when I started cleaning, so I 'magine they're playing up at the barn."

"I want them here."

She studied Ned's face for a moment. "I'll call 'em." She stepped out on the porch. "Yooouu! Top! Pepper!!! Come to the house!"

Thunder rumbled across the river. Ned glowered at the clouds building to the north and went to unharness Jake before it started raining.

Chapter Thirty-one

Ned stepped out on the porch with the .38 belted around his waist of his khakis as John slid to a dusty stop in the yard. The deputy noticed the heavier caliber pistol immediately.

The look on Ned's face told of another problem afoot.

"John, we got more troubles. The kids are gone and we ain't seen them since dinner."

"They ain't up at the barn, or at the store? Maybe they're fooling around down at the pool?"

"Nope. James is on his way over here to help us find them, but we don't even know where to look."

John saw the scared look in Ned's blue eyes and felt his stomach lurch. "You think they been took?"

"I hope not."

"Did you tell James what we suspicion?"

"I had to. Here he comes now."

James' truck turned into the driveway almost

Center Spring Branch was the only remaining option. He remembered Top's interest in arrowheads a few weeks earlier.

"John, drive down to the creek bridge and start walking upstream on this side of Center Spring Branch. I'll cut through Dell's pasture there by the catch pen, and when I hit the branch, I'll work my way toward you. If I find them and there's trouble, I'll fire a shot and you come a runnin'."

"Yessir. They'll be there I bet."

"They better be." Fear was a great knot in his ample stomach. "And when I get my hands on those two kids I'm gonna hug them and then whip their little asses."

Chapter Thirty-two

I couldn't catch my breath. I dreamed I was drowning again. The red muddy water was deep and I couldn't touch bottom to push off. I fought to swim upward, but the Rules of the Dream were in play and I couldn't get my hands free to paddle. Even my feet didn't work and I couldn't kick for the surface.

My eyes suddenly snapped open in the darkness. But even awake I still couldn't move my hands and feet. I figured I was turned wrong in the bed and they'd gone to sleep, but then I smelled wood smoke and it dawned on me I wasn't under Miss Becky's patchwork quilts, I was laying with my cheek on damp leaves out in the woods somewhere. Birds twittered on their roosts as the wind began to rise from a coming storm.

A strange sound I'd been hearing finally cut through the fog and I realized Pepper was somewhere nearby, crying. I tried to focus in the dim light, but my left eye was swelled shut. Movement caught my attention and I blinked several times to clear my good eye and saw Pepper tied facedown over a fallen log on the far side of a campfire. Her arms were wrapped around it like she was hugging the rough wood. My stomach turned when I realized her shirt was gone and wet leaves covered the white skin of her back.

"Pepper?"

She sobbed quietly to herself.

A man stepped between us and threw a big limb onto the coals. With the fire behind him, he was a shape and nothing more. Panic rose in a great wave. My lungs closed up and I forced air in and out to release the tightness in my chest.

"Shhh." The shadowy man spoke softly. "Be quiet."

"What's wrong with Pepper?" Hot tears filled my eyes and I began to shake.

"She's mad at me." The man knelt and piddled with the fire. His voice sounded familiar, but I couldn't place it.

Thunder rumbled and a short rain squall soaked me in a matter of seconds. I found myself ignoring the rain, though. It was almost as if my mind couldn't deal with everything going on around me.

"What did you do to her, mister?" I was scared enough to start bawling, too.

"I didn't do nothing, yet." His back to me, he watched her for a moment. He kept talking to me like we were having supper together. "Oh, you mean about her shirt? That was her fault. She wouldn't quit fighting me and it got ripped off. It was a good thing, anyway, because when she lost her shirt the fight went right out of her."

I rolled onto my side to get my hands free, but it was useless. My fingers worked around and I felt smooth, hard metal.

Handcuffs.

My wheezing was even louder. "I need my puffer."

"No, you don't. Learn to breathe like a man."

"You don't understand. My puffer *helps* me breathe."

"I understand perfectly. Ned babies you kids too much. But you're gonna have to tough it out for a little while, hoss, and pretty soon it won't matter no more."

Despite my terror, I was amazed at how casual our conversation had become.

He threw a wet stick on the smoldering fire. It flared up and shifted with a crisp sound. But even then, with one eye swollen shut, I still couldn't see his face.

Panic took hold and my kicking heels made him furious. "Dammit!" He rushed to my side in demonic fury, flipped me onto my stomach and put his knee on my back. The monstrously heavy weight knocked all the air out of me.

"Be still, you little shit!"

Our fighting brought Pepper out of wherever she had withdrawn. "He needs his medicine." Her voice was high and scared.

He ran his hands over my jeans, found the puffer in my front pocket and yanked it free. He threw it into the fire. The rubber bulb immediately melted and belched black smoke.

"Now, shut up about that damned contraption."

I gasped when he took the anvil-heavy pressure off my back. Pepper turned her head to see us better. A huge mouse pushed her cheekbone out of shape. I was scared of what the other side looked like.

The wind rose, bringing the sound of gurgling water and the smell of clean mud, not like a stock pond in the summertime when the sun beats down and turns it hot and sour. I knew we had to be near the creek, because the river had a completely different sound.

Lighting sizzled overhead and in the colorless glare I saw the steep rocky bank of the creek's opposite shore and the nearby sandbar. I knew then where we were.

The Rock Hole.

Shadow Man stepped past the fire and straddled the log behind Pepper. He grabbed her wet hair and yanked her head backward. Mouth opened in pain, she gasped. He leaned over her bare shoulder to whisper in her ear. Pepper fought her bindings like a trapped animal.

Dropping to his knees on the wet ground, Shadow Man laid his head between her shoulders and rubbed his hands up and down her bare arms. He turned and grinned at me, and now the light was on my side. I sucked in my breath.

"Raymond!"

"Shhhh."

Lighting ripped again with a sharp report, and it began to rain in earnest.

Chapter Thirty-three

Ned saw the light-colored muslin bag hanging from the tree limb as soon as he reached the low water crossing. He was right. They had been there, hunting arrowheads. Biting down rising panic, he forced himself to stay calm.

Dusk was already making it difficult to see. Thunder rumbled and lightning lit the distant clouds. Ned directed his flashlight toward the bank, and quickly located their footprints on each side of the branch leading toward the creek.

Although he wasn't a tracker, the prints were for the most part easy to follow. Ned followed the tracks at a fast walk, weaving in and out of the sand and gravel bars. He lost one set for a while when they led up the bank and into a dense growth of berry vines, but he went back to the stream to follow the other set. Within a minute the first pair returned and he continued his search.

He almost didn't see the print that alarmed the

kids. He'd have missed it completely if the track hadn't been pointed at right angles with the other, smaller marks. But there was no way he could have missed the area where they'd been taken. Only yards away, the sand dug deep with the imprint of struggling feet and bodies told the story of a vicious fight.

Top's new BB gun lay in the water. He was proud of the gun and would have never intentionally left it in such a way.

Ned's fear mounted and he fished it out with a sick, sinking feeling. He walked the area, trying to make sense of the scene. He found leafy branches and twigs that didn't match the nearby plants. He couldn't make heads or tails of the smoothly cut branches. Someone had obviously had fought with the kids. But what tore up the surrounding brush?

Was there a machete involved, a sword? Maybe an ax?

"Where you at, Ned?" The deep voice came from downstream.

"Here!"

In minutes John's flashlight flickered through the underbrush.

"What did you find?" Ned asked.

John's shoes were muddy and sheep-burrs stuck to his clothes. "I didn't see nothin'."

"I found tracks. Footprints. Somebody stole my kids, John."

"Was it Raymond?"

"I can't tell. I'm no tracker. But I know they're gone."

They shined their flashlights on the sand and trickling water. To the north, the thunder deepened and rolled closer. The wind freshened and rustled the leaves overhead.

"Well, he didn't bring them downstream or I'da found something. He's taken them somewhere."

Ned waved his arm north toward a faint dirt road that was once the low water crossing over the stream. "He had to have gone that way. There's no way he could carry two kids to the south. It's nearly two miles of boggy country to the nearest road."

"Yeah, but it's only about a hundred yards to the growed up stagecoach road over there. Come on."

They rushed through a landscape lit by flickers of lightning, dodging through the strip of trees bordering the branch and then charging across the rough pasture. Minutes later they broke out onto the road, breathing hard. Their twin flashlights revealed a set of tire tracks and, when John moved his light over the grass thrashing in the wind, Raymond's vehicle backed into the woods.

Searching the ground, John saw more footprints and drag marks across fresh gopher mounds. Heart pounding, he pointed east. "He went back out toward Gilbert's hay grazer, where the road comes out on the highway."

A sudden gust of wind threatened to take Ned's hat. He pulled it down tighter. "Do you think he went across the bridge toward Arthur City?"

Frustration mounted, because he had no clue. "I don't know."

"C'mon John. Help me here!"

"I cain't. I don't have any idy where he went. You know Raymond. Where would he go? To his house? Down toward the river somewheres? Maybe Ike's cornfield again."

Ned thought about what could have transpired. He attempted to recreate the events traumatic enough to render two kids incapable of fighting back. Pepper was a fighter, so getting her under control would be more than a skirmish. His stomach clenched at the thought of what it would take to restrain the little tomboy. And Top, he'd fight back as long as his lungs could take it, and then…

…the recurring nightmare of suffocating…

…drowning in red muddy water…

…down by the river somewheres.…

…he wouldn't go back past Ned's house, so the only other direction was across Sander's Creek bridge…

A crack of thunder rolled over the creek

bottoms as the storm arrived. They felt the vibration through the air. Seconds later, a brief deluge soaked their clothes. Ned studied John's face for a moment in the glow of their flashlights as rain poured off their hat brims. John saw the constable's eyes widen.

"I know where they are. We have to get to the Rock Hole."

He prayed he was right.

Chapter Thirty-four

I was drowning in fresh air.

Fighting the handcuffs had exhausted me. The whipping wind kept me in woodsmoke for minutes at a time, closing my lungs. I was close to passing out.

Pepper no longer cried on the other side of the fire, but she whimpered quietly to herself. The sound was unnerving. Pepper had never whined a day in her life and I couldn't believe my tomboy cousin wasn't fighting back. I wasn't sure if she was still awake or not, but I kept drifting away, never knowing how long I was out each time.

The rain poured on us for minutes at a time, only to slack off and then fall again.

The contrary fire sputtered and smoked badly, frustrating Raymond, who kept muttering to himself and poking at the burning sticks with a big two-handed screwdriver. He closed his eyes and turned his face toward the approaching storm.

"I like rain." Dropping the screwdriver beside the fire, he took off his shirt and threw it onto the ground. "That was the only time we cooled off in the Nam, kids. Rain, beautiful rain. Rain is clean. It washes away the blood, and you know what the preachers say: water purifies us, and I have no sin after I'm washed in rain."

Terrified, it was all I could do to simply inhale. "Please call Grandpa. Use your radio and we won't tell."

"I can't talk to Ned anymore now since you shot me." In a flash of light, I saw the bruised hole above Raymond's eyebrow. It still leaked blood. "You're pretty good with that air gun and you damn near shot out my eye. If I show up with this BB hole in my face, Ned will know what happened, and I can't have that. It's all your fault that I have to leave, but I was almost done anyway. It'll be time to go when I'm finished tonight."

"Please?"

Raymond's face went blank. Then without expression he mocked me in a frightening grown man's baby voice. "*Please, please.* You whiny little shit!"

Pepper was tied up and couldn't take care of herself. I'd never seen her when she wasn't full of piss and vinegar as the old-timers would say. I wanted to be tough, and not whiny. Something in my gut rose into my throat. Before I knew it, I spat out words I had never spoken before, but heard many times from my Grandpa. "You son of a bitch! Let us alone, goddammit!"

In three long strides he was across the fire and gave me kick in the side. It felt like I'd been hit with a sledge hammer. It knocked out what little breath I had left and I started seeing sparks.

"I'll be back with you in a few minutes, just as soon as Pepper and I are done."

The fight was out of me.

He crossed back to the log and rubbed his hand on her back. She whimpered like a scared puppy, but I barely heard her. "Please let us alone."

Overhead, the bottom fell out and the world turned to water.

Chapter Thirty-five

Ned and John pushed their way through the thick woods bordering Sanders Creek. Flashlights did little to light the way in the heavy rain, and between the percussion flares of lightning, they fought through darkness by feel alone.

Thick brush and wet dewberry vines caught their ankles, tripping them at nearly every step. Huge stands of grapevines blocked their way, costing them precious time. Soon both men were cut and bloody.

Ned grunted with each step and his lungs burned with exertion. His age and the months of worry finally were catching up with the old lawman. "John, go on. I'm slowing you down."

Carrying his shotgun at port arms, John used it to push thorny vines out of the way. "Come on Mr. Ned. It cain't be far now."

"I don't know if I'll make it." Ned stopped to catch his breath in the rain. If not for their hats, the downpour would have blinded them. "I don't know if I have the strength to make it."

"Ain't we almost there?"

"It's not far ahead. They may be on the other side of the creek and if they are, we'll have to decide what to do then."

"I want a clear shot."

"I just want to see my kids alive."

John kept bulling through the wet brush. "We got to get there first."

Chapter Thirty-six

I thrashed and fought the cuffs, knowing what Raymond had in mind for Pepper. But I couldn't imagine what he'd do to me until I recalled tortured dogs and the goat's teeth in the culvert and skinned people hanging on fences.

Raymond is The Skinner.

He kept whispering in Pepper's ear, ignoring me. With his knees in the muck, Raymond slid his hands around her naked waist and pulled her toward the end of the log. She screamed as the rough bark tore her skin. I recognized the position from what I'd seen bulls do in the pasture.

Mud covered Pepper's jeans and Raymond's khakis until they had no color at all in the flickering firelight. Raymond pushed closer and put his lips directly against her ear.

Pepper didn't move, terrified and completely defeated.

He quit whispering and straightened up,

still on his knees, to howl like a wolf. The insane sound was muffled by the rain, but for a moment it startled Pepper. She turned her head to see him and the movement caught his attention.

"I've got something for you two half-breed kids." He stood up and picked something up from the fire.

I remembered Uncle Cody's dog.

I remembered the goat in the culvert.

My blood ran cold.

Raymond held up a long, smoking stick. He'd wired one of the largest arrowheads we'd found that afternoon onto the end. "Here you go Pepper. I found this in your pocket. See? Just having this proves you're half-breed kids of that Indian, Becky Parker. I bet you're gonna like what happens next."

He hunched over Pepper and touched the arrowhead against the back of her right shoulder. Even in the rain, I heard the sizzle of burning flesh and smoke briefly puffed up. The sound Pepper made was not human; she twisted, fighting whatever was holding her against the log. Then she shrieked again because he kept pushing it harder and harder.

I would have shrieked with her, but my panic was silent.

"It'll be all right." Raymond put the arrowhead back in the fire. "The rain will wash away the pain.

Just wait and see." He turned and grinned across the fire at me. "Hey, Top. *You* get the spear point."

It was too much. It was too hard. I didn't care that I cried like a baby with the smell of scorched flesh in my nose.

After a few minutes, he quit paying attention to me and got down behind Pepper and started kissing her blistered shoulder. "Does this make it feel better?"

I finally quit crying and thought about rolling downhill because he hadn't tied me to the ground. But the creek was too close and if I went into the water I'd drown. I couldn't swim with both my hands and feet tied.

I wasn't sure, but it felt like my ankles were tied and not handcuffed like my wrists. Something gave when I moved my legs. After a couple of weak breaths, all I could do was roll under a bush and wiggle into a tangle of thick berry vines. I didn't even feel it when they stuck me. Raymond didn't notice I was gone.

A minute later I thought about the spear point in my jeans, but it was gone. Then I remembered the pocketknife Uncle Cody had given me months ago. It was there! Raymond had missed it.

I wriggled around and fished the knife out of my back pocket with only my fingertips. I felt with my thumbnail until I found the slot in the blade.

From there it was easy to open. I bent backwards and went to sawing on whatever it was holding my ankles together.

I was making good time at it when something crashed through the vines toward my hiding place. For a second I was paralyzed with fear and thought it was Raymond until I felt a warm and wet tongue on my face. Hootie had tracked me through the rain to the edge of the Rock Hole.

"Top!" Raymond's voice cut through the rain. He finally realized I was gone. "Where'd you go boy? C'mon out! I have something for you."

I sniffled and sawed at my ankles while Hootie licked the tears from my face.

Chapter Thirty-seven

As Ned had feared, they chose the wrong bank and found themselves on the high side of the Rock Hole. Frustratingly close, yet too far away, they crouched in the brush across the storm-shrouded creek.

"There they are!"

John looked over the edge. "I never seen no water come up this fast. It's already too wide here to try and jump. The only place to cross is back up at the bridge."

"That'll take too long." Ned panted and squinted at the circle of fire light through the falling rain. "Oh god, John. Looky there at what that son-of-a-bitch is doing."

They saw Chase pick something up from the fire and hold the end against Pepper. She screamed and writhed in pain. Through the veil of rain, Ned gave a hoarse cry and aimed his pistol.

Behind him, John wrapped his big hand around the revolver and pushed it down. "Hush,

Ned. You cain't shoot. Your hands are shaking too much, and you might hit one of the kids."

"He's branding them!"

"I know he is, but hush now and be quiet before he hears us." The branding cut John deep and he recalled the scars on his great-grandfather's back. "They're still alive. That's what matters."

"Which one is it?"

"Cain't tell, but we have to get over there to the other side." John looked back over his shoulder. "We have to go back a little bit and wade across where it narrows."

"Goddamn it. Let's go."

Chapter Thirty-eight

When my ankles were free I dropped the knife and rolled over to get onto my knees. Excited and thinking we were playing, Hootie barked and jumped up on my back, nearly knocking me over again.

"Top! I see you in there," Raymond called in a sing-song voice and the beam of his flashlight caught me in the brush. "Who's with you? Your friend? Hey, I have an idea. I'll show you what makes Hootie work and then we'll see what makes Pepper work."

I sobbed and pushed back through the brush. Getting to my feet, I ducked my head and pushed through the vines. Thorns ripped my soaked clothes, scratching me deep and sharp, and then I was free. The rain hit me even harder in the open. Hootie jumped at my legs, nearly tripping as I stumbled. I thought I had gotten away when a hand grabbed my collar and yanked me off my feet.

I lost the will to fight. "Don't, please don't." Hootie barked and growled, but he didn't sound mad. *Stupid dog,* I thought. *You should be trying to save me.*

A voice whispered in my ear. "Shhh."

"Please, Raymond." I opened my good eye and was shocked.

Uncle Cody slapped his hand over my mouth and pulled me into another thicket as lightning split the darkness.

"Top? Where are you little buddy?"

Hearing Raymond, Hootie left us and loped toward his friend.

I heard a shot and Hootie shrieked.

"C'mon Top, and let's look in your puppy." Raymond called to me as if we were on the porch back at the store. "Irish 'taters. He may be full of Irish 'taters. Let's see."

Cody's hand cut off even more of my air to keep me quiet.

Can't breathe…

Chapter Thirty-nine

Ned's heart almost stopped when the muffled shot echoed across the bottoms. He held the pistol high above the chest-deep water, half way across the creek. "We're too late! He's done killed one of 'em!"

John pulled the old man through the increasing current. "Maybe not!"

They splashed onto the bank. Ned's leather shoes slipped, and only John's strong arm kept him from falling back into the creek.

Lightning flashed, and they climbed high enough to gain better traction. Both men charged toward the sound of the shot.

Chapter Forty

"Stay here," Cody whispered in my ear. He lowered me to my knees and disappeared.

Raymond held Hootie's limp body by the back legs, his head flopping back and forth in the flickering firelight. Rain ran down Raymond's naked chest. A knife glinted in his hand and he gave a horrifying grin that looked like one of them Halloween masks.

I roused up and my head cleared some, but I was far from all right. Light sparkled in front of my eyes, and I felt close to the edge of a dark pit.

Uncle Cody charged across the smoky fire and body-slammed Raymond before he knew what happened. They went down in a heap and Hootie splashed onto the soaked ground without moving. The men quickly got back up facing one another in a strange fighting stance.

Uncle Cody kicked at Raymond like he did when he was fighting Calvin Williams and his boys at the store, but Raymond dodged back out of the way, blocking it with a downward swipe of his hand like he expected it. He immediately lunged with the knife, but Cody blocked it with his forearm and slid around and punched Raymond in the side. I heard his air empty in a whoosh.

Uncle Cody jerked upward on the arm holding the knife and Raymond's shoulder looked like it came out of the socket. Cody twisted it so hard the knife splashed into the mud. Raymond threw himself backward and hit the ground, rolled, and came back up, covered in mud that immediately began to wash off in the downpour. Then they went at it too fast to follow in the darkness and flickering lightning. The kicks and punches landed hard as they do when men fight, while they blocked others with their upper arms and forearms.

Sometimes lightning stopped the action like a flashbulb. Other times they were shadows fighting by firelight. I fell forward, shivering from cold and fear.

Rain beat on my back and it all went black.

Chapter Forty-one

Ned and John finally broke free of the soaked underbrush, expecting to find Raymond at his blood work. Instead, a fight raged beyond the fire. Ned's heart missed a beat when he recognized Cody.

The two young men fought with grunts, wet slaps of hands and fists hitting knotted muscle, and muddy sucking sounds as their feet sought for purchase. Neither had been out of the military so long they'd forgotten their skills.

Cody's sodden clothes slung water in the brief flashes of lightning. Though fueled by anger, he fought methodically, confident of his skills.

Shirtless, Raymond's muscular upper body looked slick and lethal. Insanity powered his aggression and proved almost equal to Cody's hatred for the man who stole his nephew and niece.

Raymond lashed out with his foot and Cody blocked the kick with his left forearm. He drove in with his shoulder, trying to knock Raymond off balance. He missed and dodged backwards, away from a blocked return kick.

Relieved they'd found the kids, Ned knelt beside Pepper's shirtless body lying limp and still over the log. He choked back a sob of relief. "I believe she's alive. Oh, god. He's burnt her shoulder. John, do you see Top?"

"No, sir. Not yet."

On rubbery legs Ned played his flashlight around them.

Big John kept one eye on the fight. He leaned his shotgun against the log and touched the seemingly unconscious little girl's cheek. She jumped at the contact and turned fearful eyes toward him.

"John?" Her normally bright eyes were dim.

"I'm here."

"Can you help me?" Her soft voice could have been that of a four-year-old asking for help to tie her shoelace.

Nerves jangling and muscles twitching in tension, John knelt on one knee, removed his shirt and covered Pepper's naked upper body. "You done helped, baby." He opened a switchblade knife with a push of his thumb and reached around the log to cut her bonds as he blinked tears from his eyes.

"Grandpa?"

Startled, Ned pointed his flashlight toward the sound. Not twenty yards away, Top lay handcuffed facedown in the thick loam. Ned stumbled forward and held the gasping boy, feeling for the wound he knew would be there. "Thank god, we got here in time."

Ned half carried, half dragged Top closer to John's protection and knelt, utterly exhausted.

The brutal fight took Cody and Raymond beyond the circle of firelight near the roaring creek. A violent kick from Raymond slammed Cody backwards. He landed flat, his head banging into an exposed tree root. Lights flared behind his eyes. He instinctively rolled to avoid a follow-up attack.

Instead, Raymond grinned through bloody lips and waited for Cody to stand once again. "Come get some more."

Cody slowly regained his feet and crouched as his combat instructor taught him. He stepped forward with his left foot and moved his right the same amount of distance to maintain his balance.

Then he smiled.

Unnerved by the sudden change, Raymond's own grin faltered.

With both children finally safe, and suddenly, incredibly tired of the battle, Ned rose. He crossed the short distance to the creek bank and grabbed Cody's arm just as he was about to launch another attack.

Without a word, Cody paused beside the

constable, breathing hard. He glanced at him and was taken aback by the look in the old man's eyes. No one in those woods besides John had ever seen the old man so full of fury.

Ned drew the revolver from his side.

Raymond had violated everything dear to Ned; the law, right, and his family.

With absolute certainty, John knew what was coming. He turned to Pepper and gently shielded her with his big hand. "Close your eyes baby. Top, you still with us?" He softly patted Top's skinny back with the other hand as the boy lay on the muddy ground. "Look a-here at me, son."

Raymond raised his hands for the cuffs. "Here you go, Ned."

Ned didn't intend to arrest Raymond.

Ned shot him.

The young constable looked down in puzzlement at the tiny hole in the bare skin of his chest. A small amount of blood trickled out of the wound and was immediately diluted by the rain.

He fell face down into the sand.

Emotionless, Constable Ned Parker stepped past Cody who dropped to his knees in exhaustion at the shot. "Ned?"

"In a minute."

Lying facedown with one foot digging into the mud, Raymond moaned quietly. "Help me."

Instinctively knowing it wasn't over, John almost lay over Pepper and moved his hand upward to hold Top's face away from the creek.

Ned aimed his pistol downward.

Thumb-cock.

The short hair in the back of Raymond's head fluttered around the small hole that suddenly appeared.

Thumb-cock.

Another shot and dark hole and black gouts of blood mixed into the mud and rain.

Thumb-cock.

A chip of something flew into the creek and Raymond's head rippled.

"There's only one way to deal with a mad dog," Ned said.

Cody wiped watery blood out of his eyes. His mind raced. "All right, then. Y'all go on. Y'all get Top and Pepper to the doctor. Those kids need help. I'll take care of this."

Ned's tired blue eyes rested on his nephew.

Cody nodded. He knew what to do. "It's all right now. Just remember when they ask, he got away."

"I got 'em!" John called over the storm. "I believe Pepper's in pretty good shape even though he burnt her, but Top ain't. We got to go!"

Astonishingly quiet, Pepper stood in the rain

with downcast eyes, clutching John's shirt closed at her neck. John knelt and lifted the almost unconscious Top, his head resting on John's bare shoulder. Holding the boy like a sleeping toddler, John turned to Pepper. "C'mon, baby." The big lawman picked up the shivering girl and draped her over his other shoulder like a sack of feed.

"I can carry one of them." Ned fumbled the keys from his front pocket and unlocked Top's handcuffs, releasing his arms.

Lightning cracked overhead, bathing them in a cold light. Thunder hammered immediately behind.

"No, you cain't. It's too far and we have to run some more before this boy gives up the ghost." Tears glistened in his eyes. "Let's go, Mr. Ned. You know the way, so lead us out of here."

They ran through sheets of rain, and neither man looked back again, though they both heard Cody calling. "Remember, he got away! Say he got away!"

Chapter Forty-two

Big John Washington carried the kids out of the wooded bottoms in his great arms, jogging all the way. When they reached the deputy's car parked on the side of the highway, John let Ned open the back passenger door, and he fell inside. Barely able to control his trembling muscles, Ned used John's radio and told the dispatcher to send an ambulance to his house. Then he made a quick u-turn away from the creek, and with his last reservoir of energy, punched the accelerator and shot down the highway in the rain.

Miss Whitney's party line was hot and everyone in town knew there had been trouble. Despite the storm, people filled the porch and the well-lit house to wait and make themselves available to help.

Miss Sweet, Big John's aunt, had been in Center Springs acting as a midwife for a colored family living in a dirt-floor shack near the river. Since the newborn arrived without incident with all twenty fingers and toes, she didn't see any need to spend the night.

She and Ralston were in a car borrowed for the visit. She'd found him loafing around Chisum after he got out of jail on bond. He was behind the wheel, and they were turning off the gravel road onto the highway when Ivory Shaver passed and tapped his brakes. He shifted his old truck into reverse and backed up to stop beside the car.

Ralston cranked down his window. "Where you going so fast, Ivory?"

"Going to get Willamena and then head up to Mr. Ned's house. Hi-do, Miss Sweet. It's a good thing you're here. They's something wrong with Mr. Ned's grandkids, and they might need doctoring."

"All right, then. Get out the way and let's go." Miss Sweet punched Ralston's arm. "Get going."

"But Miss Sweet, I cain't go to Mr. Ned's house, not after what I done."

"It don't matter none to him what you've done in the past. Miss Becky is gonna need me right soon. Now you drive us there, or I will."

Knowing Miss Sweet had never driven in her life, Ralston turned onto the highway. They pulled into the yard seconds ahead of Ned and Big John.

Top's eyes had already rolled up into his head when Ned slid to a stop beside the back porch and a yard full of cars. The men waiting at the house rushed to help them out of John's sedan. Isaac Reader opened the back door and Big John stepped out, still holding the children on his shoulders.

Half a dozen pairs of hands reached out to help. *"Get back!"* He intended to get them safely into the house and wasn't going to tolerate any other ideas or arguments. Unsure what to do and having never had a black man speak to them with such authority, they stepped back.

Miss Sweet didn't bat an eye at the sight of John holding the children. "Sweet Jesus, them po' little things." Realizing the seriousness of the situation, Miss Sweet struggled out of the car and took charge, despite all the white people standing around. "John, you get them babies in this house and out the rain. Ralston, you bring my bag in for me."

Ralston looked as if he wanted the ground to open up and swallow him, but the two people he respected most in the world were standing right there, and when either John Washington or Miss Sweet told him to do something, he did it.

Miss Becky pushed through the crowd and onto the porch. "Sweet, thank God you're here."

"They're both in bad shape and Top's barely breathing," John declared.

"What happened?" She took one look at her grandson and knew he was in trouble.

John spoke softly and stood free of the car. "They was took."

"He's worse than I've ever seen him. Oh my god, what did he do to Pepper?"

"We'll fix 'em directly." Miss Sweet made a calming motion with her hands and rocked toward the porch in her gaited walk on creaky knees. "Lawdy mercy, I'm old and cranky, and if these young fellers don't help me up the steps I'm gonna commence to *whoopin'* on somebody."

Jolted into action, Ty Cobb and Jimmy Foxx stepped forward and took her large arms to help Miss Sweet up the steps. She grunted, taking each riser one at a time, making everyone wonder if her knees could take the strain.

Miss Becky offered her hand. "Sweet, come on in, hon'. Tell me what to do. Isaac, you men need to help Ned out of the car, too, and get him in here out of the rain."

"Yessum, listen, y'all help me." Isaac and two others assisted Ned, who slumped exhausted with his head leaning against the steering wheel.

Following Miss Sweet's orders, John stomped up the porch steps and turned sideways through the door, tracking mud and water onto the linoleum floor.

Miss Sweet was still in charge inside the house. "Y'all get them in the bed and I'll tend to Ned directly, after I see to these babies. I know these people mean well, but y'all need to get out the way. I got work to do."

A few people sucked in their breath, seeing a black woman issuing orders in Miss Becky's living room.

"Listen, she ain't a-lyin'." Isaac glared around the room, daring anyone to speak. "Y'all heard her. Go on, now, and let her work."

Miss Becky made shooing motions with her hands. "Y'all get out of the way. Follow me, Sweet."

Top roused up when John carried the kids past the table full of food brought by those who waited. He went limp and drifted away again as they passed through an ocean of concerned people.

James pushed through the crowd and held out his arms. John gave Pepper over to her daddy. Ida Belle kept crying. "My baby girl, my baby girl."

James pulled John's uniform shirt closed around Pepper's scratched stomach and chest, and carried her into the front bedroom. He laid her on the bed and left her with Ida Belle and Miss Becky. They closed the door behind them. It opened again several times as the tiny hall bustled with ladies going for soap, hot water, spirits of camphor and rags.

John's arms trembled when he gently laid the boy down in the back bedroom with his head toward the foot of the bed. Miss Sweet sat her flour-sack bag on the dresser and extracted half a dozen jars containing leaves and herbs.

"John, set yourself down at the table 'til I can look in on you too." She glanced around the crowded room. "Somebody fetch me some boilin' water and a coffee mug and then y'all thin out in here. We don't need everybody in the way."

John left without argument.

Hot water appeared and after crumbling the dried herbs into a cup, Miss Sweet poured the steaming water on top.

"I need a couple of men in here."

The number of volunteers who stepped forward and lodged in the door would have been comical at any other time. They stepped back to let Neal and Walt Simms through. The worried men sat with Top on the bed and held him upright.

Miss Sweet made a tent out of a pillowcase and put it over the boy's head, then held the steaming cup under his nose. "Breathe this in, hon'."

Miss Sweet's steaming mug woke Top enough to inhale the vapors for a couple of minutes. She made him drink the mixture and then repeated the process two more times.

The weakened boy kept slipping back into unconsciousness at first, but she wouldn't let him go. She and Miss Becky kept talking to him and wiping his forehead with cool washrags to keep him awake. Before long, his lungs relaxed and he slipped into a normal deep sleep.

When she was satisfied that Top was out of danger, Sweet hurried across to the other bedroom on painful knees to check on Pepper. At the same time, two strong men helped Ned to his rocking chair beside the heater where he rested in exhausted silence, shaking with a deep chill.

Ty Cobb knew about Ned's smokehouse and returned with the most recent jar of liquid Evidence. Though mortally opposed to drinking, Mrs. Ida Wade poured a little of the white lightning into a cup of coffee and brought it to Ned. He swallowed it down in long draughts. She poured a second, stronger dose. The third cup was mostly Evidence with a little light coffee color. Ned finally leaned back, settled down and spoke quietly to those around him.

Near collapse from fatigue, uncomfortable and shirtless, Big John trembled at the table. "Here, John." One of Miss Becky's quilting buddies Alma Fant cut an apple pie in half and put it on a plate. "You eat this and drink some of this hot coffee. Let me put something in it for you, if that's alright."

"No, thankee, ma'am." John felt awkward at being inside with all the white folks. "I don't need nothing but coffee in my coffee."

"Have some pie, then."

"I don't think I ought to."

"I didn't ast you, John, I told you." She touched his arm. "We owe you a lot more than this."

Chapter Forty-three

Ned could do nothing more than slump wearily in his rocker and talk quietly to himself while the country grapevine worked its magic. The storm intensified as Ivory's family arrived in a truck that struggled up the hill to the house.

Despite the presence of John and Miss Sweet in the house, Ivory and his folks stayed outside on the porch. They anxiously watched John through the window. Ivory found a patched and tattered shirt in his truck and sent it in with a youngster. It was too tight but John wore it without buttoning it up.

A group of women and men went outside and knelt with Ivory's family to pray for the children. After a while, Ralston joined them and, gingerly taking a knee, bowed his head. Still standing, with one hand on Ralston's head, Ivory raised his face, closed his eyes, and they all talked to the Lord. Across the pasture, the Assembly of God church was open and several cars were parked in front.

Despite the rain, the south windows were open and someone played Just as I Am.

Alma Fant stuck her head into the hall. "The ambulance is here."

"Well, they ain't taking anyone anywhere." Miss Sweet placed her stocky body in the door and refused to move.

The ambulance driver worked his way through the crowded house and stepped into the hall, looking worried. "We been told to get them."

"You can't have neither one of 'em." Miss Becky joined Miss Sweet in the hallway.

"We're still going to have to charge you for coming out here." The driver tried to look past the ladies, but Walt Simms put his hand gently on the man's shoulder and held him still.

"Get you hands off me."

Walt gave his shoulder a squeeze. "Why don't you wait outside?"

"Why don't you make me?"

Doc Heinz arrived before the ambulance driver and Walt came to blows. Everyone in Lamar County respected Doc, so they listened when he spoke. In the course of his fifty-odd years as a country doctor, he liked to say he'd delivered right at three-quarters of the population of Center Springs.

"You men hold it. Sam, go wait in the ambulance and I'll call you if I need you. Now, everybody else get out of here so I can check on these kids. Howdy, Sweet. Who's in which room?"

"The boy is in thissun, and the girl is there." She pointed a crooked, arthritic finger toward Pepper's room. "The boy weren't hardly breathin', so I figgered he needed help the most. His lungs have eased up some, now."

"All right. Miss Becky, was the girl bleeding or having trouble breathing herself?"

"Not that we saw. She's in there talking just fine. She was burnt…branded, but I couldn't see anything else."

"All right." Doc went into the back bedroom first and listened to Top's chest with his stethoscope. "You sound pretty good. What happened to them ribs?"

Top drew a long, shuddering breath. "Raymond Chase kicked me."

Doc's face hardened. He gently examined the boy's side, but didn't find anything of concern. "Your eyebrow is gonna need a stitch or two." By the time he deadened the area, Top was so out he hardly felt it.

Doc was most interested in Top's breathing. "Did you do this, Sweet?" He poked his forefinger at the soggy leaves in the mug.

She nodded, but wouldn't look away. "That little feller was tryin' to die when he got here, and

I did what needed to be done." She stiffened her back in anticipation of a dressing-down.

Doc Heinz latched his bag and stood up. "I couldn't have done better. Hell's bells. I've had eight years of medical school with more than forty years of practice, and all you did was fix this boy up with a little dab of soggy leaves. You need to tell me what you used."

She relaxed. "It weren't just me." She raised her right hand. "I'm always helped by the sweet warm presence of Jesus."

"I must have missed that course in college." Doc glanced around the room. "All right. Well, I reckon he'll live. Come with me and let's look at Pepper."

They left and went into the other bedroom, ran all the women out despite their complaints, and closed the door. Half an hour later he emerged and sent Aunt Ida Belle back in to be with her daughter. "She's scraped up and has a bad burn on the back of her shoulder, but she's fine."

"Was she...did he?"

"You women always ask me that and naw, she's just fine like I done told you."

Miss Becky and Ida Belle broke down and sobbed like their hearts were broke. Seconds later, O.C. Rains blew into the house like black vengeance, dripping rainwater everywhere.

His white hair stuck up when he took his hat off. Two of his deputies followed close behind and stopped in shock at the sight of John Washington sitting in Ned's house. O.C. raised his eyes at their expressions, and the look on his face backed them off to wait beside the door.

When O.C. saw Ned in his rocker, the tension went out of his shoulders. James brought him up to date. They were talking quietly when Doc shoved through the crowd to check on Ned. He knelt beside the rocker and leaned close to listen to his chest.

Ned exhaled, and Doc started in surprise. "Why, he's damned near drunk!"

"You would, be too, if you'd swallered half a quart of Doak Looney's best whiskey," Jimmy Foxx told him.

Everyone within hearing distance laughed, the tension finally broken.

"You'll be fine, Ned. You 'bout run yourself to death is all. You rest, now." Doc gave him a pat on the shoulder and went into the kitchen. He rested his hand on Big John's wide shoulder. "You need anything, John?"

He shook his great head and leaned his elbows on the table. "I'm 'bout full up of pie and coffee. I just need to rest a bit."

Doc leaned over to speak softly. "I don't aim

to charge no one any money tonight. You feelin' all right?"

"I'm wore plumb out." John gave the side of Doc's leg a pat. "That's all."

O.C. joined Ned and knelt beside the rocker. He put a hand on his knee and leaned forward to whisper in the old constable's ear. "Ned, was it Raymond Chase for sure?" He turned his good ear to listen to the soft reply.

"Yes." Ned felt his stomach start to quiver and shoved down the tears that started to rise.

"Did you do for him?"

"Yes."

"Where is he?"

"With Cody."

O.C. looked at his old friend for a long a while. Ned closed his eyes and rested.

"Is Cody all right?"

"Yes. I'm supposed to tell you something."

"What's that?"

"Raymond got away."

O.C. thought for a moment about the conflicting story. Then he slowly nodded. "It's over."

"Yes."

"But Chase is gone."

"Yes."

"This can't come back."

Ned opened his eyes. "Cody said. I believe him."

"All right, then."

"Something else."

"What?"

"Cody weren't there...because of what was done on the creek."

O.C. thought for a long time and then creaked to his feet. "All right, then."

John and Doc were still sitting at the table, so O.C. took a chair beside him and leaned in. Doc dug in on his own piece of pie and pretended he didn't hear their whispered conversation, their heads close together.

"Them little kids was near dead, and it was raining hard, Mr. O.C. The las' thing I heard when we was running out of the bottoms was how Raymond Chase got away. I reckon it was Mr. Ned hollering he'd got away from us. Ain't nothing else to it."

O.C. stared hard at his deputy. Satisfied, he stood and waved the two deputies outside. He followed them to the porch to give them instructions. They finally got in their car and drove off.

Once more in the house, O.C. called to the crowd. "Y'all, come here and gather 'round, cause I don't intend to tell this but once." He threw his hat onto the table between a plate of cold chicken and a half a coconut cake and ran his fingers through silver hair.

"Constable Raymond Chase did this to these young 'uns in there. He's the one they call The Skinner. It's a damn sorry shame to have to tell you since he's one of mine, but those are the facts."

A gasp went up from the crowd both in the house and on the porch.

"Now he got away, but I've instructed my deputies to put out an all-points bulletin and to call those FBI boys back in town. We'll find Raymond and deal with him when we do. Now, I don't want none of y'all to go running around out there waving shotguns around and bollixing things up. Let my boys and the feds handle it. Let's all be grateful we got these kids back, and there won't be any more hurtin' done around here anymore."

"Listen," Isaac Reader stepped out of the crowd. "You sure it was him and weren't any of them circus people from across the river that's been doing it?"

"No, Ike, it was Chase."

"All right. You know I hate them clowns."

"We know, Ike." O.C. went back to sit with Ned.

Engines started outside as neighbors left to spread the word.

"Ned, you and John did all right, and don't

think you didn't 'cause Raymond didn't come out of them woods. I'll have my men down there in the morning and they'll start looking for him, but I warn you all," he raised his voice to be heard. "With all this rain, I doubt there'll be many tracks. We'll do our best, though."

Chapter Forty-four

After John and Ned left with the kids, Cody sat by the fire to rest. The steady rain threatened to drown out the blaze, but Cody threw the entire pile of wood on the surviving coals. Despite being wet, the flames flickered to life and finally generated some warmth.

His ribs ached and a jaw tooth was missing. Cody spat blood onto the ground and stuck his tongue into the hole. He looked sadly at the little dog's body lying in the mud. If it hadn't been for Hootie, he might never have gotten to the kids in time.

By coincidence, Cody joined the search after dropping by for a visit with Miss Becky. When she met him on the porch and told him the kids were gone, his heart dropped. He had a long moment of indecision until, in the background, Hootie's howling and whining from the corn crib caught his attention.

"Did you put the dog up?"

Miss Becky looked toward the pasture. "I never, but somebody put him in there. Turn him out and he'll run to the kids."

Cody rushed to the corn crib and turned the Brittany out. The young dog ran around the yard for a few moments with his nose to the ground and then took off like a shot, leading Cody along the kid's path and straight to the Rock Hole.

Despite the fire, Cody shivered from reaction and the chilly rain. He reached out to rub Hootie's wet hair. His first touch smoothed the soaked coat, but the second elicited a shocking response. A muscle twitched under his hand. He slid closer through the wet leaves and picked up the limp dog, thinking the twitch must have been his imagination.

Blood covered the left side of the dog's muzzle, but instead of finding a large hole in Hootie's head, Cody realized the bullet glanced off at a very shallow angle, knocking out a large chunk of scalp without penetrating. In the firelight, he saw a thumbnail chip of the dog's skull was missing, but the wound had already stopped bleeding.

He gently shook the young dog. "Hootie? Hey, boy, you with me?"

Hootie's tail feebly wagged, and he sighed deeply. Cody took off his shirt and wrapped the young dog. He laid him close to the fire and sat back, thinking. In the flickers of lightning Cody could see Raymond's cooling body, his feet now in the rising waters of the creek.

"You missed out on it all around tonight, you son-of-a-bitch."

Cody remembered the sunken remains of a Depression-era dugout house not far from the Rock Hole and with a sigh, forced himself to his feet. He walked the short distance and found a few rotting boards protruding from the caved-in shelter, illuminated by Raymond's flashlight. Assisted by the near continuous lightning, Cody pulled them out of the wet ground and used one of the short planks as a shovel to enlarge and deepen the dugout.

When he was satisfied, he used Pepper's bindings to tie a loop around Raymond's ankles. He roughly dragged the corpse from the creek bank through the rain and rolled it into the hole. Throwing Raymond's shirt in afterward, Cody collected several large rocks and dropped them in on top of the body along with a number of broken boards. He kicked in a couple of feet of sand, then added more large rocks to ensure nothing could dig up Raymond's remains.

Rain settled the wet sand around the rocks and the body. To ensure the grave would never be found, Cody returned to the roiling, rising waters of the creek and searched the bank. As the batteries in Raymond's flashlight grew weak, he finally found a young tree washing out into the current. It came free of the wet ground with a couple of good tugs.

Cody returned to the grave and planted the tree in the mud, backfilling around the roots and trunk with sand until the ground was once again level. He stood there for a moment in the diminishing rain, facing west where he could faintly see the lights of Ned's house. The water quickly washed away all evidence of the activity.

"You killed my dog, too, and I never liked you anyway." Cody unzipped his fly and finished watering the grave.

Incredibly weary, he returned to the sputtering fire. Hootie thumped his tail weakly at the sight of Cody who loved on him for a few minutes. Then he gathered up Raymond's revolver, knives, and screwdrivers and threw them all in the deepest part of the Rock Hole. He knew the strong water would eventually bury them in silt forever. Finally, he twisted the arrowhead free from the bailing wire branding iron and threw it into the creek, also.

The fire was once again out when Cody finished. He knelt beside Hootie and gathered him in his arms. "Let's go, little buddy. And remember, Hootie, Raymond got away."

◇◇◇

Rain fell for days. For the first time in over twenty years, the Red River broke free of its banks and spread across the bottomlands, inundating Sanders Creek and submerging the Rock Hole under nearly ten feet of water. When the flood receded over a week later, the bank was as pristine as the day the first Indians found the deep hole.

The flood completely obliterated Raymond's grave, rendering it impossible to tell the young tree hadn't grown there from an acorn. It was as if the good Lord swept his hand across the creek bank to forever seal their secrets from prying eyes.

Chapter Forty-five

I was good as new when Grandpa's term as constable ran out. He didn't run again. Folks had finally quit talking about the flood and Raymond Chase, and went to talking about Uncle Cody and Norma. Her divorce from Calvin finally came through and she married Uncle Cody. After the ceremony, they climbed on a plane at Love Field in Dallas and flew to Las Vegas.

The new constable took office when he came back from his Vegas honeymoon.

The FBI finally gave up and left when they couldn't find hide nor hair of Raymond Chase. They worked on me and Pepper pretty hard, but for all they knew, we told everything that happened. I don't mean they weren't suspicious. Those old boys knew the truth and a couple of kids weren't going to pull the wool over anyone's eyes. But they never got us to say what they wanted to hear, because either Grandpa or Mr. O.C. kept a tight rein on our answers.

Cody's name never came up at all, and they never knew what happened that night, because Uncle James carried him up to our house the morning after Raymond took us. Cody kept apologizing as soon as he got out of the car about not being there because, truthfully, the flood covered the Sanders Creek Bridge and folks had to drive clear around to Forest Chapel to come in the back way.

He had Hootie with him and told how he'd found him walking down the highway. "He must have run off in all the excitement."

I broke down and cried and cried when he jumped up on the bed with me the next morning. I'd seen Raymond kill him, but when he licked my face, everything seemed like a horrible nightmare.

It was funny. The FBI never did ask Miss Becky any questions about that night. If they had, she wouldn't have lied, because she's not like that, and they'd have gotten everything they wanted.

Pepper went through a long, hard spell. For a while she wasn't herself and didn't have much to do with anyone. From time to time Miss Becky would find her standing in front of the dresser mirror, looking over her shoulder at the scar shaped like an arrowhead.

A year later Pepper and I decided to finally

go swimming at the Rock Hole with Uncle Cody. I found her in her bathing suit just before we left, looking at the scar in the mirror again.

For some reason it seemed like the time to ask what Raymond whispered in her ear that night. Staring at her scar, I just had to know. "He said some things to me that I didn't understand, about rain and looking inside things. He was gonna brand me, too. That feller was nuts."

She wouldn't give me a straight answer and didn't take her eyes off the mirror. "You ain't a-woofin'. He was talking nasty and saying other stuff too, about everything being full of Irish 'taters. Full of 'taters. Shitfire, that man was crazy. If I'd remembered my knife that night I'da cut Raymond's throat and this never would have happened."

But it did happen, and now it's over except for our scars, inside and out.

Today Grandpa and I went down to the river, and the water was flowing calm, strong and thick, but I knew that depending on her mood, the Red can turn mean. That old river has a hold on us and is part of who we are. These bottoms are our home, and we take care of ourselves here.

You see, we're from up on the River.

To receive a free catalog of Poisoned Pen Press titles, please contact us in one of the following ways:

Phone: 1-800-421-3976
Facsimile: 1-480-949-1707
Email: info@poisonedpenpress.com
Website: www.poisonedpenpress.com

Poisoned Pen Press
6962 E. First Ave. Ste. 103
Scottsdale, AZ 85251

CPSIA information can be obtained at www.ICGtesting.com
226374LV00002B/1/P
9 781590 588857